THE MAN WHO COULDN'T DIE

RUSSIAN LIBRARY

The Russian Library at Columbia University Press publishes an expansive selection of Russian literature in English translation, concentrating on works previously unavailable in English and those ripe for new translations. Works of premodern, modern, and contemporary literature are featured, including recent writing. The series seeks to demonstrate the breadth, surprising variety, and global importance of the Russian literary tradition and includes not only novels but also short stories, plays, poetry, memoirs, creative nonfiction, and works of mixed or fluid genre.

■ □ ■

Between Dog and Wolf by Sasha Sokolov, translated by Alexander Boguslawski

Strolls with Pushkin by Andrei Sinyavsky, translated by Catharine Theimer Nepomnyashchy and Slava I. Yastremski

Fourteen Little Red Huts and Other Plays by Andrei Platonov, translated by Robert Chandler, Jesse Irwin, and Susan Larsen

Rapture: A Novel by Iliazd, translated by Thomas J. Kitson

City Folk and Country Folk by Sofia Khvoshchinskaya, translated by Nora Seligman Favorov

Writings from the Golden Age of Russian Poetry by Konstantin Batyushkov, presented and translated by Peter France

Found Life: Poems, Stories, Comics, a Play, and an Interview by Linor Goralik, edited by Ainsley Morse, Maria Vassileva, and Maya Vinokur

Sisters of the Cross by Alexei Remizov, translated by Roger John Keys and Brian Murphy

Sentimental Tales by Mikhail Zoshchenko, translated by Boris Dralyuk

Redemption by Friedrich Gorenstein, translated by Andrew Bromfield

The Tale of
an Authentic
Human Being

OLGA SLAVNIKOVA

THE
MAN WHO
COULDN'T
DIE

Translated by Marian Schwartz

Columbia University Press / New York

Columbia University Press
Publishers Since 1893
New York   Chichester, West Sussex
cup.columbia.edu

Published with the support of Read Russia, Inc.,
    and the Institute of Literary Translation, Russia

Library of Congress Cataloging-in-Publication Data
Names: Slavnikova, Olga, author. | Schwartz, Marian, 1951- translator.
Title: The man who couldn't die: the tale of an authentic human being /
    Olga Slavnikova; translated by Marian Schwartz.
Other titles: Bessmertnyæi. English
Description: New York : Columbia University Press, 2018. |
    Series: Russian library
Identifiers: LCCN 2018022924 (print) | LCCN 2018027118 (ebook) |
    ISBN 9780231546416 (electronic) | ISBN 9780231185943 (cloth : alk. paper) |
    ISBN 9780231185950 (pbk.)
Subjects: LCSH: Veterans—Russia (Federation)—Fiction. | Perestroæika—
    Fiction. | Soviet Union—Politics and government—1985-1991—Fiction.
Classification: LCC PG3488.L35 (ebook) | LCC PG3488.L35 B4713 2018 (print)
    | DDC 891.73/5—dc23
LC record available at https://lccn.loc.gov/2018022924

Cover design: Roberto de Vicq de Cumptich
Book design: Lisa Hamm

CONTENTS

INTRODUCTION

Ressentiment Monsters

MARK LIPOVETSKY

I met Olga Slavnikova in 1987 or 1988. Back then we both lived in Sverdlovsk (now Ekaterinburg); she worked as an editor at *Ural*, the local "thick" and respectable literary magazine, and I was publishing my first articles in it. She had just finished a journalism degree at Ural State University (my alma mater too) and was launching her literary career, both as a prose writer (her first novella, *A Freshman Girl*, was published in 1988) and as a literary critic. We had many common interests—primarily the culture wars that were roaring around us—and quickly recognized each other as like-minded. The circle of young literati to which we belonged was mesmerized by the newly discovered continent of Russian underground and émigré modernist and postmodernist literature—from Vladimir Nabokov to Sasha Sokolov and Venedikt Erofeev—which started to appear in print after decades of censorship and about which we talked all the time.

This was the peak of perestroika, and Olga was an active participant in the literary innovations of the time. One such innovation was a "special" issue of *Ural* (1988, no. 1), which published a few pieces of nonconformist prose and avant-gardist poetry along with a radical (for the time) political-economic article. Although it was the latter that brought national recognition to this issue (according to rumors, it was resold on the black market at a vastly inflated price), *Ural* continued to publish less conventional literature in a "magazine within a magazine" entitled *Text*, with a belatedly Structuralist chic. Although not entirely independent from *Ural*'s management, *Text* published exciting prose and poetry by young and not-so-young writers who would otherwise never have appeared on the pages of any Soviet journal. The novelty of this literature was not political, it was aesthetic—most of the works published in *Text* not only deviated from Socialist Realism (which nobody took seriously anyway) but also disregarded social realism and the classical realist canon— which in the eyes of readers and the literary establishment was a much greater sin than being anticommunist.

At that time, however, nobody yet saw Slavnikova as a leader of the new literature from the Urals (or from *Ural*). This changed drastically after her first major novel, *A Dragonfly Enlarged to the Size of a Dog* (1997). Published in *Ural*, it was included on the short list for the Russian Booker Prize. Furthermore, *A Dragonfly* became the year's greatest literary sensation—critics and readers alike noticed the novel and praised it as one of the brightest debuts of our generation. This was the work where Slavnikova found her original style. Valentin Lukianin, a critic and editor-in-chief of *Ural* in the 1980s and 1990s, aptly writes:

> Everybody knows that a photo of the head belonging to a fly, mosquito, or dragonfly, when taken through a microscope, reveals a horrible and even fantastic monster. But this monster really exists, although we don't recognize it in a small insect. In the same manner,

Slavnikova placed normal and ordinary relations between intimates under a microscopic lens, and through this device, she discovered everyday Russian reality from such an angle that nobody has ever experienced.[1]

Slavnikova's newfound style paradoxically fused the lessons of traditional realism and radical modernism. On the one hand, Slavnikova is attentive to the everyday life of poor and socially marginalized people, especially women. On the other, she enlarges the details of their ordinary existence with such a powerful "microscope" that they turn into surreal symbols, and through this metamorphosis her prose exposes life's frequently morbid undercurrent. This approach, however, excludes a necessary component of the Russian literary tradition, the writer's compassion for her characters. Slavnikova is truly mesmerized by her monstrous "everyday people," but with the fascination of a scientist, she keeps her narrative distance, never allowing readers to identify with any of her characters. Her "coldness" stands for an unblinking analytical position, for an acidic skepticism hostile to any sweet illusions. Such a distancing is critical for all her works, but especially for *The Man Who Couldn't Die.*

Almost all of Slavnikova's subsequent novels would gain recognition and win literary prizes—the new style discovered in *A Dragonfly* proved flexible enough to absorb diverse themes and stories, all invariably associated with contemporary Russia. Her subsequent novel, *Alone in the Mirror* (1999), written while she still lived in Ekaterinburg, appeared in the prestigious Moscow journal *Novyi Mir* and won its award for the best publication of the year; her slightly dystopian *2017* (2006, translated into English by Marian Schwartz in 2012), which Slavnikova wrote after her move from Ekaterinburg to Moscow, received the Russian Booker Prize. Two of her latest novels—*Light-Headed* (2010, translated into English by Andrew Bromfield in 2015) and *Long Jump* (2018)—were both short-listed for the largest Russian literary prize, The Big Book, and the latter still has a chance to win it. The only exception is the novel that you are holding in your hands, *The Man Who Couldn't Die* (or *The Deathless* in Russian), which first appeared in 2001, in the Moscow magazine *October*. Although it didn't win any major literary awards, many critics consider it Slavnikova's best and most accomplished work of literature—her true masterpiece.

Furthermore, *The Man Who Couldn't Die* has a cloud of a scandal around it—and what could be better? Slavnikova claimed that the authors of the famous German film *Good Bye, Lenin!* (2003) plagiarized her plot. Both works juxtapose dramatic scenes of early postsocialist transition with the figure of an immobile elderly person—the paralyzed grandfather, a former wartime scout, in Slavnikova's novel, and the comatose mother, a former Party activist, in Wolfgang Becker's film. In both works, relatives try to protect their weak-hearted elders from the shock of the revolution and its consequences by maintaining the illusion that things are the same as before in the USSR and GDR, respectively. To support this illusion, both Slavnikova's and Becker's characters produce fake newsreels for home TV.

Frankly, I don't share Slavnikova's concerns: I believe that the metaphor juxtaposing physical immobility and being stuck in the past and/or awakening in a different country was too obvious to anybody living through the postsocialist transition not to become a common trope. Furthermore, the radical differences between *The Man Who Couldn't Die* and *Good Bye, Lenin!* are much more significant than their similarities. The latter is full of optimism and excitement around the long-awaited revolution, which is why the film became so popular worldwide, while Slavnikova's novel tangibly delivers a sense of bitter disappointment—of what Nietzsche called *ressentiment*—in the fruits of the same revolution.

The concept of ressentiment—inferiority and weakness compensated for through hostility toward others, be it the authorities, immigrants, liberals, or Americans—has been frequently used to describe the situation in post-Soviet Russia. In the words of the philosopher and cultural historian Mikhail Iampolsky,

> The peculiarity of the Russian situation lies in the fact that the entire society, from Putin to the last pawn, in an equal degree bears a sense of ressentiment. For Putin, ressentiment stems from the lack of acknowledgment for Russia and him personally as equal and respectable players in the world arena; for the pawn, it stems from a sense of helplessness before police, government officials, judges, and bandits. I think that the ressentiment-based fantasies of those in power at a certain point came into resonance with the ressentiment-based fantasies of ordinary people. And the world began to transform. The Ukrainian affair appeared to be a noble war against imaginary fascists. Russia's isolation—its re-establishment in the rank of superpower and the plummeting of the economy— the growth of wealth and happiness.[2]

Slavnikova wrote her novel in the very beginning of the Putin era, in 2000–2001, but the atmosphere of ressentiment that she captures allows us to detect seeds of the future resonance between "ordinary people" and post-Soviet authorities. The novel's plot develops along two parallel lines. One follows the meager life of a family fully dependent on the pension of its patriarch—the paralyzed and bedridden Alexei Afanasievich. The other traces the semilegal and outright illegal schemes and tricks accompanying elections in a small industrial town—probably somewhere in the Urals, but, actually, anywhere in Russia. As is clear from today's perspective, these two plotlines diagnose two major sources of social malaise indicative of post-Soviet ressentiment: nostalgia for the Soviet past and popular revulsion toward democracy and democratic procedures.

Marina, the stepdaughter of the bedridden veteran and a journalist trying to win herself a place among the new power elite, connects both plotlines within the novel. But this link is almost mechanical; Slavnikova's rich metaphors and leitmotifs establish much deeper connections between these two dimensions of the story.

Each of the three central characters in *The Man Who Couldn't Die* has their own web of leitmotifs; taken together, they manifest the existential, rather than the political or psychological, "taste" of the post-Soviet nineties. Nina Alexandrovna, Marina's mother and Alexei's wife, is shell-shocked by life under capitalism and perceives everything outside the walls of her home as a chaotic confusion of phantoms and chimeras. She lives as if sleepwalking, and even the people she sees on the street look "blurred and slightly translucent." Although her daughter, Marina, is much savvier about the new ways, she also perceives people as being "like shapeless specters." Despite all her futile efforts to gain a stable and decently paid position as a journalist, she remains alienated from reality. The metaphors surrounding her variegate the motif of the void: "She was surrounded by a strange, lifeless emptiness"; "The world around her was surprisingly empty"; " 'There definitely isn't going to be any money today. Beyond that, I don't know,' Marina said in a raspy, muffled voice into the nearest microphone, feeling an emptiness behind her"; "The emptiness before her was infinite, and she could only wade into it further and overcome the familiar resistance of a dimension without qualities"; etc.

Lost in the fog of ressentiment-bound nonreality, Nina and Marina join efforts to create—ostensibly for the paralyzed Alexei but in fact for themselves—a comforting illusion of Soviet "stability," of things remaining unchanged forever under the portrait of Leonid Brezhnev (whose tenure in power exceeded Stalin's but was shorter than Putin's). Despite its obvious cheesiness ("It's a prop right out of a Hollywood movie about Soviet life"), this home spectacle has a tangible effect on its participants. Alexei acquires a visible similarity to Brezhnev, growing into a symbol of the past era himself: "It turned out that Alexei Afanasievich had *always* been the creator and center of Soviet reality, which he'd managed to hold onto a little longer; and now this reality, squeezed to the size of their standard-issue living space, retained its permanence, inasmuch as its pillar had not disappeared." The force of her stepfather's "encapsulated time" helps Marina realize that nostalgia for the predictable monotony of Brezhnev's Stagnation has already emerged as a powerful and wildly popular political force among the post-Soviet "electorate": "Apofeozov's chief opponent in the true elections . . . was, of course, not Krugal but Leonid Ilich Brezhnev." Furthermore, while trying to strengthen her loyalty to the election campaign, Marina "voluntarily made herself the heart of the paralyzed era, the heroine of a Soviet film; in retrospect, she almost came to love the Young Communists and her fictional Party membership."

The novel's subtitle is a reference to a famous Socialist Realist novella from 1946 about a wartime pilot who continues to fly despite losing both legs to amputation after a battle injury. Marian Schwartz has translated this phrase as "The Tale of an Authentic Human Being" rather than "A Tale of the Real Man." I can understand her choice—the epithet "authentic" (*dopodlinnyi*) and its derivatives frequently appear in the Russian original of the novel in association with the paralyzed veteran. Even Brezhnev's portrait becomes more authentic in his proximity: "the general secretary, whose death had here been reversed and whose longevity had become a natural feature that only kept increasing, had somehow borrowed an *authenticity* from Alexei Afanasievich that Brezhnev himself had never possessed."

Seemingly resonating with her characters, Slavnikova does not spare the satirical details in her depiction of post-Soviet public life—and especially of the elections—as a parade of clumsy simulacra. In a particularly hilarious scene, a charlatan named Professor Kuznetsov runs a "healing" séance in support of an election candidate. (I have a strong suspicion that Slavnikova wrote this scene "from nature"—a certain Kuznetsov enjoyed incredible popularity in the Ekaterinburg of the 1990s for selling various torture devices, such as clusters of small but very sharp plastic nails intended for standing or even lying upon—promising to heal all ailments and pains.) However, despite its "factographic" nature, this episode reads like a paraphrase of Mikhail Bulgakov's famous séance of black magic from *The Master and Margarita*: the same barrage of lies and illusions, the same willingness of the audience to accept any phantasm for truth. Slavnikova's explanation of the impact of these illusions is different, but the tone she adopts in this section is recognizably Bulgakov's:

> Professor Kuznetsov's experiments (his female patients, after spending time with him in the hotel, returned covered in gooseflesh, as if they'd been rolled in semolina, and for a while would express themselves exclusively in verse) promised each person not only longevity and an extended youth but in essence the rescinding of their past life. Each could now start over, from childhood if they liked, which is what happened with many.

Unsurprisingly, against the background of post-Soviet political chimeras and childish phantasms, the Soviet past starts looking more real, more trustworthy than the current reality. But this is what people *want* to see, this is exactly how the optics of ressentiment works. Slavnikova's text goes beyond this optical illusion. She tries to expose the nature of this "authenticity."

What is so authentic about Alexei Afanasievich? His wartime past? It is embodied in the image of the noose made of strong silk rope with which he strangled a large number of German soldiers during his night raids. He carries this noose around his neck like a cross and never washes it, so that "the scout had a raw red stripe on the back of his neck, where the filthy noose rubbed his spine . . . In damp weather, Alexei Afanasievich would itch terribly from that crude mark forever after." Alexei preserves the skill of re-creating his deadly noose out of any string as the last reflex of his paralyzed body.

Another motif associated with his wartime glory is the huge, gilded German bed that he brought home as a trophy and upon which he lies for the fourteen years of his paralysis. We learn that on this luxurious bed, Alexei also repeatedly raped his wife, Nina. The motif of rape in connection with the German bed serves to point at the unnamed by Slavnikova, but well-known to the Western reader, rampage of sexual violence during the Red Army's victorious raid across Germany at the end of World War II.

It turns out that the authenticity of Alexei Afanasievich's postwar experience is also quite questionable: "In all the decades of their life together, the Kharitonovs had never reminisced about anything together. They hadn't accrued any symbolic property in common, such as any love, however brief, immediately tries to acquire."

Eventually, Slavnikova's analytical gaze reveals that the old scout's *authenticity* has only one real foundation—his association with death: "There was something odd and even sinister to Alexei Afanasievich's abnormal longevity." A continuing reversal of meaning between life and death, blurring the distinction between these states, permeates the entire novel. Death is present not only in Alexei Afanasievich's wartime past but also in his ice-cold family life after the war, and of course, in his present half-dead condition. A thick web of motifs associated with death surrounds this character, just as themes of sleepwalking surround Nina and themes of emptiness—Marina:

> He was already a failed product of death, a defective good from whom death had taken a step back without dispensing with the continuity of life in his illuminated consciousness. The veteran had not reconciled himself to this and was now planning to *make death* by his own hand—to repeat the mirror image of what he had done to others with such ease.

Husband and wife had tacitly admitted the possibility of death and its legitimate proximity. After this chaste barrier fell between the Kharitonov spouses, death for Nina Alexandrovna and Alexei Afanasievich became something much less shameful than their clumsy nighttime lovemaking, no hint of which had been permitted during the sensible daytime hours.

The similarity between death and sexuality in these passages is not a Freudian slip of the writer's pen. Rather, this is the true meaning of nostalgia for "Soviet authenticity," of the post-Soviet attraction to "Soviet glory"—it elevates death as the only authentic truth, the supreme social and individual value. In short, nostalgia is self-destructive, as the novel's plot vividly demonstrates.

The interweaving of motifs associated with the novel's characters as well as with the satirical representation of hidden electoral mechanisms produces a surreal effect that transforms Slavnikova's seemingly realistic close-ups into a parade of monsters. Her text is inhabited by people who look like smaller copies of themselves, foreheads covered with natural wooden patterns, faces reminiscent of minerals: "His large face was made up of parts that looked sanded, without any wrinkles whatsoever, and between these broad patches of youth lay winding darknesses that also looked sanded, darknesses that retained the professor's age, like soil in the cracks of a polished stone." These transformations of the human into the nonhuman are coupled with opposite metamorphoses, when objects act like living beings. Consider "an awful old leather bag sewn from scraps that looked like a creation of Dr. Frankenstein's . . . She'd hoped that the shapeless monster, to which she would never entrust even the smallest denomination of currency, would digest everything she didn't want to remember during her tense daily labors and especially at night." Or "the heavy bus, which kept dropping on its ass," or the "shuddering elevator, whose buttons had turned into black ulcers long ago," or the door, "which had occasionally dropped rusted-through wallpaper nails, like rotten teeth." These monstrous creatures are the embodiment of ressentiment; they visibly materialize what is brewing inside people and inside the country. They manifest phantasms that occupy reality, taking control of time and space.

However, these spectacular metamorphoses add a supplementary dimension to *The Man Who Couldn't Die*. Despite their depressing direct meaning, all these metaphors fill the novel's style with wit, playfulness, and joyful estrangements. They establish tangible connections between Slavnikova's novel and great literary predecessors—not only Bulgakov but also Andrei Bely, Dostoevsky, and Gogol. Through these links, Slavnikova situates post-Soviet ressentiment within a long (and wonderful) tradition of the Russian grotesque. This purely artistic twist offers a different perspective that overcomes the phantoms of the given time and suggests examples of productive distancing from contagious illusions shared by the majority.

Nietzsche argued that ressentiment "itself turns creative and gives birth to values."[3] *The Man Who Couldn't Die* shows exactly what kind of creativity and values the post-Soviet ressentiment gave birth to. Hopelessness and cynicism, a readiness to deceive and a willingness to be deceived, the valorization of death over life and of the past over the present (and future)—taken together they constitute the soil on which the aggressive nationalism and jingoism of the 2010s would breed. The art of distancing appears to be another value born out of ressentiment, and it offers a productive alternative, both intellectually and aesthetically, as Slavnikova's novel dazzlingly demonstrates.

Olga Slavnikova has a very serious view of literature, comparing it with the hard, fundamental sciences and treasuring its complexity of vision above popularity. She says in an interview:

> In my understanding, literature as an art form requires the same attitude as fundamental science. The uninitiated may find it incomprehensible. But one fundamental work of a mathematician, which, in the best-case scenario, only a thousand like-minded scholars understand, can completely change the picture of the world.[4]

Obviously, this is her ambition as a writer. *The Man Who Couldn't Die* accomplishes this maximalist program. The novel will stick in your mind like a splinter. It is as discomfiting as it is invigorating and provocative, yet its multifarious effects can change the picture of contemporary Russia by shaking numerous stereotypes and, at the very least, by eliding sweeping generalizations and oversimplifications about its past, present, and future.

NOTES

1. Valentin Lukianin, *"Ural": zhurnal i sud'by* (Ekaterinburg: Kabinetntyi uchenyi, 2018), 530.
2. Mikhail Iampolsky, "V strane pobedivshego resentimenta," *Colta.ru*, October 6, 2014, http://www.colta.ru/articles/specials/4887.
3. Friedrich Nietzsche, *On the Genealogy of Morality*, ed Keith Ansell-Pearson, trans. Carol Diethe (Cambridge: Cambridge University Press, 2002), 21.
4. Iuliia Rakhaeva, "Olga Slavnikova: 'Dialog idet mezhdu pisatelem i mirozdaniem, a chitatel' lish' prisutstvuet,'" *Druzhba narodov* 6 (2009), http://magazines.russ .ru/druzhba/2009/6/ra15.html.

THE MAN WHO COULDN'T DIE

World War II veteran Alexei Afanasievich Kharitonov had been lying in the farthest and probably coziest corner of their standard-issue two-room apartment, immured in his enfeebled, emasculated body, for fourteen years. "A very good heart, a very strong heart," Evgenia Markovna, the aging district doctor, who looked like nothing so much as a wise rat, murmured. Every month, her slender, wide-set legs took her to this apartment and this corner, where the paralyzed man was spread out under a blanket, on top of a fresh, tightly stretched sheet, wearing new, haphazardly pulled-on underpants with elastic like a machine-gun belt. "Just like a young man's," the educated old woman murmured as she ran a cracked sliver of cheap soap under the faucet while the veteran's wife, the young pensioner Nina Alexandrovna, held a terrycloth towel worn to patches from laundering at the ready. Both women tacitly understood that talking about his heart was no explanation.

There was something odd and even sinister to Alexei Afanasievich's abnormal longevity. Unlike most of those by now legendary war's veterans, whose numbers decreased erratically by the year,

Alexei Afanasievich had gone off to war not as a boy but as a grown man who had already graduated and worked in a school for a while. And if those relatively young old men who gathered time and again under new red banners, banners papery in the light, seemed like the offspring of the young men who had once gone off to the front— totally different people born out of life's long dream, in which they had died, succumbing to its intolerable duration, the true bearers of the war's memory—then Alexei Afanasievich, on the contrary, was striking for his *authenticity*, which had carried forward through the troubled and vividly illuminated years. By his mere presence he authenticated himself so thoroughly that, although he had never joined the Party, it would scarcely have occurred to anyone invested with power to ask for his ID. Each of this man's positions and actions had lasted exactly long enough for him and the people around him to fully realize and remember what he had accomplished; the fif- teen or so men he had once killed, as an army scout, without noise or weapon, were probably among the few who had come close to solving the riddle of death while still alive. Alexei Afanasievich had given them this knowledge, and blessed with it, their legs dancing, madmen looking vaguely past their own temple, they had dropped their submachine guns, bowls of soup, and dirty postcards to the ground. Alexei Afanasievich's favorite weapon was a noose made of strong silk rope, which had an advantage over a knife: even on the darkest of nights, light of unknown origin would be caught and cast on a blade. That silk rope had never once failed him, and the scout himself, while stifling the fascist's porridge-warm bellowing with his fist, palpably felt the moment when the soul quit the body with a jolt as gentle as a kitten's jump. In intervals between dangerous jobs, so as not to lose his instrument, Alexei Afanasievich carried the noose around his own neck, the way other thoughtless men wore crosses in war. Occasionally, the worn cord was actually assumed to have a cross on it. Whether out of a manly distaste for snot-nosed washing, or out of concern that he would wash the patina and luck off the glossy silk, Alexei Afanasievich never rinsed the rope in any of the putrid bathhouses where he had occasion to steam away his own salty, frontline dirt—and as the rope became infused with his body, it became more and more a part of him. The scout had a raw red stripe on the back of his neck, where the filthy noose rubbed his spine, which was as skinny as a bicycle chain and slippery from sweat. In damp weather, Alexei Afanasievich would itch terribly from that crude mark forever after.

After demobilization, Alexei Afanasievich, though he had eight medals and countless other minor decorations, did not try to become any kind of boss, devoting himself wholly (as the factory newsletter wrote) to peaceful work in a technical archive; however, the look from his cold eyes, with their stony streak of green, contained a warning, and his movements were such that an observer couldn't help but think how much his sun-scalded arms, his lame leg, and his healthy leg weighed *separately*. Because of his frontline lameness, Alexei Afanasievich marched as if the left half of his body held an additional, ever-present burden that he had to carry wherever he went, tugging and adjusting the invisible straps more comfortably. Each subsequent step, taken as he leaned on his sturdy, far-reaching cane, depended not on topography but exclusively on the habit of his unhurried, twisted gait and the burden of himself (the burden of his heart, which thumped relentlessly on the left, under his shirt). Alexei Afanasievich lived without ever explaining anything to himself but rather as if remembering himself one part at a time—and because of this, everything he'd lived through stayed with him, as if the veteran's existence simply couldn't end because some part of his consciousness never dozed, reliably combining the present and the past, where he was always and forever alive. His *authenticity* seemed to guarantee his immortality, at the thought of which Nina Alexandrovna, being younger than her husband by exactly a quarter-century, felt a mute, superstitious question arise deep inside her and saw a clear picture arise of her own funeral, as if it were to take place the day after tomorrow—and how strange it would be for her, who slept on a cot beside her husband's tall bed, to suddenly find herself lying higher than Alexei Afanasievich, on the dining room table, in her dress and shoes, under a funeral sheet.

Fourteen years ago, Alexei Afanasievich's procession across the earth had been cut irrevocably shorter when, after dinner, as he was smoking on their cramped, curly blooming balcony, his intrepid cane staggered under his considerable weight and started to shake. He himself remained standing briefly, perfectly erect, as if weightless, before collapsing onto the empty cans and basins, filling the entire wrecked patch of balcony. Nina Alexandrovna ran out from the kitchen at the terrible glass tocsin but couldn't get onto the balcony because there was nowhere to step without stepping on Alexei Afanasievich, who had turned drastically white, like a belly half fallen out of a body, and she couldn't see his face, just a lock of hair, perfectly still in the air, that had poked straight up when the back of Alexei Afanasievich's head slipped, unconscious, down the balcony doorjamb. While the emergency crew was on its way and Nina Alexandrovna's daughter Marina and her son-in-law Seryozha Klimov—at the time only a fiancé who spent the night—came running from friends' and were able to tie towels together to drag the stuck body—which looked like it was trying to hug itself with its long outstretched arms—off the balcony, at least an hour and a half passed. Half of Alexei Afanasievich's face was pulled down and oddly smeared, as if someone had tried to crudely wipe off his plain, soldierly features. His bristling eyebrows, which had always looked like two roosters, had now shifted in opposite directions, and his left eye, half-covered with a weakened eyelid, shone weirdly, a strip of bloody white.

And so it remained, this *half* face, a mere profile of something human, no matter the angle. During periods of inexplicable improvement, which would come on suddenly, for no apparent reason, Alexei Afanasievich, pulling his lips back crookedly as if trying to chew on his creased cheek, occasionally emitted awful, long, viscous sounds reminiscent of the shouts of a drunkard gripped by indignation or a plaintive song. Sometimes his left arm would come to life, and he would drag it back and forth over the blanket and even hold objects, picking them up with a cautious, creeping movement, but the objects, turned oddly or all the way over, still couldn't fill the emptiness of his stiffened hand. This *overturnedness* of the things in Alexei Afanasievich's senseless hand expressed his loss of the verticals and horizontals of normal space. Once upon a time, Nina Alexandrovna, a petite woman with a girlish fluff of hair, had taken pride in her husband's heroic height, six foot three, but now that number, which had probably not changed, had no physical meaning. Nor did his clothing sizes (Nina Alexandrovna simply bought whatever was roomiest from the assortment flapping in the wind at the wholesale market). Alexei Afanasievich's lameness, which previously had elevated him even higher above the level crowd, had vanished: the absence of all the toes on his left foot except for the squeezed woody knot of a pinky toe looked like the damage to a statue for which the mind can so easily compensate. In the end, the paralyzed man's body, still authentic in its presence, which occasionally even suffered ordinary human illnesses (a cold, gastritis), had no spatial dimensions at all, just weight, beneath which the old trophy bed, which looked like an iron carriage, *would never clank again.* Unless Alexei Afanasievich was touched, weight, that invisible property of immobile objects, was merely his means of interacting with the Earth's equally abstract astronomical center. When Nina Alexandrovna turned his body, well-tended by a paralytic's measure and marked by old scars like the pale, flattened stalks you see under boulders, it felt like she was moving by a millimeter the entire *invisible* earthly mass—which had taken the veteran for a natural part of itself. This daily effort took such exertion that sometimes Nina Alexandrovna had to sit out the taut blackness that pumped into her head and made her feel how flimsy the skull's bindings creaking behind her ears really were. When she came to and found herself in the same place, though, she resumed her labors as if nothing had happened—with a light-mindedness that combined oddly with her short height and fine gray hairs, which you couldn't see, actually, in her airy, very fair hair, and which only made it shine all the harder under the invariant light of household electricity. She also continued to care for Alexei Afanasievich's former clothing: his brown boots, whose aged layer of shoe polish looked like chocolate, stood in the front hall beside her dusty shoes; his puffy gabardine suit, which looked like it had inflated due to idleness, hung in the closet with mothballs in each pocket—readied long since for its final burial mission, in which, however, the veteran's family both did not and did not want to believe.

■ □ ■

The fact was that the immobility permanently occupying the apartment's far, dusky corner was more potent and vibrant than all the rest of their walking and talking family life put together. In the new era that had suddenly overtaken them, the Kharitonov family, which had not been handed any party favors at capitalism's kiddie party, survived primarily on Alexei Afanasievich's veteran's pension. Heedless Nina Alexandrovna, who had spent her entire life in a quiet design office beside a nice clean window that was always decorated, like a scarf, with either frost patterns or fancy maple branches, had never worried about the future because for so many years each new day had been no different from the day before. Any small happiness, such as a length of stiff dyed Yugoslav wool or her coworkers' wedding—two engineers, no longer young, identical in height, who for many years had not admitted their relationship to anyone and had finally found their way to the Registry Office—would completely obscure the future's vagueness. Later, when all the air in the new life had become like it can be in a room where the windows are broken out and all the familiar faces have strangely drained into themselves, like water into worn sand, Nina Alexandrovna suddenly realized that now it was impossible, forbidden, and foolish to be happy for *someone else*. At that point her own joys suddenly seemed utterly insignificant, as if what she saw in her hand were cheap spangles, colorful rags, and crusted coins. As for actual money, using it took a special knack now. While inflating to incredible sums, it simultaneously deflated and melted away in her hands so that economizing made no sense. Nina Alexandrovna tried to lay in stores when she could. Once she bought a whole sack of incredibly cheap, coarse macaroni, which cracked woodenly in its paper bags and took an hour to cook, at which point the pot's contents became an inedible paste. There were other food purchases as well, sprinkled with the poppy seed of insect excrement and splotched with greenish mold. Once, Nina Alexandrovna had her wallet stolen from her right in the store, in the cramped lines that stretched like anchor chains around the clattering cash registers, but instead of horror she experienced the only true relief she'd felt in years.

She quickly ceased to understand altogether what it meant to earn money now. When she picked up her pension, she occasionally ran into people she'd known who everyone had once considered crafty and clever at getting along and who were now fussy men in big-assed Chinese down jackets and ladies with imploring eyes wearing balding Astrakhan fur and remnants of metal-intensive Soviet jewelry, crude rhombi of scarlet and cornflower blue stones that still sparkled. If these *practical* people hadn't been able to adapt to the new goods-and-money reality, which had the metabolism of a shrew and always seemed to have swallowed something greater than its own weight, then what could you expect of Nina Alexandrovna, who had always been too timid to understand how life actually worked? Basically, she had to rely on others, in exchange agreeing to do work that was the same day in and day out. Had she stayed on at the job to which pensioners who had greatly overstayed their time continued to cling, listlessly turning voracious pencil sharpener handles for entire days at a time, she could never have withstood the abrupt change in the frenzied bosses, the bickering over the rare paid orders, the quiet gambling with office shares, thanks to which the former director, who'd been fired for renting out space as a chemical storeroom, suddenly returned as the owner of all six now quiet floors of the building. As it turned out, Nina Alexandrovna had left at exactly the right moment and now could look after Alexei Afanasievich without asking her bosses for twenty extra minutes at lunch. She kept telling herself she wasn't lonely and her family needed her more now.

Her son-in-law, Seryozha, who one would think would become the modest family's breadwinner and head, hadn't been able to put his two incomplete degrees to any use, though, and worked as a guard at a parking lot one day out of three, always returning with the fresh, though no stronger than usual, smell of alcohol. This thirty-three-year-old, medium-tall, smooth-shaven, and already practically bald man looked strangely like an anatomical plaster cast, a kind of popular-science example of man in general. To his wife's caustic comments made every time her husband rashly set his small, elegant hands to housework, Seryozha responded with the placid smile of that anesthetized shade that one sees on models in anatomical atlases displaying their crimson interwoven musculature like Laocoonian snakes. On his days off, Seryozha preferred to quietly disappear, sometimes not showing up until dawn, cautiously fumbling with his keys and the loose-fitting locks. He would turn on the stealthy light in the front hall that penetrated the rooms around the corner, from time to time leaving under the mirror some money of unspecified origin, which Marina, before going to work, would disdainfully scoop into her wallet. A few years before, Seryozha had tried to go into business, threading wooden "talismen" that looked like wormy mushrooms onto leather cords and trying to sell them in the wet-leafed square in front of the city's only picture gallery, where they sold all kinds of rubbish—from pulpy landscapes in polished frames heavy enough to be called furniture to wire rings with teardrop stones complete with horoscopes. By way of encouraging this crafts business—not that she had much of a choice—Marina even wore a piece of jewelry her husband had given her for a while—a lacquered semblance of a quasi-human ear that rubbed rust-brown warts on her white synthetic sweater. Naturally, his trading—out of a dilapidated painter's case (borrowed from one of his distant acquaintances to serve as a counter and to create the right atmosphere)—came to naught. Now the leftover goods, wrapped in old newspaper that had dried out like birch bark, were lying under the bed—and the failed artisan had yet to demonstrate the slightest inclination for taking up anything else.

Of the entire family, only Marina had not given up. One day Nina Alexandrovna turned around and her plump blond teenager, whose face had always seemed to be smeared with berry juice, had become a shapely young woman swathed in a black, cheaply shiny, synthetic business suit. Marina had always been a top student in high school, university, and journalism school, but there was always something important missing from her top grades and her extensive journalistic articles, which always began, as she was taught, with some lurid detail—the way a clumsy draftsman, wishing to depict a standing figure, starts with the nose and eyebrows but then it comes out wrong and just doesn't fit on the page—but for many of Marina's fellow students who had no idea where to put their commas, their careers had yielded exceptional results. People who had copied off her during tests, devotedly breathing over her shoulder, now had jobs on newspapers generously patronized by the authorities and had even become dapper little bosses, whereas Marina, with her special "Red" diploma, toiled away freelance in the news department of a third-rate TV studio located in a bankrupted House of Fashion, where bolts of thick brown woolen cloth moldered away on wooden shelves in the storerooms and a pink mannequin with breasts like knees gathered dust. Marina put in a full workday, the same as staff—three or four stories plus editing—but they paid her only a fee, which came out less than what they paid the spiteful, muggy-eyed janitor who was constantly grumbling about all the cables on her floor. Marina tried to do a talk show interviewing local and visiting crazies on a generic orange set left over from some old kiddie show that was unclaimed due to the walls' radical color, which made the commentators' youthful faces look like scrambled eggs. All the set had were big plastic cubes interspersed with collapsing cardboard equipment boxes, half-liter cans filled with cigarette butts, and a shabby bracket off which square women's jackets hung, like pillows with sleeves. But Marina devised a way to use the wretched interior. During the broadcast, she and her guest kept reseating themselves from one cubic meter to the next (the camera dispassionately registered Marina rocking from side to side, freeing up her skirt), and goggling puppets would pop out from behind the other colored cubes and make comments, their mitten-like knit faces gasping for air. Unfortunately, this original project, which poor Marina, on the air *herself* at last, took pride in for a few weeks, didn't attract any advertising, and Studio A's director, a fat, angry young man by the name of Kukharsky, who had a beard like a wasp snarl (his uncle, whose name was Apofeozov, headed up a fairly powerful municipal department), gave Marina's show the ax.

That evening, Marina was a dreadful sight—especially to Nina Alexandrovna, who hadn't dared touched her daughter in a long time and didn't know what her hair—dyed so many times, now just bits of yellowish chaff remaining from what used to be chicken fluff—felt like now. Marina sat at the kitchen table in silence. Her eyes were coated with the same ghastly film as the untouched bowl of soup in front of her. She sat without moving a muscle, but there were changes brewing in her, and for a minute Nina Alexandrovna even thought that Marina's immobility had the same quality and was filled with the same mysterious, immured will as the immobility of Alexei Afanasievich, who lay three walls away with a clump of oatmeal in his mouth and an overturned baby doll in his twisted hand. Marina's husband Seryozha, evidently sensing something similar, silently stretched out from behind the crowded table, one part at a time, flashed past in the front hall, and threw on his raincoat, as if trying to cover himself from head to toe. Marina turned her large white face only slightly and blankly watched him go—and Nina Alexandrovna abruptly remembered seeing Marina and Seryozha as a solemn wedding couple, brand-new out of the box, as it were, and because of that immediately realized they were never going to have children.

At that moment, as she was not shy to explain at home, Marina joined battle for her place in the sun, a battle every self-respecting person ought to wage. Continuing to hold on at Studio A (by the skin of her teeth, clinging by just her long nails and steel-tapped stiletto heels), she recruited contributors and intrigued against young Kukharsky, whose removal required bringing down no less than Apofeozov himself—over whom billowing clouds of financial scandal were gathering with the change in the local weather. Mixed up in this was an investment fund that had soaked up every last drop of a multimillion ruble government loan, and a pair of other nephews loomed up, too, obscure figures of unproven kinship but very much alike, with ugly saucers for faces on which something resembling assembled features were drawn only in the middle, the rest being free space—and both had been caught stealing. The opposition press dragged in the nephews—whom they referred to as "businessmen"—for interviews one by one, but essentially nothing came of it. Clever fellows who repudiated each other nearly to the point of refusing to believe in each other's existence, they turned out to be like the two reels of a tape recorder with the tape running between them and broadcasting a recorded text. Apofeozov himself, a thoroughbred of a man, although rather dog-like in appearance, who had wrapped himself up in menace, suddenly became captivating and marvelous. Ornate shadows played on his broad face, a face made of some rich material, turning first to the left and then to the right; his double-breasted suits fit superbly, and his amber, slightly prominent eyes gazed out so penetratingly that TV viewers lost their sense of the materiality of the television and screen that separated them from the politician. While giving interviews exclusively to his own people, Apofeozov appeared on air so often that he saturated the air, which when he exhaled it became strangely itchy and astringent. Time and again, Apofeozov's invisible presence sent a noisy, gleaming wave out over the tree leaves, and even when there was no wind, it was as if some spirit were whirling up a tail of dust from the asphalt and solemnly kissing the dusty surface of an enervated pond as heavy as a velvet flag. Apofeozov's spirit hovered everywhere, as if he himself had died; love letters poorly disguised as political statements started filling his mailbox thick and fast, to the secret annoyance of his longstanding secretary, who looked like an aging Pinocchio and was totally sexless.

A worthy enemy was even found for Apofeozov: someone named Shishkov, a politician and PhD, long-legged and long-faced, like a chess king, who previously had raged at exams and thundered on perestroika discussion tribunes and who now owned a chain of pelmeni shops where he himself demonstratively ate the little dumplings, dabbing at his thin but vivid lips with a vast number of napkins taken from plastic cups. Ever the top student, Marina felt a spiritual kinship to this crafty and crazy professor who had bet an uncompromising experiment on his own ailing stomach—to say nothing of the fact that Shishkov had definitely promised his former student, if he won, the position of deputy director at Studio A with a nice percentage from advertising and a salary of six hundred adjusted rubles. By the most modest estimates, this promised money was more than twenty paralyzed Alexei Afanasieviches could bring the family. Marina (who didn't know that the studio's future director had already been readied in the provinces, a grim, unrecognized poet determined to redo everything according to his own lights) had something to fight for. All means were now good: at secret meetings over brown tea and soggy crackers, realistic compromising material was developed out of the raw material they'd gleaned, material that asserted, for example, that through his nephews Apofeozov personally had stolen more than seven hundred thousand American dollars (in reality it was three million three hundred, which no one knew for certain, even Apofeozov himself, who rather embarrassingly couldn't add a million four hundred and a million nine in his head). Using money from a friendly bank, they placed specific, conjecturally toned articles in the central press that were then rerun in local papers, which cited the authoritative source. Marina had a lot on her plate. Now she would come home in various cars that cautiously pulled up to the front door closer to twelve o'clock, and something truly reptilian appeared in her grin. She paid no attention at all to her husband, whether present or absent, while strangely, as Apofeozov's enemy, she became alluringly pretty. Even before this she'd been proud that her suit was two sizes smaller than the sweaty denim things she'd worn as a university student, but now she'd grown quite thin and she'd hung around her waist a wide black patent leather belt with a buckle that looked like the lock on a respectable firm's door. Now, when she passed through the studio halls on her scuffed stilettos, breathing shallowly through her inflamed, hastily lipsticked mouth, lots of men took a second look—and one time Shishkov himself, sitting one empty seat away at the secret conference table, ceremoniously pulled her over sideways and allowed himself one fatherly kiss that smelled of pelmeni.

Nina Alexandrovna looked at Marina through new eyes, too. This harassed woman she only half knew, who it had become almost impossible to touch physically, had become a kind of vision, a domestic apparition. They seemed to be showing her daughter on television but never allowing a visit, when she could quietly fix her daughter's unattractive black collar or just stroke her hand, which lay heavily on the oilcloth until her half-bent middle finger suddenly started jumping, like a key on a broken player piano, at which point Marina would make a fist and gather it firmly into her other hand— but the tic would skip to her face, where fine, sensitive threads took to dancing. "Mama, lay off," she would mutter through her teeth, even though Nina Alexandrovna hadn't said anything. She silently heaped up pan-fried patties made from sticky cheap ground meat and suddenly remembered, for instance, ten-year-old Marina flying in from the yard with her hair ribbon in a tangle and a black busted knee shouting from the doorway, "Mama, leave me alone!" Nina Alexandrovna very much disliked these new nerves and the artificial thinness and flaccid shadows, and she couldn't stop her imagination from convincingly ascribing a whole set of hidden illnesses to her daughter. But she didn't dare ask Marina to spend time on doctors, who in the heat of battle she could perceive only as new enemies. Meanwhile, Nina Alexandrovna's imagined ulcer became as much a reality for her as her husband the paralytic with whom she had to live. Occasionally at night, as she lay on her crooked cot, which smelled like old canvas, and listened to Alexei Afanasievich's body close by, above her, to his soft, bubbling snore, Nina Alexandrovna allowed herself to dream that everything might still work out and she might have a grandchild. Sometimes she heard odd noises coming from the next room, sounds Marina and Seryozha were obviously producing together. Nina Alexandrovna couldn't explain the nature of those sounds, which suggested nothing organic or bodily and definitely not human speech, just iron squealing, wooden creaking, a pencil cup clattering to the floor—as if the four-legged pieces of furniture were battling and butting each other in their owners' absence (although they were in fact there).

The heartrending emptiness, which pressed in and gnawed at itself, frightened Nina Alexandrovna so badly that she crossed herself under her blanket, clumsily planting her pinched fingers on her wrinkled brow. And in the morning the faces of her daughter and son-in-law were *different*, as if they'd never seen each other before. Leaning against the window, which was covered with rain, like bird poop, Marina gulped down her unsweetened kefir and ran off to work, leaving her cloudy, dripping glass on the cold windowsill. Only then, nicely steamed from his shower and blotchy red from the hot water, did Seryozha come into the kitchen wearing a clinging t-shirt—and Nina Alexandrovna, pushing toward him the plate of turnovers Marina had totally ignored, thought that the only reason her son-in-law hadn't become a real drinker was that for some reason his exemplary, never-ailing organism wouldn't let him. Separated from the world by an insuperable physiological sobriety, her son-in-law apparently kept running into a transparent wall and was quite incapable of breaking his habit of drinking the same weak beer and ironing his own worn-out synthetic shirts so that they smelled like scorched loneliness. Sometimes, attentive Nina Alexandrovna noticed her son-in-law trying to take an interest in his surroundings: he would run his eyes over the lines of the fat books opened in front of him at a right angle that seemed to be leaning into the corner of some separate room, or tune in the transistor radio, which sounded like it had a cold, and force himself to listen to what was happening on every elusive station he caught through the thick of the static. Every so often, Nina Alexandrovna thought that her son-in-law was making a conscious effort, tensing his gaze, and was on the verge of having a good talk with Marina, and her heart would melt sweetly, as if a declaration of love were in the works. But the moment would pass, the spark would go out, and Marina herself would invariably spoil the occasion, bestowing a sarcastic grin on her husband or demonstratively starting to wash dishes so that the abruptly turned-on water would bubble up and spill into the sink along with the grease and food scraps. In those moments, Nina Alexandrovna's son-in-law's mirror eyes seemed to see everything twice as big as it was; she had also noticed for some time that Seryozha had acquired the habit of shrugging his shoulders even when no one was talking to him.

■ □ ■

It had been Marina's idea. Keep Alexei Afanasievich from finding out about the changes in the outside world. Keep him in the same sunny yet frozen time when the unexpected stroke had cut him down. "Mama, his heart!" Marina had pleaded, having grasped instantly that, no matter how burdensome this recumbent body might be, it consumed far less than it contributed. Initially, clear-eyed Marina may have been moved by more than primitive practicality. There had been a period of infatuation between her and her stepfather, when the little girl would crawl all over Alexei Afanasievich, who seemed as big as a tree to her. She would go through all his pockets and invariably find chocolates planted there for her. Alexei Afanasievich taught her how to fish and how to toss plywood rings on a post. Once the two of them had cleaned out every last gaudy toy with the digger claw on a Czech grab-n-go. All that lasted about a year. For a while, the dragonfly pond out back of their brand-new nine-story apartment building had sucked on their two red-and-white fishing floats as if they were pacifiers; by the next summer, the pond had turned into a swamp plastered poison green with plants—and now there were stalls on the spot. Marina couldn't forget this entirely, at least not until that rather bizarre moment when, a month after Brezhnev's television death, she hung a medal-strewn, beetle-browed portrait of that official paragon on the wall.

In retrospect, Nina Alexandrovna could only wonder at young Marina's perspicacity. You'd think she had nothing on her mind beyond Seryozha and her synopses. Yet, at the first historic tremor, she had divined in the decrepit general secretary's replacement by a younger, more energetic one not a pledge of Soviet life's continuity but the beginning of the end. She immediately began preserving the substance of the era for future use and purging it of any new admixtures, no matter how harmless they seemed at first. So it came to pass that their good old Horizon television—on which only impressionistic bursts of static were still in color—showed the farewell to that great figure of the modern day (the richly beflowered tomb, wreaths made to look like medals, the craned neck and half-face of a watchful man lined up to view the body)—and then went stone dead. Marina temporarily forbade anyone to buy another, but she did take out a subscription to *Pravda*. No one could say for certain whether Alexei Afanasievich could read now. He had always carefully worked his way through the newspapers, holding his place with a school ruler, as if measuring the quantity of information by the millimeter, but now he looked at the newspaper page that Nina Alexandrovna held at half-mast without moving his eyes at all. It might as well have been a bedsheet she'd picked up to mend. Nina Alexandrovna was charged with reading the paralyzed man specific articles, which Marina made fat deletions in and supplied with hand-written insertions. Nina Alexandrovna carried out these instructions, although she was embarrassed by both the articles and her own voice. She had to tilt the newspaper very slightly to find the end of Marina's almost indecipherable sentence—and sensed vaguely that Alexei Afanasievich's immured brain, with its dark bruise from the stroke, was sending her staticky, buzzing bleeps in reply. Every once in a while she imagined (she couldn't bring herself to verify this) that if she just leaned closer to this desiccated head with the crookedly stretched mask where his face used to be she would be able to talk to Alexei Afanasievich without using any words at all.

Very quickly, *outside* time became so altered that there wasn't even anything in *Pravda* for Marina's pen to rework. By the time they started knocking out windows in the stuffy Soviet rooms (overnight, the still relatively young and full-cheeked Apofeozov went from being first secretary of the Party district committee to being a democratic leader who had publicly torn up his Party card), *inside* time had come to a standstill, and this was the time maintained in Alexei Afanasievich's room, which had a faint smell all its own that lacked an objective source, like the acrid trace of a burned match. Everything in the room manifested a tendency to stand still, to doze off in an uncomfortable position. Nina Alexandrovna would catch this special quality of autonomous time, at the boundary between wakefulness and sleep, when suddenly she *merged* with her surroundings and felt nothing but her own weight—which was bliss, but spoke to Nina Alexandrovna of her weariness even more than an attack of hypertension could. In the afternoons she noted how good it felt to hold the weight of most objects in the room.

Something suggested to Nina Alexandrovna that this stopped time knew no essential difference between order and disorder. She couldn't help but see that things in the room would accumulate and then shed their ordinary meaning. This loss of meaning was especially obvious while she was cleaning. Nina Alexandrovna battled resolutely against the thick and amazingly even dust that eagerly settled on a wet spot where tea had spilled, quickly becoming a fuzzy patch. She was endlessly wiping and feeling everything like a blind woman, whether she needed to or not. Privately, Evgenia Markovna, the doctor who came to check on the patient, must have wondered at the sterile chaos maintained around the sick man. The china figurines on the sideboard looked like products of Nina Alexandrovna's housecleaning, shiny knickknacks sculpted by hand and rag. Here, too, were crowded empty prescription bottles that should have been tossed long ago, also freshly wiped and clear right down to the medicinal tear at the bottom. The glassed-over Brezhnev portrait, which the doctor never examined but always turned to look at as she left the room, also bore the rag's traces: a violet rainbow from cheap window cleaner. Each time as she finished with the portrait, Nina Alexandrovna would cautiously lower her bared leg with the swollen tendons to the floor and climb down from the wobbly chair in two moves, and Alexei Afanasievich would shut his big right and small left eye in approval, as if he were seeing precisely what he thought he should see.

Klimov the skeptic, who had opposed the entire scheme (at the time he hadn't yet lost all his rights and had tearfully defended himself against his mother-in-law's slightest digs), remarked more than once that if they wanted to retain the *atmosphere* of the seventies, then they should hang a portrait of Vysotsky, but Marina, guided by instinct, ignored her husband's advice. There was something false, of course, alien, even, about this *particular* portrait of Brezhnev. As Seryozha, who was busy with his then wildly lucrative (despite the sewer smells) video store at the train station, said, "It's a prop right out of a Hollywood movie about Soviet life." Yet this encapsulated time, which had survived its own violent demise in this one individual room, obviously possessed properties no one had ever observed in its natural state.

These properties had something to do with immortality. The general secretary's rejuvenated photo—half documentary print and half retouched and clearly made during his lifetime—was striking for that very *quasi-drawnness* you see only in a dead person's features. So precise was this impression that, when she realized exactly what the impotent fold of Brezhnev's mouth and the sepulchral tidiness of the hatched-in hair reminded her of, Nina Alexandrovna began wiping the portrait with anxious deference and avoided turning it over and seeing the half-erased inventory number on the back. But what was amazing was this: the general secretary, whose death had here been reversed and whose longevity had become a natural feature that only kept increasing, had somehow borrowed an *authenticity* from Alexei Afanasievich that Brezhnev himself had never possessed. If Brezhnev had been a cardboard figure in whose name books were written and on whom mutually exclusive medals had been hung, like a game of tic-tac-toe, then now there was no reason to question his existence, if only because the general secretary could no longer die—even if he were to admit his desire to do so. Also a veteran of the Great Patriotic War, he was now, in *outside* time, not dead but missing in action. Having effectively distanced himself from those veterans with schoolboy faces ruined by drink who shuffled along behind their new Communist leaders and continued to live in the present day, he had attached himself and even begun to bear a certain iconic resemblance to Alexei Afanasievich, who had never belonged to the Party. Anyone entering the room (though in fact they let in almost no outsiders) could see the paralyzed man's forehead, as worn as a coin, and the two needly, low-hanging eyebrows—and see the same thing on the cheap wallpaper covered with teacup flowers. Even Nina Alexandrovna somehow succumbed to the reassuring illusion that Brezhnev in his official portrait was not the former head of the Soviet state at all but simply a distant relative.

Naturally, as the project's author, Marina had to decide whether this spectral time had any need of events. She had outlawed the principal natural event (death), thus rendering any event related to it (illness, injury, leadership changes, and so forth) impossible— and any attempt to add to this list made even the decisive (she had decided so much!) Marina uneasy. One got the feeling that the list permeated life so deeply that it might eventually include anything, even something no one had ever connected with death—as if, at the slightest attempt to pull out the plant, the roots would suddenly pull hard sideways and down and lift a little, like a seine loaded with every kind of dirt that ever comes under men's feet. One way or another, Marina prohibited anything that might arouse negative emotions (in this sense, *her* stagnation had achieved perfection). She cut short any attempts by Nina Alexandrovna to inform the patient of anything personal—about an apartment in the next entryway being robbed, for instance, or Alexei Afanasievich's nephew poisoning himself with rotgut vodka. "Mama, the money!" Marina would exclaim in an anguished voice, obviously referring to Alexei Afanasievich's heart but at the same time clutching at her own, the plump heart beating in her chest. "Daughter, dear, does it hurt?" "Mama, leave me alone!" Upon receiving this familiar rebuff, Nina Alexandrovna felt on her left side, under her ribs, a subtle ache, which she experienced as a heaviness in her fingertips. Aware that, with the consolidation of *inside* time, any illness of hers had simply become impossible, though, she took all this back with her to the kitchen. She now pictured Alexei Afanasievich's heart—which had to be safeguarded as the family's principal treasure—as a large crimson tuber for which his paralyzed body had become something like a vegetable bed entwined with engorged blue roots.

■ □ ■

It was strange to think that that heart had ever loved her. Had it really? Nina Alexandrovna had been beautiful once. Hers was a regular, rather insipid beauty so devoid of any color that the eye had nothing to latch onto. Her oval face, constituted in the refined, old-fashioned manner of penmanship lessons, simply could not withstand that inner darkness where an ordinary person might store and reproduce visual images—and so was not preserved in the memory even of people who knew her quite well; you could feel no emotion for her in her absence. There was probably some secret connection here to her fear of simple physical darkness, a fear Nina Alexandrovna had never been able to overcome. As a result, no one had ever really seen her high, virtually satin-stitched eyebrows, or the sweet outline of her lips, which were always chapped, like slices of apple left out on a saucer—but Nina Alexandrovna's figure was quite ordinary, and her appearance on the street demanded no effort of attention whatsoever from passersby. No one had ever once tried to meet her, or asked for her phone number, even when she had purposely taken evening strolls through the Park of Culture, where the benches overflowed like seats on public transportation and tiny lights ran conscientiously down the garlands decorating the central paths, like ants down their trails. She had lived, unremarked, with sickly little Marina, who had been stricken with every ailment known to man, in the workers dormitory where she, the accidental mother, was always being yelled at by the superintendent's wife, Kaleria Pavlovna, a large woman with a tiny mouth. One soft winter's night, Kolya Filimonov, her neighbor down the hall, threw himself out his window and lay swelling up from the snow for several hours, in the shadows, resembling nothing so much as a parachutist's bulging cupola, now deflated. A marriage proposal from an elderly, childless widower, who immediately gave her a light beige blouse in crinkly flat Syrian packaging, was an absolute lifesaver for

Nina Alexandrovna; on her wedding day, she and her things were thrown out of the dorm.

So had that happened or not? Alexei Afanasievich had never permitted any romantic nonsense (which he called *literature*) between himself and his young wife. His rare kisses, mainly in public, on holidays, had been as dry as a toothbrush. Alexei Afanasievich had strict rules about not touching Nina Alexandrovna at all during the day, as she scurried about her household chores, as if touching her would implicate him in women's work. If he did take her by the arm at an evening gathering at the institute, say, then he held his gabardine elbow out, thereby denoting and maintaining the distance between himself and his spouse, which left her to mince along, her stubby, polish-dotted fingers resting on his undemonstrative woolen sleeve. Even at night, looming over his wife at an angle, nearly crosswise, as if he were a plane dive-bombing someone fleeing a routed echelon, Alexei Afanasievich made no attempt to talk to her and would not let her make a sound. Nina Alexandrovna had only to moan ever so softly and he would immediately cover her mouth and half her face with his salty, leathery palm. Nina Alexandrovna's swollen lips retained that salt long after, making all her food seem tasteless and insipid, as if she were eating something still alive.

On the other hand, he never brawled and never drank, the way other veterans did whose memories of the war had become symbols. Unlike them, Alexei Afanasievich kept it all in his mind, fully preserved, link upon link (the inevitable elements of secrecy in reconnaissance work had probably given this chain its special strength). On Victory Day, the former scout tossed back a single shot poured to the brim—without spilling a drop—and took his family, all dressed up for the occasion, to enjoy the fireworks. Loudspeakers everywhere blared verses about the immortality of great deeds. Brass bands blew hot marching music that sent sparks flying. And little Marina, all excited, her summer sandals flapping, raced ahead and scrambled up everything in her path, including railings and lampposts, raising hot bumps on her silly furrowed brow. When at last the dull, friable salvo rang out and sparkling bouquets were set off above the oohing crowd, leaving a faint burning ember in the pale sky, a laughing Nina Alexandrovna knew moments of utter feminine happiness alongside her hero, who in honor of the holiday had his arm around her plump little shoulder. At those fireworks she felt happier than the real heroines of May 9th, the sprightly aunties with their white curls and gold teeth shuffling along to the jangle of medals and the yapping of squeeze-boxes held chest high. "They don't make people like that anymore," murmured Alexei Afanasievich, as he greeted yet another frontline woman, who planted a pursed carnation of red lipstick on his well-scraped cheeks. Nina Alexandrovna, standing modestly back, thought that someday she would prove to her husband her full value, her feminine selflessness, maybe even her valor—but now the years had flown by and he had had a stroke.

The Kharitonovs never really got the hang of love. Now the traces of her former beauty had become more noticeable than the beauty itself had ever been; the years seemed to have applied a crude layer of stage makeup to Nina Alexandrovna's face and neck. At times, Nina Alexandrovna thought that her paralyzed husband not only didn't love her but simply didn't realize that she was she. Maybe this was because Nina Alexandrovna was often embarrassed to talk to him; it felt like talking to herself or, even worse, a cat or a dog. Given the limitations imposed by her daughter, any sentence had to be fully composed in her mind before it could be spoken; sometimes

Nina Alexandrovna would start out smartly and gaily, right at the door, but then she would forget a word, instantly forget everything else, blush, and get mixed up, exactly as if she'd been caught out in a lie—and as a result fewer and fewer words remained. Relief came only when she did something *physical* with the patient: fed him his cereal and strained soup, having wrapped an old sheet around him (on which half his dinner would be left in curdled patches), like at the barber's; or scraped off his stubborn, salty, fish-scaly stubble (once she dreamed of Alexei Afanasievich in a salt-and-pepper beard that sucked up his eyes and cheeks, and she awoke in tears). The harder the job, the more natural it felt. If during these ablutions Alexei Afanasievich's body, which had accumulated a shapeless layer of fat on its sides, was especially hard to turn over, Nina Alexandrovna would shout smartly at the sick man, as if she were a stranger—a nurse or an aide.

Evidently, nothing from outside time could serve as an event for inside time anymore; communication between the two times had ceased. Inside had its own daily routine, which was defined by task: feeding and shaving him, plumping his pillow, slipping a bedpan under his bursts of defecation, wiping his body down with rubbing alcohol-soaked cotton balls that quickly hardened, covering him with a blanket for modesty's sake. The fact that Alexei Afanasievich's body was also laboring (when it swallowed, its throat expanded more powerfully than any athlete's muscle) created the illusion of a shared life that even had a kind of temporal goal. These *daily* events weren't enough, though. Inside time demanded a broader scope as well, and even Nina Alexandrovna sensed that every scene played out between her and the paralyzed body required context for plausibility.

As a result, something arose that could be likened to the pseudo-metabolism in a feeding vampire's organism. After she decided to invent pseudo-events (honorably shedding her own blood first), Marina one day announced—ostensibly to her mother, who was sitting near the sick man—that she was applying for membership in the Communist Party. During this open-ended period of candidacy, Marina, who had learned a thing or two over the years, acquired a cheap Korean television (which within twenty-four hours was white with dust, as if it had been draped with a cloth) plus the most basic VCR, which they concealed from the paralyzed man under a stack of desiccated newspapers. At the TV station, making use of the archives and the not altogether selfless help of secret allies discontent with Kukharsky's internal policies, Marina edited the "evening news" for the sick man. The monotonous pictures consisted of collective applause, the kind of long shots of state workers that smudge not only hands but faces, a row of tall, smoke-belching, grated-window factory workshops, and summit-meeting kisses where the general secretary's profile subsumes his partner's oncoming profile, the way a processing machine subsumes its material. Soon Marina had teamed up with computer whiz Kostik (who fell in love with Brezhnev and asserted that using a program he had found on the Internet and downloaded illegally he could factor the general secretary's voice into its female and male components), and they got so good at it that they were able to create the Twenty-Eighth and Twenty-Ninth Congresses of the Soviet Communist Party for the paralyzed man. Serving as material, in part, were black-and-white Duma sessions, which they spliced in (there was something artificial about Chernomyrdin, who flashed across the screen a few times and bore a distant resemblance to Brezhnev), but the general secretary himself delivered a speech many hours long, as if doing so were the most natural thing in the world, efficiently setting the text out in two stacks. Marina nearly believed she was actually hearing every word of the speech being delivered by the two-voice chorus. Meanwhile, the text suggested that there had been an increase in international tension, and the deputies in the audience listened meekly, like troops seated rather than standing in straight lines.

No one could say for certain whether their playacting was fooling the sick man, of course. Nina Alexandrovna, at least, thought she picked up a certain agreement, a semblance of approval in the signals emitted by his asymmetrical brain. Of course, Alexei Afanasievich had always not so much liked as considered it proper that his innumerous family wait on him hand and foot, so he may simply have been pleased with their efforts and the theatricalized fuss occasioned by his illness. The pseudo-events, those spectral parasites, began to take increasing hold over the Kharitonovs, though, and feed on them. It was like a change in focus that reveals at least two landscapes in one. Nina Alexandrovna sometimes took fright at the distinct sensation that Brezhnev's funeral had indeed been a deception, a film someone had spliced together, that the years were still divided into five-year plans and the country, with all its heavy industry, was continuing to build communism in the heavens above—where it was already half ready, its façades glittering. She did get out of the house, of course, and her own glutted eyes did observe the changes: the colorful litter on the street from imported wrappings, which her dream book said meant riches; the abundance in the shop windows of all kinds of meat—from mosaic slivers of pork to candy-pink Finnish sausage— which meant an advantageous marriage; the abundance of private commerce in all kinds of little things, including amazingly cheap Chinese pearls as white as rice, a strand of which Nina Alexandrovna dreamed of from time to time with hopeless emotion—but which the dream book said meant copious and bitter tears. The fact that she had seen all this in her waking hours only intensified the prophetic qualities of the objects that snuck into her field of vision. One day, on her way to the nearby market, Nina Alexandrovna suddenly saw, instead of the elegant minimart, the old grocery's empty window (a bare bubble routed by competitors the day before yesterday), and on its skewed doors a fresh flyer for a candidate for deputy, a stern comrade with the handsome face of a Saint Bernard, a manager by the looks of him, with a perfect rectangle of biographical text beneath. This remarkably resurrected scene—the fat, sluggish cleaning woman at the back of the store, the black-and-white flyer, the sticky spot and curved glass from a broken vodka bottle on the front steps, which smelled like grapes in the autumn air—suddenly overwhelmed Nina Alexandrovna with such undeniable reality and the reliability of simple things that at the actual market, which seemed like a mirage with empty waving sleeves and buzzing flies, she obliviously paid whatever they asked and returned home to her angry daughter with her purse flat empty.

■ □ ■

In addition to the lady doctor, Evgenia Markovna, who maintained her neutrality and, if she did mutter something under her breath, then it was strictly to herself, there was one other person in the outside world—an extremely dangerous person—who had to be allowed to see the paralyzed man. This was the benefits office representative who brought his pension. Unlike the lady doctor, she was awaited by Marina with nervous impatience. She was the first thing Marina asked about when she came home from work, and if the pension was held up for a few days, Marina's passionate desire to catch sight from the balcony of the familiar, barrel-shaped figure on tiny feet mincing through the front door brought to mind an intimate love such as Marina had not felt for anyone in the family since everything had ended between her and Seryozha. The benefits rep—whom Marina, in revenge for the conflicting emotions the woman elicited in her, had dubbed Klumba, which means "Flowerbed," because she always wore flowery prints—had become essential to the family, her face dear to the point of automaticity. This massive lady, whose white collar opened like two notebook pages on her chest, seemed to play a critical *personal* role in the Kharitonovs' fate.

At the same time, Klumba's penetration to a place where a *different* time murmured, as if from a loudspeaker and the nasal and erratic clock, inflicted palpable losses on that time, which her visits diluted somehow. Each time, Klumba demanded to "look at grandpa" before handing out the money—she said because these days lots of people were cunning, and in her personal practice there was an instance when a family took money for a dead man for four months. Shaking out her onion-skin-colored curls at the front hall mirror, she walked importantly, following Nina Alexandrovna's gesture of invitation, to the far room, where she stood in the doorway perfectly still for a minute—after which she returned with a raspberry flush on her porous cheeks and, still not looking up, counted out the bills, letting the money fall into separate piles: a pathetic one for Nina Alexandrovna, and a substantial one for the veteran. "I don't know how you can live in this smell," she said in the end, as she stuffed her work papers into her large, messy bag.

Naturally, there was no smell, nor could there have been. Nina Alexandrovna scrubbed Alexei Afanasievich's bedpan better than her cooking pots, and his laundered sheets, which were always hung out on the balcony, may have had tiger stripes from old urine, but those stripes had no more smell than the printed roses that decorated the benefits rep's crimplene dress. Evidently, though, it really did smell here as far as Klumba was concerned: her inflamed nose found the smell of a room sprayed before her arrival with harsh streams of flowery air freshener highly suspicious. Apparently, she feared getting too close to illness and misfortune and had to overcome this fear dozens of times a day, heroically maintaining the crude mosaic of her *work* face and tapping out her feminine assault with her heels. "My work is nothing but germs," she said angrily, seeing a sticky spot on Nina Alexandrovna's gleaming kitchen. In reality, the spot was just a pretext for a fight. On the most carefully cleaned surface, Klumba saw pathogenic microorganisms, whose mere existence—which was, in contrast to the little green men alcoholics see, a scientifically proven fact whose objectivity could not be denied—was quietly driving the woman out of her mind. Nina Alexandrovna frequently noticed the benefits rep stealthily lick her manicured index finger and peck at imagined crumbs. The paralyzed man's room, where sunlit dust lay on things rendering them both fit for writing with your finger and also oddly empty, like blank pieces of paper, must have seemed to Klumba like a graphic image of the world as she imagined it. More than once after Klumba left, Nina Alexandrovna would uncover stealth commas left by her visitor's finger in secluded places. Something in this pensioner's home bothered Klumba, something that had to do with her basic frustration at the everyday, which was why, having just hurried Nina Alexandrovna to sign off, since she still had eighteen more addresses today, she suddenly got stuck halfway into her raincoat and made up for her dismay with loud tirades that she tried to pass off as perfect models of good sense. This went on until the humpbacked old woman from the apartment upstairs, who had been "waiting on her pensun" since six that morning, took the two flights of stairs, measuring the height of each stair with her cane, and started ringing the bell, reminding them there, inside, of a photographer and his camera, both covered with a black cloth and aiming a radiant look at the expressionless object to be photographed.

Klumba may have viewed her contact with people as an exchange of microbes, and in this sense microbial life was for her a phenomenon more spiritual than medical—what is otherwise called "fluids" or "aura"—only Klumba, a down-to-earth person with a higher education, did not recognize mystical words. Looking at her conventional little mouth, drawn like a cock's comb (while the old neighbor lady, wielding the pen like a crochet hook, fished up the lost thread of her signature that she'd started, and straightening her scarf with a motion like a kitten washing itself, deposited the money in her purse), Nina Alexandrovna thought that for Klumba, a kiss was probably unsanitary and consequently immoral. In her own way, meanwhile, the benefits rep was not devoid of human emotions. She understood Klumba a little when, beset by monetary worries, Nina Alexandrovna forgot her boiling kettle, which was rattling quietly on the flooded burner, and Klumba grabbed it, boiled dry, with her bare hand. Desperately trying to shake *her* heavy hand cool, Klumba shouted at Nina Alexandrovna so loudly that the rubber burn that instantly covered her retracted palm felt unbearably icy.

Klumba's sympathy mechanism must have worked differently from most people's. Another person's pain completely bypassed her soul (which, although it was carried from place to place by this well-balanced, firm-stepping body, was, one had to suppose, a rather small and underdeveloped structure, crowded out by a ponderous liver nearly the size of a saddle) and acted on Klumba *physiologically*, that is, immediately dropped from the other person's ailing organ into her healthy one. Although scarcely capable of imagining another person's loneliness or the agony of unrequited love, Klumba served as the ideal mirror for the sufferings of the flesh and in this respect was defenseless. As she visited disabled and half-destroyed old people in the course of her job, Klumba bore their ailments like fluorescent marks and went on and on about her wards, who inhabited the musty burrows of their disability, as about biting microbes inside a large anthill. At the same time, evidently, Klumba was utterly pitiless. In her faceted eyes set exactly a centimeter apart one read such impatience that the neighbor lady, fumbling along the wall and accidentally turning the light on in the bathroom, preferred to get out before Nina Alexandrovna could get free and drag her upstairs, like a broken bicycle. Sometimes Nina Alexandrovna got the impression that Klumba went from apartment to apartment visiting the old and destitute with the secret goal of destroying this little world, like a parasite infiltrating the city's healthy organism, as if her *knowledge* of a disabled person robbed him of his individual existence. Klumba seemed to be fighting unwholesome human wreckage, attaching it to herself and fostering its dependence on her own heroic persona— and by no means just financial dependence. The regime seemed to have robbed pensioners of certain important human characteristics.

As a rule, Klumba arrived morose and cleared out even more so: her black bag clattered its bottom metal and her nose burned like a lump of coal. But if the benefits rep was in a good mood for any reason, the danger for the *next* time multiplied. For some reason, raised spirits in her always found expression in loud, abusive tirades against the authorities, which neither respected nor pitied unfortunate old people in the least, forcing them to starve on their miserable crumbs. This heat was stoked by the fact that Klumba was, as a woman and a citizen, a supporter of Valery Petrovich Apofeozov. When she saw his figure at the center of things, the intertwining of national and local branches of authority created an unexpected drawing rich in imagined profiles and—like in magazine picture puzzles—hidden pirates, so much so that the enthusiastic Klumba really did have something to talk about. For her, Valery Apofeozov was not merely a goal but also a means for hating everyone else, especially Muscovites: his existence seemed to give Klumba many additional rights. The voice of a visitor, younger than her by ten or fifteen years, compelled her to rattle and clatter teacups in the kitchen; indeed, the voice itself rattled, borne off toward the sick man's room on pointy red kitten heels. Breaking off in the middle of a word and convinced that "grandpa" was watching (Alexei Afanasievich's gaze became perfectly intelligent), Klumba continued without commas from where she'd left off—after which, leaving the door flung open, she could be heard throughout the apartment for a good fifteen minutes. Nina Alexandrovna could only hope that the paralyzed man would take the berated politicians for superintendents or repairmen who had become characters in that humor magazine *Crocodile*.

■ □ ■

No one knew what season it was in the sick man's room. In outside time, as has been mentioned, it was autumn. Nina Alexandrovna's shoes had worn thin and now soaked through in the lightest rain,

turning her wet mesh stockings purple. In the evenings she sometimes noticed the same kinds of stains, only black, on her daughter's feet when she wearily pulled off her wet Italian boots, which
had softened to a semblance of stewed prunes—though they'd
been bought quite recently. A cold wind had come up very early, in
the first few days of September, and started rinsing the earth; the
grass, not yellow as yet, became pickle-juice green, and street ven-
dors covered their goods with moisture-dotted clear plastic. The
feet of mother and daughter were defenseless against the inclement weather. No matter which pair of shoes, even their winter boots,
deep *barefoot* imprints formed inside. The September pension was
marked by the purchase of shared (primarily for Marina, of course)
light boots. Waiting for Klumba's appearance on the twentieth, Nina
Alexandrovna sensed a lethargy, a minty numbing, a fist under her
left shoulder blade that steadily turned her toward uneasy thoughts
about her daughter's illnesses.

Klumba showed up looking very businesslike, her makeup damp
as if it had been affixed to her focused face with spit, and wearing a
soggy wool suit that smelled of sheep. Having glanced as usual into
the pale washed room with the paralyzed man in the bluish bed and
then returned to the kitchen with her list at the ready, she noticed
in passing that "for some reason the grandpa in the bed had a rope."
After counting out the long-awaited money and seeing out her visitor, who spent a long time tucking her smashed curls into her sack-
deep velour beret, Nina Alexandrovna hurried to the bedroom,
overcome by a strange unease. Nothing special: just the belt from
her green robe, which had become a rag long ago. Evidently it had
been lying around somewhere and landed on Alexei Afanasievich's
blanket, dragged in by something during housecleaning. Before,

too, Nina Alexandrovna had had occasion to leave various things in the paralyzed man's bed—to say nothing of the fact that Alexei Afanasievich always had a few of his toys there with him: a couple of small dolls and a stuffed rabbit. Nina Alexandrovna had learned long ago, by trial and error, that most ordinary objects were too small or too flat for her husband's hand and required some dexterity. If he was to pick them up with his mitten-hand, they had to be mainly china figurines: the German beauties and shepherdesses with little flowerlike faces he'd brought back as trophies. Alexei Afanasievich dropped one of them, and it broke into four pieces, and the head, its little cheeks gleaming, rolled under the chair. For some reason, it upset Nina Alexandrovna that when her husband stretched an empty hand out of its imprisonment, a hand that was like a prosthesis compared with his entire dormant body, he could master not real things but just likenesses, the little substitute figures the outside world derisively slipped him, avoiding contact. She took the hint, though. She replaced the china with plastic dolls that Alexei Afanasievich raked up, like a cannibal, and dragged under the blanket headfirst until the smiling little person slipped from his awkward, weakened grasp. Also good were toy rubber whistles that sometimes, in his claw, emitted a raspy, half-stifled squeak, announcing the paralyzed man's ultimate victory over the inaccessible matter that surrounded him. Today Nina Alexandrovna had planned to buy Alexei Afanasievich something new and as amusing and sweet as possible: the little Chinese dinosaur with the apronlike flannel belly she'd seen the month before in the little girls' department at Children's World. Tucking in the sick man's blanket (his left hand, placed on top, traced out something like a welcoming gesture, although his brain was clouded), Nina Alexandrovna quickly gathered her things, took a little money, slipped her feet into her now dry, round-toed shoes, and left.

Meanwhile, the sun had peeked out, and the puddles on the wet blue asphalt were like cleanly washed windows. Next to the underground passage, old grannies were selling their last oily-soft brown cap boletus mushrooms bruised from fingers and pine needles, sturdy little white-bellied cucumbers, and cheap, stiff asters that smelled like a pharmacy. A fair-haired, bent-over bicyclist rode by all shiny, sending his wheels rippling through the little puddles, and the sun spilled all over him, including his spokes and whooshing glass windshield. Hurrying, stepping on her buckling soles as if she were pressing on unresponsive pedals, Nina Alexandrovna headed to Children's World, outside of which, to her bitter joy, there were always several strollers filled with bouncing babies all asleep. This time, next to the polished porch, there was only one stroller, covered in brown checked fabric like a rolling suitcase—and exactly the same stroller, only empty and lined in oilcloth, was displayed in the window, under rattles hung on invisible silks, as if it were a Garden of Eden filled with colorful plastic birds and fruits. Unable to resist the temptation to peek, Nina Alexandrovna stealthily leaned over the baby's eyebrowless face, as soft as clabbered milk, where its little closed eyes were like flat wrinkles—at which point a squat young mama in gilt eyeglasses ran down the front steps, kicking at and scaring away her own purchases. Nina Alexandrovna stepped back and apologized, and the mama, without saying a word, tilted the stroller back on its wheels, turned it and let it bang down, and wound off decisively through water and fallen leaves.

Upset, Nina Alexandrovna quietly entered the store. The little girls' department was partitioned off by a rope strung with crude pieces of paper: scribbled on one in large faint purple marker letters was "Inventory." In the little boys' department, school uniforms in the same official navy blue as work records hung single file. There was also a gentlemanly little white jacket hanging separately at the unthinkable price of fourteen hundred rubles, and the toys were represented by silvery tanks with rasping working motors, a large array of cold steel and firearms, and some robot soldiers with matching plastic weapons as miniature as Christmas tree lights in individual square boxes. Nina Alexandrovna was horrified as usual by the ever-present thought that she might suddenly lose her mind and bring Alexei Afanasievich a toy tank or submachine gun, or one of the blunt little armored cars possibly made from repurposed real armor and painted authentic army green.

Right at that moment she began feeling unwell, uneasy, again. She must have been examining the windbreakers on the hangers too closely because a young saleswoman, a professional smile on her large, inkily painted lips, hurried toward her. All of a sudden, though, Nina Alexandrovna decided that anyone who got close to her now would tell her some bad, depressing news. Hastily pushing past the checkout lines, she found herself back on the mirror-shiny front steps. Strangers were passing on all sides, their collision seemingly precisely calculated for where Nina Alexandrovna was cautiously descending the stairs. The people were in so much of a hurry and weaving in and out, sideways, holding their purses close, sometimes slamming into each other and their coat hems sticking together for a second—yet no one looked anyone else in the eye, and their faces, once they'd flashed by, disappeared faster than the dark leaves that teemed in each gust of wind. Nina Alexandrovna thought that it had been a long time since she'd seen so many people at once—or at least a long time since she'd been aware that hundreds of people were flashing by, and suddenly she realized that despite the specificity of each person who appeared before her—a specificity that was utterly unattainable when she was sitting in her apartment—she perceived them all perfectly in the abstract. It didn't take even hundreds or a dozen for strangers to become an abstraction. All it took was two. As long as those two were just coming closer in the crowd, you could make out a curly head of hair, or a black knit hood, or a finlike rubber elbow, but the instant these two coincided, to say nothing of spoke, her mind erased them.

Still holding onto the railing, Nina Alexandrovna was struck by the fact that lately the city's population seemed to have increased dramatically. There were so many people, automobiles, and rocking buses with advertisements on their sides stratifying the transportation stream. All this poured and meandered through the streets like the green-mica cast from half-stripped trees. She didn't know why she didn't read the papers or watch the *real* news at all. Everything Nina Alexandrovna saw around her was lacking *film* or being shown on television. Without that, her surroundings felt inauthentic. They lost their status as the primary reality and seemed like a film in which Nina Alexandrovna felt uncomfortable, as if she were in front of a TV camera, and she moved as if she were constantly trying to encircle or circumvent something.

With a shaky step that demonstrated to one and all her failure to coincide with reality, Nina Alexandrovna headed toward the market to buy food. In the glass sarcophagus at the front of a furniture showroom, a gingerbreadish armchair revolved very slowly, its tempting armrests making it look like something someone would want to take on its arm, like a lady; two young men efficiently overseeing the sidewalk were presenting passersby with announcements of some kind, and the one who blocked Nina Alexandrovna's way was wearing tiny, pincerlike rings in his ears and in one large fleshy nostril. There had been none of this before—nor was there any in the life Nina Alexandrovna continued to lead within her own four walls. Here, in the outside world, she was surrounded on all sides by new objects that no book of dream interpretations could have explained—and she shuddered to think what kind of events would have to occur in ordinary human life to justify the presence in her dream of this armchair, grandly unoccupied under cold, bright-white clouds, or these long buses trailing their low tail sections, like half-paralyzed animals trailing their hind legs, or the *computers* being sold everywhere whose electronic entrails seemed to be glowing and swimming on their screens, like an X-ray. Before, no one could have imagined so many things going unbought; their four- and five-figure prices seemed to make them dangerous to have in circulation, like a gun kept dangerously at home. This was the first time Nina Alexandrovna had felt so depressed outside. On the other hand, since she knew nothing about her surroundings, it was all relatively simple. The main thing was knowing her way. Beyond that, she could ignore the colorful façade.

From a distance, the market entrance was denoted by a pair of sparkly tall poplars. Their leaves, nearly invisible in the sun-filled air, looked like splotches on a mirror's detached amalgam. At the sight of a familiar beggar with his one empty eye socket that looked like a navel and his bedraggled squeeze-box gasping greedily for air, Nina Alexandrovna felt a little better. Not far away, directly behind the market's latticework fence, angry music pounded out from a newsstand, rendering the beggar's squeeze-box as mute as a fish gill.

Only very close, almost flush to it, could its vague growlings be heard—but Nina Alexandrovna still tossed a soundless new ruble into the cap that lay at the beggar's feet like a black lozenge. The narrow aisles, drunk on sun and juices, were messy, as always; the sticky puddles had a muddy, visceral liquid at the very bottom, and their spots attracted the ferocious flies that buzzed everywhere and, when they stuck to your face, turned out to be unexpectedly cold, almost metallic. But for Nina Alexandrovna, everything here was familiar, and the fact that she had already heard the music coming from the market stalls many times at other markets added to her self-confidence. In no hurry, Nina Alexandrovna bought vegetables for soup, a little fresh sausage, freshly cut, a can of meat and a can of sardines, a firm onion in crackling gold, and a bloody-silver bream as big as a shovel painstakingly selected from the several offered her. Unlike the street chimeras, all these objects were at least related to humans because of their edibility; something told Nina Alexandrovna that she needed to limit herself to things like that. Nonetheless, she did stop by the Chinese fur and plastic toy stand. There, the deft salesman, whose high cheekbones reminded her of a Russian kettle, happened to be demonstrating some simple fun to some kids in filthy jeans: he would squeeze a rubber pear, which inflated a shiny spider through a long tube and made the spider—a stiff patty with dangling dead legs—hop clumsily. Imagining how much Alexei Afanasievich would like controlling something at a distance, Nina Alexandrovna immediately bought the spider, wound the tube around it, and stowed it neatly in her bag. By now she was almost totally calm, and even the scary spider, which when wound around looked like a medical device, a tonometer or stethoscope, evoked confidence in her. She told herself that she simply was finally developing the habit of paying more attention to her surroundings. As if to confirm that, she immediately noticed on a metal pole of the green market gates the portrait of a respectable man who looked like a good dog—the same portrait she'd seen on the doors of the vacant food store. The pole's roundness magnified the portrait, like a loupe, making the candidate's face look like it was constantly approaching the voter. Nina Alexandrovna smiled involuntarily in response to his wide-stretched smile.

Continuing past goods stalls with thinning sales (the beggar leaned over his squeeze-box, held tight in his lap, and took bites from a crumbling potato and a pickle), Nina Alexandrovna noticed two of those portraits pasted up in a row, like stamps, on a steel booth, together increasing the object's cost, even if it couldn't be mailed to anyone. All at once it became crystal clear that she'd already seen the dog-man flyer: in the underground passage, at the Children's World register, and on her own building's front door, which looked like a broken-down washtub and where the flyer efficiently covered the biggest dent and so in and of itself didn't immediately catch her eye—and lots of other places, too. The thought that the director's good face, pasted to many objects whose purpose was beyond Nina Alexandrovna, nonetheless made this puzzling thing ordinary and simple enough, and Nina Alexandrovna felt a grateful warmth. She even felt comfortable enough to allow herself to perch at one of the plastic tables on the street, where a puddle of spilled coffee was being sucked up by the wind, place her order with the androgynous teenager who rushed over, and be served a plate with an American sandwich so big she couldn't get her mouth around it. Disassembling the sandwich into its soggy, reciprocally stained components and glancing at the people running in different directions, which the stormily flying leaves signaled in vain with bursts of light, Nina Alexandrovna felt she could relate to it all perfectly calmly. On her way home, the director-man's face flashed by and drew her along, like the moon in a dense forest, until it brought the pacified Nina Alexandrovna to her front door, where it finally smiled with just its glossy eyes over some new, crookedly pasted-up paper loudly announcing a major recruitment of paid canvassers at such and such an address.

■ □ ■

Marina's day had become so overloaded that she couldn't steal even a minute to call home and find out whether Klumba had brought the money. Sitting in campaign headquarters—in a dank half basement with splotched boards in the corner that had been rented for a song—she was registering in a soggy notebook the many many citizens who had shown up in response to the announcements that all of Shishkov's personal staff had spent the past week pasting up throughout his voting district. District 18—where primaries for the regional Duma were being held (the previous deputy, a financially Russified man from the Caucasus, had been shot in the brand-new box of his suburban home, where his blood had looked like cocoa in the construction dust)—did not have much going for it. It was a sloping, bloated area, the cheek of the large Southwest District, and stretched from downtown to the industrial swamps, where the horizon seemed to be rotting away from fumes and the earth's fabric seemed holey, rolled into feathery hurds: a ball-bearing factory and the nine-story gray Khrushchev-era apartment buildings attached to it, whose numbering would drive any normal person insane; building after building after building; two private-sector streets poorly connected by falling fences, with dingy little scarlet flowers in age-warped cottage windows and dahlia beds like graves in scraggly front gardens; a narrow, polluted stream in banks slick even in winter, under the snow, the stream wet with dark soaked spots that ate through the light flakes, and come autumn, empty, as if it had been turned off, without a single shape on the black water; a small section of a good block where, however, the unavoidable difference between the new prosperity on the street and the poverty of the apartments hidden from view had reached the point of metaphysical incongruity; and, finally, the main attraction, the Palace of Political Education, one of those concrete and glass giants amid the paved rectangles of windy squares for which there are absolutely no words but that reign over an area, occasionally attracting chains of tiny human figures to some second-rate pop concert. Since eight-thirty in the morning, district residents, smelling of wet wool and their own kitchens, had crowded in front of Marina's wobbly table. They handed her their life-bedraggled passports and leaned over the notebook to use the official pen to add their chicken-scratch signature next to their passport information. After that, the recruited person was given a folded piece of paper, "Canvasser's Instructions," inside of which a fifty-ruble note was pleasantly and firmly stapled; then he was presented with another, tidier notebook, where opposite his freshly entered name the sum of 120 rubles was entered: this was the bonus the canvasser would get after the election victory of the Salvation bloc's candidate, Fyodor Ignatovich Krugal.

Marina's present situation was nothing to be envied. She'd been fired from Studio A, after all. Some five-year contract Marina had managed to forget about had ended, and now young Kukharsky had remembered and ultimately did not deny himself the pleasure of calling Marina into his office and, sprawled out in his upholstered leather armchair, his lemon-yellow tie falling to his navel, and with a caramel behind his hairy cheek, telling her off in no uncertain terms. While Marina was shrinking in front of Kukharsky, her colleagues managed to clear out her modestly inhabited, utterly innocent desk, put her belongings in sticky black trash bags, and set them outside the door. She had no choice but to go home, lugging a thin bag split by sharp corners in each hand; downstairs, the guard demanded she show him the contents and discovered an *unwashed* Studio A mug, so she had to call upstairs and sort that out. For some reason, the pain and fear were exactly like the time when she and her Mama were driven out of the dormitory. The superintendent's beautiful wife, working her hands like a doctor *palpating* a belly, checked their opened suitcase. Her Mama had been beautiful, too, with long curls and wearing a new blouse with candy buttons—but now she couldn't go run down the dark, sweetly scary corridor whose linoleum had a watery wave from a distant window. That she had experienced all this before made it harder rather than easier for Marina. She felt somehow Kukharsky had seen in her that awkward creature who asked everyone for presents (the present *box* contained buttons, stamps, colored chalk, a wrapper folded like a candy that Marina considered a prettily made toy and was very afraid of crushing), that dorm starveling she had been—wearing a dress made from foot-binding flannel—before she learned to despise her own childhood and be a top student.

Now Marina depended utterly on Professor Shishkov. Shishkov had spared a whole twenty minutes on personal sympathy for Marina, had patted her in a fatherly way, dabbing at her welling eyes with his impeccable handkerchief and giving her little shoulder a penetrating squeeze. *Important* work had been found for her that marked the final stage before she became deputy director and justice triumphed. The felonious Apofeozov, who needed deputy immunity so as not to be brought up on a number of charges, had plunged into the elections when they cropped up—and the professor, rejecting perfect symmetry at this stage of the struggle (in general, he shunned the symmetrical, seeing in it a dangerous duplication of things and equality of sides), ran against Apofeozov not himself but a loyal man with the full approval of the interested banks. Mr. Krugal, the director of that very same Palace of Political Education—whose architecture resembled a ball-bearing factory in the Communist future, thereby attracting the working electorate's heart—was a man with a failed past either as an actor or a TV newscaster. At the same time, he was so ignorant that this rare quality of his, which somehow permeated his entire staff, came across even in the posters and advertisements hung on the Palace in numbers no fewer than the bedsheets on neighborhood apartment balconies. Everything Krugal had to say, including "Hello, dear comrades!" had to be written down, so there was much work to be done. As the new speechwriter, Marina was warned that any text presented a number of natural obstacles for the candidate—line breaks, for instance. She also had to avoid more than two epithets in a row and the word "reconstruction," which the candidate couldn't say due to an old dislocation of his jaw. As he issued his final instructions, the professor looked so deeply into Marina's soul that, as if for the first time, she herself saw his frozen eyes behind which it was like white fish flesh with fine bones, and she saw his disagreeable nose shaped like a pike's head. For the first time the thought that today Professor Shishkov was the person closest to her in the world made her uneasy.

The concept of "responsibility" simply moved Marina to selfless labor. After just a few days she felt comfortable with Mr. Krugal, a short man with a big head, a squeezed, pseudo-Roman profile that fell lower on his face than normal, and an exceptionally tensed forehead that looked like it was being stretched and that came out in black-and-white photos as a splotch. A magisterial and even massive person in his flyers, Fyodor Ignatovich in life made the impression of being a reduced copy of himself. Krugal had been chronically at odds with Marina's predecessor, who had been exceptionally touchy with regard to Russian language and style and therefore exceptionally thin-skinned; and the moment anyone felt Krugal had insulted them, Krugal took offense, too. But now, inexplicably, the candidate had picked up his dismissed consultant's faultfinding and was latching onto all kinds of niggling details in the prepared texts. Crossing his legs and twisting in one direction, munching cookie after cookie and twisting in another, and squinting at pages in a third, he would analyze and reanalyze sentences that seemed dubious to him until they lost any spatial or semantic meaning; a thing as simple as bringing natural gas into private homes—which because of the tanks, among other mundane reasons, often burned to charred kebabs— seemed to Fyodor Ignatovich filled with danger and ambiguity, and the fateful word "reconstruction," which had ended up in his speech after all and become attached to something he was going to have to promise, made the candidate wince and cautiously wiggle his off-center jaw, which clicked smoothly behind his ears. The web of fine pencil marks Krugal conscientiously spun around Marina's paragraphs flummoxed her until she realized she could just erase them. All this notwithstanding, she was doing well, according to the fatherly professor. Unlike Krugal, Shishkov, who signed off on the texts, made sure to praise Marina at every staff meeting. Imagine her surprise when she unwittingly discovered they were paying her approximately half as much as the most unimportant person in the campaign headquarters, young Lyudochka, who was forever giving herself manicures and admiring her ten mirrorlike nails, occasionally removing a stuck-on hair from her precious work of art. Actually, the imbalance could be explained away by the fact that Marina was the last hire, paid some remainder salary. Moreover, unconsciously she felt that the less she got in the present, the more she was building up for the future: now her salary of fourteen thousand seemed as inevitable as a top exam grade following a sleepless night.

Meanwhile, victory in the elections was far from a fait accompli. Apofeozov's headquarters, pumped full of money like fully inflated biceps, was working wonders. Apofeozov was truly omnipresent. Five of his videos were playing continuously on every TV channel, deftly interspersing the candidate with a popular Moscow politician of similar political coloration, so that the voter really did start thinking that Apofeozov and the Muscovite—whose doughy bald spot and charming smile made him a carbon copy of everyone's favorite yellow spherical cartoon creature Kolobok—were in fact like peas in a pod. No matter what paper you picked up, it was plastered with a portrait of Apofeozov, like a hundred-ruble bill; there was an unprecedented concentration of Apofeozov in the air, which trembled feverishly with dingily green, immature falling leaves. At times, Marina (who for more than a month had been playing old news for her stepfather, news which due to the repetitions had acquired the hypnotic power of a commercial) began imagining that Apofeozov, having become the form and essence of the *present moment*, the embodiment of the realest reality, was the opposite of the *immortal* little world she was defending. Apofeozov's chief opponent in the true elections (of which the District 18 elections were a by-product, a crude material form concocted of haphazardly printed flyers and ballot urns wrapped, like coffins, in cheap red cotton cloth) was, of course, not Krugal but Leonid Ilich Brezhnev. Continuing (in Marina's news) to fly abroad and welcome delegations—entire festivals of Hindus made white by their clothes and Negroes of various tribes with open miners' faces and buttery Asians in knee-length military tunics—Brezhnev undoubtedly lived on in the collective consciousness of District 18 voters, who were still wearing their Soviet-era coats. Not that they'd admit it, but they continued to carry around this image, worn to holes here and there, but made to measure for them and still connecting them to the wide world more reliably than nutritious Snickers bars and American Terminator movies. However, in his fantastic vitality (which was nothing more than the indomitable will to eat, drink, build a suburban home that resembled the ogre's castle in the fairytale, and open secret accounts in Switzerland), Apofeozov had become an increasing temptation for voting women, who suddenly entered a second youth with the help of margarine lipstick and cheap hair dye, though the gray roots showed straight through under even a dim 10 watts. Intense specimens who had obviously come to believe, along with Apofeozov, in the miracle-working characteristics of nourishing creams and rejuvenating serums were already noticeable on the streets under his wardship and becoming more and more numerous. Marina was worried that their sudden thirst for life would go haywire and bring Apofeozov a decisive voting advantage.

Krugal worried about the exact same thing. His artistic soul keenly sensed voters' unfavorable disposition. Nervous and capricious now, one day he raised quite a stink with his impresario, during which Shishkov's secretary, fearfully cracking the door open, the way one lifts the lid on a boiling pot, thought she saw a flying jacket through the crack—after which Krugal stepped out in that same, messily hitched up jacket, holding handfuls of torn paper and with unshed tears, like in a child's sad little eyes. After the row, the now sterner Shishkov let him go first, like a woman, and stealthily swallowed a few crimson pills from a plastic tube. The problem truly demanded resolution. Not only staff workers, depressed by the hostile pressure and aplomb, but also ordinary citizens existing between their mailbox and a television stuffed with campaign goods, couldn't help but realize that the Salvation bloc's enterprise was a beggar compared with Apofeozov's aggressive show. Thus, the dictate of common sense notwithstanding, Shishkov's personality came through: for the professor, stinginess took the place of that lost poverty which Shishkov felt deep down was the foundation of Russian spirituality. At the same time, he couldn't help but see that in the near future a cruel loss awaited Krugal, who had insinuated himself into a battle between forces he didn't understand, forces perhaps even mystical.

■ □ ■

The professor had hit on a new and surefire campaign move, though. For quite a while an elementary arithmetic thought had given him no rest, that the two thousand-plus votes he needed for victory (half of a 25 percent turnout plus one vote from the Unknown Soldier), would cost, based on the average price of a bottle of vodka, one-third of what it cost to purchase newspaper space, produce flyers, and rent auditoriums, where the entreated voters would consist of a few vagrants, whose wild hair and short stature made them look like alcoholic goblins, and a dozen or so old women bored out of their minds. But the election commission did not permit simply pulling up with vodka in secluded apartment courtyards, where at any time, day or night, you'd find people of all ages hanging out—not that there were any guarantees that someone who took a full half-liter today would vote for Krugal tomorrow. Theoretically, votes couldn't be bought at all, inasmuch as electoral law forbade candidates from rendering services to the population by whose will they could come to power—although in practical terms, of course, mutually beneficial processes went on sub-rosa. Every so often young men wearing windbreakers and caps in specific company colors appeared in the irrational spaces of District 18 glassed in by the rather murky sun, like flies on windows, and passed out groceries in the name of the philanthropic Fund A; moreover, a couple of times near garages, observers saw modest vans that said "Bread" on the side from which bottles wrapped in election flyers, like napkins, were quickly lowered into workers' poster-flat hands thrust out of their sleeves nearly to the elbow.

All this illegal, small-potatoes fuss, this waste of money, which the district sucked up like a gigantic brown sponge, actually made Professor Shishkov physically ill. His keen intellect, which knew how to use even symmetry alien to him *exactly the wrong way around*, yielded an idea as sudden as a win at roulette (at which, working his hunches, the professor seemed always to lose, drawing down intellectual resources incomparable to the rare luck of a scientific find— which comprised his private creative drama). *Instead of rendering services to the population, he should buy and pay for their services:* then it would be perfectly legal to call the corrupt voter—who basically just wanted a drink—a canvasser. Then and there, the professor sketched it out on his torn napkin (he was having dinner at his plastic cafeteria, and once he'd finished his soggy salad, he started on his sticky-ish signature dish): if each hired canvasser simply brought the adult members of his own family to the ballot box, then all it would take for an absolutely assured victory was laying out fifty thousand, at most, and, if he wanted to increase turnout, eighty thousand, before the elections. The bonus for success, should Krugal get elected, could be paid out piecemeal afterward; the scheme's elegance was that the bonus, while serving as a guarantee of the canvassers' work, simultaneously relieved Shishkov of the lion's share of the investment risk.

Leaving lumpy pelmeni covered with dollops of sour cream, like subsided soap foam, on his plate, the professor immediately dialed his secretary's mobile and called a staff meeting. A few hours later, all the wheels headquarters had, from Krugal's spit-and-polish BMW to the professor's puny heap, had been brought out by the deathly pale staff, which had been alerted and were plunging into the long, sediment-filled gullies. What a night it was! A fine drizzle, a chill, the street lamps' bright gloom, sour mouths that had the metallic taste of sandwiches and tooth decay, snatches of hard, seasickly dozing while the car taxied to its assigned objective, letting rare bright spots through its windows. Equipped with cans of paste and stuck-together stacks of announcements warm from the printer, people reluctantly climbed out into the darkness, stepped on the damp asphalt's wet, mercurial ripple, and headed out under sagging umbrellas, two by two, to post their pieces of paper on every single swollen front entrance and push them into the scorched and crumpled mailboxes, which had accumulated the kind of mess around them that trash cans do, what with the elections' imminence. That strategic night, the professor sat in his dank headquarters sleepless and thoroughly chilled. His nose, which he honked into a fluttering handkerchief, was as full-blooded as his heart, and on a piece of paper in front of him lay a few pills whose sequence apparently held the program for solving this crisis, a mysterious code known only to the professor.

As usual, Marina was assigned the most important area: the private sector. There was something inexpressively awful in those windblown backyards, where the darkness touched her face, lifted her extended arm, and led her into a deep, rustling hole. The gray spots from streetlamps, which illuminated everything under it as if through the thick bottom of a glass bottle, only got tangled underfoot. Low-slung calico windows hung directly over the flowerbeds, and rather than pick out objects, the meager light seemed to produce unconvincing copies of them. Marina and sleepy Lyudochka, whom the feverish professor had foisted on her, often couldn't tell where they were pasting the announcements, which kept trying to roll up and lick their frozen hands with smeared paste. The desertedness and silence (only dogs barking and jumping behind a slab of timber, creating the impression of a nighttime zoo) doused Marina with a bad presentiment—and indeed: from one of the lightly banging gates there suddenly emerged, drunkenly thrusting a bluish knife in front of him, a shapeless man wearing a long, unbuttoned leather coat and some kind of crazy hat with earflaps that looked like work gloves sculpted directly on his head. Lyudochka flapped her arms, as if to catch the wagging blade like a fly, screamed, and ran. So did Marina.

They could barely remember racing from the receding obscenities to their car, which was hidden behind a rise. Their umbrellas kept banging into each other and skipping in the air like inflated balls, and the stack of announcements Marina was now holding to her side rather than close to her chest kept trying to slip apart and float away. Their dingy white heap, tucked in under a large cloud-shaped birch, was closed and dark. Glacial. The driver and his girl-friend from bookkeeping probably hadn't come back yet from the other end of the lane, where a solitary light blinked and teared, as if viewed through the wrong end of binoculars. Lyudochka, her makeup smeared, was hysterical. Hiccupping, she tugged at the rick-ety door and then picked up her coat hem and tried to sit right on the filthy hood. Marina was barely able to drag her partner to the nearest damp stall, crooked and black against the light birch leaves. She felt no regret making a seat of the announcements and poured a full lid of harshly and crudely fragrant brandy from the reserve flask the professor had given her. "I hate him. I hate him!" the trembling Lyudochka whispered after sipping from the threaded vessel, as if she were downing a raw egg, and Marina guessed that this wasn't about the guy with the knife or even the driver doing who knew what with the plump-cheeked bookkeeper but about the professor himself. Looking sideways at Lyudochka (eyes like stars, a smear under her nose), Marina thought maybe she would take her on as her secretary. Once more she thought without any surprise that in fact she wasn't interested in Lyudochka, nor was she, for example, in the girl she didn't know with the crudely knit face and the fantastic braid that fell well past her waist, generously adorned, like a horse's tail, with cheap barrettes, who had been making out with Klimov a week ago at the wet streetcar stop—while Marina sat above them at a streetcar window. They'd been making out below, not even hid-den by the limp umbrella dripping down the girl's back—and appar-ently hadn't bothered to hide, as if there were no such person as

Marina. An unfamiliar ring burned on the man's ring finger like a glassy rash—not an engagement ring, not a man's ring at all, a ring that obviously meant something in their relationship and that obviously was kept in one of his moldering, trash-filled pockets. Marina, languishing in secret impatience to run home, was trying incredibly hard not to lose her compulsory enthusiasm. Her husband, from whom not a peep had been heard for seven days, might have shown up to spend the night—but there was no way she could abandon this effort, even though home, which was also in this district, was a stone's throw away and seemed even closer through this pure rural darkness. She could even make out the small thumbtack of the satellite dish on the roof of the nine-story building next to hers.

"I hate everyone I see," the bleary Lyudochka stated, more calmly now but also more convincingly, and to Marina her turned face, oddly eaten away by the profound darkness, looked like an ear. Her partner's abrupt lunge when she went to screw on the lid—as if trying to look at her watch, which was on her other arm—made it clear that Lyudochka was drunk; shining a little light on her own watch, which kept rolling away from the streetlamp like a doll's eye, Marina could only make out the minute hand, which caught the light, and realized she had no hope of seeing her husband today so that she could officially kick him out. At last, she heard leaf-kicking on the small rise: the bookkeeper descended first, huddling and yawning, and the driver, sliding down pigeon-toed, hurried behind her, grinning and toting a crumpled newspaper full of a pungent mass of mini-apples picked with their withered leaves still attached. The couple had no paste or flyers at all; in response to Lyudochka's tragic tale of the guy with the knife they magnanimously shared a tight fistful of stolen fruit with each of the victims. It was utterly absurd;

you could only pretend that this was purposeful work. Taking a bite of the withered wilding, which had hardened like batting, Marina decided that the only way she could go back and get the others back to reality was to write up the bookkeeper and driver objectively.

■ □ ■

The day after that expedition, their sacrifices appeared to have been in vain. The announcements, white everywhere, having suddenly flown out like clouds of moths to live for a day, had yielded no result whatsoever. But as evening came on, pandemonium ensued. Once they'd sorted out the hundred "instructions," the population came to believe, as they did in God, that the Krugal campaign was handing out free money. In the back room at headquarters, where a low lamp lit only the hands on the wide, fabric-covered table, making it look like a gambling den, additional packs of bills were opened; sluggish Lyudochka took a long time placing her ruler and grasping a pencil in her sharp manicure in order to draw lines in a new record book. Quite a few unexpected problems had arisen. Having clarified that there were now definite restrictions, people lined up to be canvassers by the family-load, which substantially reduced the efficacy of the planned investments. Marina personally attempted to refuse a culti-vated married couple with panicked eyes behind whose back in ad-dition languished a puffy offspring of the male persuasion squeezed into a jacket with a great many zippers and fasteners who obviously had ID. They amicably agreed that only the head of the family would register—and he wouldn't stop apologizing while Marina was pro-cessing his decrepit ID, which was as flat as a flyswatter. As it later turned out, though, his patient spouse, who quietly disappeared two steps away from Marina's table, registered herself and her child with another registrar—and there were similar instances every day.

The women over forty who had obviously fallen under Apofeozov's spell but who had come to his opponent for their fifty rubles made a strange impression. Slightly embarrassed but as presentable as generals in their pink and cream greatcoats of cheap cashmere, they hurriedly wagged their pen in the notebook, as if effacing their own signature, and immediately detached the banknote from the instruction, holding the latter at arm's length and haughtily surveying the office in search of a trash can. The chipped steps leading to the headquarters were blanketed with these instructions, like paper snow. The wind dragged these same flyers—fresh and bumpy from the large raindrops, with smeared footprints that looked as if they'd been licked—into the narrow wells of half-basement windows, where they jammed the shaggily rusted window grills along with freckled birch leaves and hung like humid clusters on moist, wadded spiderwebs.

Now representatives of the district, of all its sloping streets and muddy layers, passed before the headquarters workers every day, and it was strange to think that the announcement's text, like a spell, had brought this entire misbegotten population to life, drawn them out of hiding, that the voter, ordinarily invisible and anonymous (and therefore by implication mysterious even for the out-and-out PR types calculating their conduct with astronomical precision), now, before voting for a candidate, appeared in person, showed himself to the campaign headquarters life-size. Meanwhile, the guy in the wrinkled full-length leather coat smeared with pale, dried mud showed up. That morning, he'd found the tempting flyer, as uneven as a zebra's stripes, on his rise by the fence and just didn't connect this sudden gift from Father Frost with the previous night's incident—not that he was likely to remember any of that anyway. He turned out not to be so scary, after all, just unkempt and nervous. His forehead was twisted by some tragic worry, his teary little eyes shone like pearls in a mollusk's flesh, and he was constantly crumpling and straightening the cozily shabby mohair scarf at his throat. In the light of day, it was hard to imagine this unkempt intellectual knifing anyone, especially since his muffled voice, punctuated by a soft, breathy cough, was so pleasant. After introducing himself as a "well-known artist," he roamed a little among the tables, delicately glancing at the papers being drawn up. Then he ran off for a couple of hours and, with someone's vague permission, hauled in several pictures wrapped in Apofeozov campaign newsletters. Marina didn't care for his masterpieces. The things they depicted were disagreeably damp and shapeless compared with their authentic originals; they pressed up against each other with a density characteristic of organs lying in a living creature's opened interstices. The contrast between a work that has obviously spent its every square centimeter on elaboration and the paltry prices on the pictures was so provocative that many immediately reached for their purses. Lyudochka, for example, bought the small square of a pinkish painting in a board frame: the abundantly daubed canvas depicted some unbelievable liver, the mother-of-pearl swellings of which were quite unlikely to be identified as a tea service and table lamp.

As for Marina, she was among the few who didn't succumb to the cheap goods. She'd been keeping especially careful track of her wallet for a while. She knew for a fact how much was there and in which denominations, and how much was left at home, in the cheap box decorated with broken shells made to look like plaster nostrils that was well hidden under her old, gray-worn slips. Somehow the accuracy of this reckoning (which gave Marina a quiet high and with that high a vacillating pain) was linked to the fact that Marina was on her own. Without Klimov, who had brought some in and spent some without asking, creating total indeterminacy and leakage, Marina could now control her budget wholly and entirely. Previously, her chaotic husband, carried away by the notion of future profits, might, for instance, buy a can of terribly expensive Finnish varnish (two-thirds of which, unused and haphazardly closed, later dried into hard, solid pieces) to finish his wooden creations. With Klimov around, to do something to protect what was hers, Marina had set money aside for a rainy day: sometimes the pockets of her old clothing, where you could still find stiffened pre-reform small denominations, were stuffed with money, and her winter coat, adorned with a crumbly, half-disintegrated fox, was occasionally as rich as Gobseck. Now, locked into her own expenditures and calculations, Marina kept her cash in one monitored place; taking and spending any sum out of that had become significantly harder.

Marina may have been economizing for a future life of freedom, or for some consoling purchase; but more likely, for the first time she had conceived a vague doubt that she really would occupy the deputy directorship at the newly won TV studio. She couldn't say where the ill wind was blowing from. Krugal, now perked up, was more welcoming than ever and at the sight of Marina good-naturedly wiggled his face (thus suddenly resembling an oven mitt)—and Professor Shishkov, no matter how bothered he was by the unplanned increase in the estimate, always found a second or two, in passing, to place his cold, narrow palm on the back of his protégé's head. Marina must have pictured all too often her future prosperity and lived for this too much—and of course, that couldn't happen without Klimov, without his shadowy presence. Now that Marina had realized (or harshly convinced herself) that there wasn't going to be any more Klimov, whatever she'd imagined immediately lost its plausibility.

Most agonizing of all was the fact that her cheating husband hadn't vanished altogether. Marina, up to her ears in hiring canvassers (while she also had to prepare for the TV debates, at which Apofeozov, according to rumors, might appear with some killer "Program of National Salvation" and Fyodor Ignatovich Krugal was set on appearing in a tuxedo), still hadn't been able to catch her husband at home and take away his keys. Meanwhile, the traces of his daytime appearances were getting odder and odder. For sure, he caught up on his sleep during the day—as attested by the messy bed and carelessly tossed blanket, which looked more like he'd been walking than sleeping on it; turning back the blanket, Marina failed to find any traces of his round, well-worn retreat such as her husband used to make for himself in bed every night. There was something she couldn't put her finger on, as if Klimov had flattened out. His things, which Marina kept a stealthy eye on, with a hunter's fixed gaze, would float away to wherever he spent his mysterious overnights and then return worn and shapeless, as if in that time they'd been worn by a dozen different and not very fastidious men. One time she discovered some laundry in the bathroom: stuck-together underwear hung on the line like a heavy pile of cooked noodles; a steamy, crudely knit sweater that dripped cloudy drops from the bottom like minute aquatic creatures was still warm to the touch; and the box of detergent stashed behind the basin was sodden.

It was simply astonishing the way her husband managed to avoid seemingly unavoidable encounters. One time, as she wearily climbed the front stairs, Marina distinctly heard Seryozha's oncoming steps, characteristically muffled, which, the moment they were discovered, hung suspended. Then the steps rushed up the staircase, four times lighter, as if someone had softly struck a dangerous matchbox all set to ignite from a hissing spark. It would have been easy for Marina to go up the next six flights of stairs and drive the fugitive headfirst to the attic hatch, which was closed by a lock that always hung there, but when she finally reached her own apartment, above her, right over her head, there was suddenly such a vacuum of silence that it seemed crazy to Marina to drag herself up there with her heavy bags, survey the perfectly bare landings, and herself stand alone in front of the myopic, battened-down, nighttime apartments. Once Marina thought she saw him in the bushes . . . though actually, the man, who dashed from the lit entrance to the twiggy, shadow-stirring darkness (although there was something very Seryozha-like in the conceal- ing elbow thrown over his head), may have been your garden-variety vagrant collecting bottles. Anxious to get past the curtain of lilac that tumbled from the lawn and took up half the asphalt as quickly as she could, Marina could sense the man behind the branches, as if he were something arboreal akin to that person in the wallpaper design you imagine in the tedious gloom between sleep and wakefulness— when the chimeras that steal the sleeper's reality become visible and produce a slow horror; she even sensed seeing the vague shadow, clutching a bubble of some bulky clothing to his chest, unbutton his trousers with uncoordinating hands.

Much more frightened by her husband's cheating than she could afford to be during the campaign craziness, Marina had evi- dently developed a fear of men. Subconsciously, she now saw them as degenerate creatures hiding in the dark and dirt to threaten her with an attack or some kind of *impact* that would turn her soul into a chemistry experiment heating various caustic substances in her chest. Maybe the man on the lawn and the painter with the curved knife, although real people, were equally the fruit of Marina's fear, a fear that had conjured them up out of nowhere, without any justification for their existence. Actually, this had already happened—a long time ago, in her dormitory. Marina remembered how at first she hadn't been afraid of anything and had gone into every unlocked room, even where they were drinking vodka, stupidly clinking their stupid glasses and pulling her onto their laps, which felt as uncomfortable as a grown-up's bicycle. Later she suddenly started being afraid, especially of her Uncle Kolya Filimonov, who would walk around and sit, grabbing himself, as if he were anxious to get to the toilet; his eyes were as red as ladybugs, and his right hand had been hurt and was bandaged so that it looked like a rabbit. Because he liked looking out the window on airless nights, Marina started to be afraid of the dark. This had stopped later, when her mother, all dressed up, took her from their dorm, but now it was back. Maybe Marina should have turned to someone for support, but she'd learned from experience and wasn't someone who bared her soul to anyone. In the evenings she switched off her bedside lamp, which immediately gave way to the powdery window light, and tossed and turned for a long time, shifting her two heavy pillows like sacks of memories worn to dust. In her mind, she was constantly talking to her husband, occasionally smiling a broken smile if some funny comeback got stuck in her mind. So many of these mental conversations had accumulated that, even if the girl in the halter had abruptly withdrawn, daily life would not have given Marina the chance to say all this in reality; all this—a euphoric mixture of fantasies and altered memories—had been *hopeless* from the start, and the more she worked through it, the less it could correlate with any future. As she gradually broke with reality, Marina's enlightening *daytime* dreams were separated from waking only by a cloudy, milky membrane that let through sounds and basic colors. Her husband seemed to be leaving her these dreams to *watch*, the way he once might have left her a magazine or newspaper article to read.

■ □ ■

Had Marina been able to talk to the unfaithful Klimov for just a few minutes, that would have blocked, plugged the fantastic stream of conversation that didn't let up even at work and that manifested itself in Marina's handwriting in extra segments and a swollen caviar of letters, so that even visually the voters' passport details in her notebook resembled stray thoughts. All of a sudden she discovered that Klimov's image, which Marina had long considered dulled, was in fact as vivid as a parasite that's entwined its strong shoots around the mind's every hope and movement.

Marina's feelings when seeking a meeting with the fugitive, counting the minutes to the end of the workday—living every day with ticking clockworks installed in her brain—bore a strong resemblance to her feelings in her first year of university, when she was chasing Klimov and would totally tune out if for some overriding reasons he hadn't come to class. Outwardly, the situations *then* and *now* were ridiculously alike. Even minor details were reproduced, like the sour electrolytic tingling on her wet palms or her sudden wild impatience—which became an internal scream—when a well-off voter not only put her fat-bellied purse on Marina's table but stood in front of her for more than a few minutes. Her feelings today, though—copies of her former ones—were hollow: her heart pounded, but her heart was empty. Her feelings no longer had an object and so now needed one even more than when the elusive Klimov simply cut a couple of classes or was quickly exiting a room where Marina had some need to enter—and the room became a dead end. Seeing him daily was an insurmountable need; if in her lectures they suddenly started talking about something disturbing and lofty (the Russian literature teacher, a fading enthusiast with dull, googly eyes and a slanting bang that looked like an arrow on a map of military actions, went on forever declaiming verses from the classics), Marina would turn around and look ecstatically at Klimov, who would immediately lay his shaggy head on his elbow, smearing his notes. Then, at least, there was someone to look at—although Klimov didn't like it. Now, emptiness loomed in dozens of different images, most of them frightening and unpleasant. Sometimes Marina imagined that the male shadows of the day and night had entered into a conspiracy and were coordinating their movements—all in black footwear—whereas the only reality was Klimov's rust-brown boots strolling through cheerful, nastily splashing slush.

She also observed one other unhealthy phenomenon. Unexpectedly, her past life—everything that Marina considered very far in the past, separated from the present day by many years—had suddenly turned up *here* and surrounded her now much more solidly and persistently than the reality of the crumbling streets and her basement workplace, all of which, along with the streams of public transport and the daily crowd of visitors mumbling with closed mouths, increased the pressure. *I have my whole life with me*, Marina told herself, looking off into open space (which was so narrow and had such limited sky, you could scarcely call it freedom), and right then she felt her loss, as if, although she had preserved all her morally outdated property, her most important capital had been illegally confiscated. Her attempt to save money in the battered box, under a clattering mat of glass beads, tangled chains, and cheap earrings attached like mosquitoes, now looked like a *greeting* from the past. From behind her present treasure house, its absolute prototype suddenly came forward, striking at Marina's heart: the dormitory gift box—a tea canister rough with crude rust that inside preserved its dull gold—as if breathed on—its mirrorlike walls and bottom but not the empty candy that had been squashed and now looked like a dead bug spreading its crushed lower wings. Imagine the presents and candies Marina could buy herself with the fourteen hundred rubles she'd saved to keep from frittering them away.

Meanwhile, the past's return highlighted the fact that in those fifteen years that had wiped clean away the foundational medal-wearing era that Marina had single-handedly attempted to preserve, Klimov hadn't changed one bit. The fact that her husband had suddenly hooked up with another, exotic woman—whose head had too much coarse, tarry hair for that small bulb to preserve a human brain structure—only underscored the fact that he himself had remained the same. Now Marina knew for a fact not only that Klimov had someone else but also exactly how and what was going on between them. For example, when Seryozha leaned in to kiss the woman, or ran his finger, as he once did to Marina, across her wide, charred eyebrows, which after Marina's tweezed petioles must have seemed positively masculine, Marina had been a superfluous witness. The situation was undoubtedly dangerous. Marina could only imagine how badly Klimov wanted to get rid of his wife so she wouldn't spy on him and his girlfriend through some metaphysical crack. Her sense of victimhood was immediately aroused as soon as someone's damp steps, tapping like wooden blocks, were heard under the arch leading to their courtyard (no one had brought Marina home in a long time). Marina could barely keep herself from running straight through the puddles, where treacherous pieces of brick, which looked like someone's boots left in the water, lay like dark chains, but the front door, which the lamp made watery, at the far end of the courtyard, just wouldn't get any closer.

The main danger, though, which Marina hadn't even let herself contemplate, so she wouldn't fall prostrate and could keep working at headquarters, was that Klimov and his departure might destroy her painstaking construction, created over so many years of effort. Marina would have done anything to keep from undermining her stepfather's heart, to keep it beating until better times. Klimov didn't know how she'd humiliated herself before a certain Zoya Petrovna, the sanctimonious blonde with a mouth like stewed carrots who ran the archives at the dilapidated film studio downtown. Klimov had no idea the effort it had cost Marina each time to reach an agreement with Kostik, the film editor, a reluctant and cunning creature who was fond of all his colorful shirts, his love beads, and his delicate mirrored eyeglasses, but who took positively swinish care of his titanic computer, whose white antique beauty was permanently etched with grime and whose keys looked like molars ground down by rough fodder until they'd lost their letters, uncleaned for three hundred years. Undoubtedly, ratlike Kostik (a newly fledged fan of the general secretary, he had bombarded online auctions with requests for L. I. Brezhnev's personal effects) had his own, virtual reasons for not particularly liking Kukharsky, but each time he helped the disgraced Marina "churn out some real pulp fiction," he capriciously raised the agreed-upon fee in dollars and tried to edit into the "news" his own face looking out like an ape's among the decorous Soviet faces. All this, outrageous and stupid as it was, had to be endured. Marina lied to her inevitable accomplices, saying she was preparing a surprise for that pig Kukharsky, a killer special project, an alternative post-documentary film—which was mostly the truth, because her fake news turned out to be more expressive than what was supposedly authentic. Developed socialism's special effects emerged distinctly in the material. Here, unlike in its Hollywood counterparts, nothing got blown up and no cars crashed. On the contrary, they constructed a grandiose, extensive meaning and structure that were clearly the geometry of a catastrophe lifted into the industrial air.

In order to achieve relative stability in her own district, Marina voluntarily made herself the heart of the paralyzed era, the heroine of a Soviet film; in retrospect, she almost came to love the Young Communists and her fictional Party membership. This affected her position in the conspiracy and at Professor Shishkov's headquarters, for instance, where Marina, despite her low salary, had become a significant figure, the conscience of the entire effort. Nor would Marina, hewing to purely Party principles, let her stepfather find out about the death of his drunkard of a nephew, who looked like a dead man long before his live-in lover, an alcoholic with a face like stomach contents, killed the poor guy with a classic Russian ax. Marina had gone to the scene for the Studio A crime beat personally. Still fearless, she wasn't terribly impressed by the dark little ax, with its rim of dirty sludge like you find under nails, or by the small bug-like blood spatters on the kitchen wall. Nonetheless, she refused to confirm this disgraceful death as a fact. For her anxious mother, who wasn't allowed to see the real news, either, but who somehow could tell something bad had happened, the crime story became a vodka poisoning—which was also partly the truth since, according to the autopsy report, at the moment her nephew, unsteady on his feet, was leveled by the ax, his organism was as sloshed as soup and he had barely a few weeks to live. Nonetheless, Marina had to take care to maintain this person's pseudo-life. Moreover, the newly departed lush, who, before the ax, would show up to put the touch on them for minor amounts on Red pension days, turned out to be a much more voracious parasite than the canonical Brezhnev. Even after inventing a philanthropic drug rehab for the nephew (behind which immediately loomed the two-humped shadow of the Apofeozov businessmen brothers, who now actually did run an anti-alcohol philanthropy together), Marina couldn't settle what she discovered were his considerable drunk debts, which badly taxed her reserves. For some reason, she thought it was important to fully repay what was written down on the last page of her old planner: she had to finish out the worn handwritten calendar, zero it out. But the whole business was complicated not only by her limited discretionary funds but also by the terrible vagueness that arose as a result of the alcoholic's surprise visits when, sometimes, he would be discovered in the kitchen, painfully sober, with the heavy expression of a made-up tragedian and knees pressed together femininely, agonizingly picking at the chocolate daubs from the homemade cake on his plate—and of course, without Marina's knowledge, taking some serious hair of the dog. She just couldn't zero him out—and evidently her mother, taking from the mailbox the latest transfer sent by Marina, still asked herself why her now grown-up relative didn't show his face or come visit even for the holidays that had always been sacred for him, dates for reestablishing his rights and for being with his people. Doubtless, her mother secretly suspected that brusque Marina had insulted her relative—which was also true because the deads' resentment for the living always seeps through the night and comes out on the wallpaper, and also because Marina had stashed the body.

Nonetheless, in the homemade movies, within the confines of the family, as steady as a stool, the family of four followed the simple laws of Soviet well-being. Once Marina had driven Klimov out, she had to feed yet another phantom, who, in point of fact, had long since inhabited the apartment as a reluctant vision that barely fed on human food and sat in his armchair with the newspaper as the personification of a *husband in the abstract*. Klimov had barely ever stopped by where the twisted patient lay, following his visitor with his eyes. The only thing that connected Klimov to her parents' room, which was set up like a Red Corner, a Soviet shrine, was the contents of the wardrobe, the only one for the whole family—and lately Nina Alexandrovna herself had been bringing out his half-undressed hanger, on which Klimov's sole silk tie dangled like a sword on a sling.

While trying to figure out how she was going to go on (in anesthetized moments of practical mental exertion), Marina would tell herself she could entirely compensate for her lost husband's presence only by tending to whatever clothing remained. In leaving their home, Klimov was hardly going to take everything; something had to be preserved, if only old things from their happy, distant student days purchased at the gargantuan flea market on the edge of town, where Marina and Klimov had always held hands tightly and had a prearranged meeting place, just in case they got separated: a very fat, worn birch, as white as toothpowder. Marina hoped that Klimov would never go into the attic after that and get into the big brown suitcase where their unwashed memories lay, pressed into a distressing, mutely smelly lump, and remove them layer by layer like stiffened bandages. As it turned out, by searching out and going through what her husband wouldn't want to take, Marina had restored him and herself to their best, their finest past. She felt she had equal rights to her husband's faded property, and not just because it had been paid for with her parents' money and afterward with her paycheck. It was just that, by leaving, Klimov had forfeited his moral right to create the illusion that he, the cheater, had never been there at all.

Gradually, albeit just in Marina's mind for now, there was a new, strictly symmetrical familial harmony in which Klimov's continuous absence corresponded to Alexei Afanasievich's absence, and the two *incomplete* husbands, quietly occupying adjoining rooms, presented the active women with increasing loneliness, and their vanishing difference in age, multiplied by kinship, could be discerned less and less given the drawing of identical wrinkles, whose wavy circularity resembled a tree's annular rings. Self-confident Marina thought she could easily borrow from her mother that weekly meticulousness with which she—no less conscientiously than she attended to her stepfather's body—cared for the body cavities and folds of his gray suit, which her efforts had kept so fresh and smart over the past fourteen years. With time, Klimov's wedding suit, too, now moved to the corner of the closet by the heavy press of junk, would probably acquire a well-groomed similarity to the gabardine that flaunted the war veteran's planks of medals and empty sleeves and occasionally took its owner's place on the narrow family balcony. One had to assume that the morbid similarity between both their husbands' things—the unworn clothing and the unambulating footwear that started looking ceramic—would one day create an idyll unattainable within the bounds of simple human actions. Knowing full well that it takes money to maintain specters, Marina, once she'd paid off the alcoholic's debts, might buy something fashionable for Klimov—because fashion, like a distorted transfer of real time to the mute and foolish language of objects, could exist even given her apartment's stagnation in the general secretary's shadow.

All this, actually, was the pragmatic lyric poetry of a madwoman. Deep down, Marina understood that she may have gone too far. If up until now she'd managed to construct and repair a fake reality without any particular damage to the reality of her own "I," then the new phantom—her lost husband—threatened to change all that. How was it that Marina couldn't remember herself for so many long years? She couldn't remember how, over the course of a gloomy student winter with trees in plaster, she'd desperately envied Klimov for being himself, how she'd tried to interact with him, reading her own letters to him: cherished pages from notebooks covered in the extravagant handwriting of a schoolgirl's compositions not desecrated by having been sent through the mail. Had anything changed now, when apparently the life you'd lived came back all at once and taught you not to repeat yourself—not that it predicted any kind of a future? Hadn't Marina bought herself the same thing Klimov had, a ring that looked like a sugar lump—and at the same time agonizingly not the same thing, offending the eye with the ineluctable chicanery of its construction, its deformed excess, which simultaneously wiped from memory the unfound original? Holding out her slightly trembling hand outrageously adorned with the over-large acquisition, Marina realized that she was going to have to throw herself into maintaining the spectral Klimov's life. As she looked at these people, these voters—who were in turn looking at her with pairs of brackish, infinitely patient eyes—Marina thought that if her life, her existence, were the condition for the parasite's life, the possibility of feeding it and the power to stop it all immediately would console her—but the parasite would continue to thrive when all that remained of Marina was a tortured shell. "What a cool ring," Lyudochka remarked, taking her extended hand with the confidence of a fortune-teller but not looking at her palm. Returning to reality and to headquarters, where it was lunchtime, Marina decided, first, that she would sign herself and her mother up for their legitimate fifty rubles and, second, she would call home, but certainly not to hide behind the anonymity of a trill and be taken for an Asian girl with a braid and lure Klimov out of his lackluster nap. In fact, she had to clarify whether Klumba had shown up and inquire about their finances once and for all; when she left the shouting clients for the back room, turbid potatoes were gurgling on the hotplate there, boiled to shreds, and long-legged Lyudochka was slicing a stale baguette and covering it with big slices of salami in its casing. Basically, life went on as if nothing had happened, even though all Marina heard in the receiver were long, impersonal rings.

■ □ ■

As she dragged her bag up the stairs, Nina Alexandrovna, winded, distinctly heard what she thought was the telephone tinkling, barely pushing through the taut obscuration in her head. By the time she'd sorted out the locks and the keys, which looked like dogs had gnawed them, and squeezed into the stuffy front hall, the phone was silent. Over it, looking at Nina Alexandrovna with mirror eyes hot from sleep, wearing haphazardly pulled-on jeans frayed by decrepitude, her startled son-in-law was shifting from foot to foot. As usual,

Seryozha must have slept in after his night shift and the call had awakened him, but for some reason Nina Alexandrovna imagined that her son-in-law had not been too late to get the telephone, so sedately white on its smooth runner, like in a picture, but had stood over it like that, gawking, as if trying with his outstretched arm to dampen the cascading rings and channel the assertive noise through his fingers—anything but touch the receiver. Actually, these were just fantasies that immediately flew from Nina Alexandrovna's mind when she noticed how skinny her son-in-law had grown. His house slippers looked like they were on his hands, not his feet, so slender had his hairless ankles become, and his sunken belly hung from his ribs like an empty sack. This was no surprise. After all, now he had to work nearly every night; sometimes, when he showed up at home, he could barely throw his elusive jacket on a hanger before getting into the bed that her daughter, rushing off to the TV studio, hadn't even had time to make properly. Nina Alexandrovna supposed that one of her son-in-law's relief men had fallen ill, and she was afraid they wouldn't pay him for the extra work, and Marina, who had become almost too beautiful of late, with lips like a vivid ulcer, would start ragging him again.

Nina Alexandrovna told Seryozha she'd heat up the borscht and went into the kitchen, where she put the food away in the old refrigerator, shocking her fingers on raw electricity as usual. Then, she took a generous scoop of the pink medley from the full soup pot, which had a part-circle of orange fat with a transparent tear, heaped it into a smaller pot, and put it on the gas, and the cold jelly began to bubble quietly around the edges. The borscht had turned out well. Ten minutes later, after Seryozha had thrown on a shirt and perched round-shouldered on a stool, there was a full bowl of the hot, colorful soup with a big dollop of lovely sour cream and an array of thick sandwiches on a separate plate in front of him. Looking at the dreamy smile that gradually lit up Seryozha's young face as his sunken cheeks warmed from the food, Nina Alexandrovna felt something inside her relax and soften where everything in a person should be firm. Of course, lately she'd become overly trusting in the good. The harder life got, the more pliantly Nina Alexandrovna responded to its random and weak smiles, which might not have meant anything like what she was seeing from her perspective. Even she guessed how easy it was to buy her with the mere sight of a baby in a stroller or, say, the scene of a friendly conversation, when two men who were utter strangers to Nina Alexandrovna, perfumed youth wearing expensive clothing made somewhere that had to be overseas, simply clapped each other on the shoulder—but she was willing to value herself more and more cheaply because she lacked even crumbs of kindness for her emotional moisture to soften into a warm pap. Now, too, looking at her son-in-law digging the soft, thick, whitened mass out of the bowl with increasing enthusiasm, Nina Alexandrovna believed he might find a good job soon and the family wouldn't have to stretch itself so thin waiting for pension day.

Nina Alexandrovna herself had lost her appetite; the sour bun from the street stand had settled in her stomach like a wad of heavy dough. Alexei Afanasievich was usually sleeping at this time of day—or rather, drifting into what in his unvarying existence might be considered human sleep—and snoring softly. His half-shut right eye glittered, while his brain burned like a frosted lamp, clearly delineating the spattered bruise from the stroke that made Alexei Afanasievich look like Mikhail Gorbachev, of whom he had never heard. Nina Alexandrovna usually spent this time in the kitchen, so as not to disturb the paralyzed man with her heavy, ambulating presence. Now, though, in a state of mollified good will, she had an urge to feed him. She decided to check on him first, though, so she cautiously cracked open the bedroom door. Only then did it occur to her that she couldn't hear him snoring. Standing bewildered on the threshold, Nina Alexandrovna immediately saw—but failed to understand—that something unusual was going on in the bed, whose big gilded knobs burned like headlights. The sheets, which Nina Alexandrovna had left smooth and tight, with the neat paralytic slipped inside like a pen in a shirt pocket, were now rumpled and bunched up at the invalid's feet, and the blanket was hanging at an angle over the side. Alexei Afanasievich's left arm was lying quite apart and seemed nearly as big as his entire body, whose odd bending had something armless and fishlike about it. What struck Nina Alexandrovna most, though, was the flimsy white rope fastened to the bed's latticed headboard like a monogram woven in the air. At the other end, the rope ended in a noose, which lay askew on the paralyzed man's face. Betrayed by this seemingly carelessly drawn circle, Alexei Afanasievich was looking through it wildly, and his protruding right eye blinked, while the other, half-closed, twitched like a tree's withered, raindrop-splattered leaf.

Standing there for a minute, her thoughts at a total impasse, Nina Alexandrovna realized she simply could not acknowledge this. The string lowered around the lattice and around itself in limp, empty loops represented not a running knot he had made but a graphic diagram in the air of how its intended knots should be tied. There was something *innocent* in the white, drapey silkiness of the rope, which bore some vague relation to a daintily embroidered blouse she recalled on an adolescent Marina. The first thing to do was to destroy any evidence of the crime. Cautiously, grasping it with two wary fingers, Nina Alexandrovna flipped the noose off the sick man's face, and in response the paralyzed man let out an indignant, throaty grunt. Murmuring something reassuring, Nina Alexandrovna tried to remove the deadly rigging from the bed. The knot in the noose slipped off easily, like a bead, and dropped into her hand; but her light tug pulled the half-finished, branch-like work on the headboard lattice so tight that it took Nina Alexandrovna a quarter of an hour to gnaw through the tough silk stalk with scissors and free the scratched twig. All this time, Alexei Afanasievich, lying in a cooled patch of venomous old-man urine, breathed more evenly and vigorously than usual, and Nina Alexandrovna could feel his brain pushing out dark, concentric circles, like a stone tossed on the water.

So that's how it was, she told herself, dropping into her chair. Alexei Afanasievich had attempted to hang himself. Incredible. This wasn't just about the remainder of his paralyzed days. The particular way Alexei Afanasievich was living, steadily adding minute after minute to the sum total years lived and preserved and not letting himself be distracted for a moment from increasing the quantity of his existence, meant one thing: the moment he died, all he had built would vanish as if it had never been. A distraught Nina Alexandrovna felt herself trying to form a mental picture of things that her ordinary little mind simply could not absorb; it felt as though a tight woolen cap had been pulled over her head. She had the vague sense that her gray-haired husband's life, which to the disinterested outsider was thoroughly unremarkable, like a set of unimportant archival files— not counting his heroic war—was in reality an unacknowledged act of heroism. His life had in fact been colossal and, like everything colossal, pointless. Any bit of fluff, any scrap of existence, to say nothing of larger, more valuable items, had come into play for Alexei Afanasievich now. Everything had become building material for his nest, his anthill, which he had been creating instinctively rather than according to any rational plan. It was crystal clear that this life of accumulation, which never let anything drop, could exist *wholly* either on this or that side of the line of death—but not both. Alexei Afanasievich had probably been trying to put a halt to his building before its natural completion. He was truly preparing to destroy more than his own *comfortable* future, with his velvety puréed soups, fluffy porridges, and fake newscasts; he was planning to annihilate everything in one fell swoop.

This was indeed inconceivable, monstrous, and unfair; this devalued the life he had lived. Nina Alexandrovna's hands, resting in her lap, could not lie still; they kept jumping, like writhing fish cast ashore. Had the veteran managed to stick his head through the noose, which was in fact too small, then Nina Alexandrovna's diligent marriage would have drowned in oblivion, leaving her no one's widow and no one's wife, alien and isolated. It would also have meant the disappearance of her predecessor, Alexei Afanasievich's first spouse, a stout young woman with an oval face like a large medallion and dark hair that covered the bottoms of her ears and gleamed like a record in the sad daylight that permeated the old snapshots of her that remained in her maidenly purse, which was as heavy as an encyclopedia and worn down to its gray fabric. Nina Alexandrovna could not imagine what voids might arise if Alexei Afanasievich made an exit *like this*. She had some notion of them from the light of those faded snapshots, which preserved the woman's pose-in-the-park on a backdrop of pointy leaves, deep in a star-shaped kaleidoscope of trees; speaking to the void, too, was the light of a today spent in sorrow—a sun-filled light, so resembling *that* photographic light, which gave an odd taste of the astronomical distance of its source, of just how far that light had traveled to outline the tall trees in their fever of falling leaves, the coarse sugar of the window tulle, and these little medicine bottles. This meant her husband had been planning to abandon Nina Alexandrovna to her fate. Of course, he didn't know that his handsome pension was supporting the family, and now it was simply too late to tell him. Nina Alexandrovna didn't have the words to inform him, out of the blue, about the changes, which even she found implausible. She simply wouldn't know where to begin because she herself didn't understand how or why all this had actually come about. If you looked at present-day capitalism from that distant fork in time, then this looked more like a puppet show or the nightmare of a convinced Communist who finds himself inside his own dream. The sole basis for that figure's existence, if only in men's minds, was the victory in the Great Patriotic War.

It turned out that Alexei Afanasievich had *always* been the creator and center of Soviet reality, which he'd managed to hold onto a little longer; and now this reality, squeezed to the size of their standard-issue living space, retained its permanence, inasmuch as its pillar had not disappeared; on the contrary, it was trapped along with all its medals glowing in their boxes (a Red Banner, a Patriotic War 1st class, Glory 2nd and 3rd class, and four Red Stars), which, unlike the general secretary's meaningless decorations, possessed an internal logic and event-linked significance. Now, though, the veteran, who had turned into a body, into the horizontal content of a high trophy bed, had suddenly declared war on his own immortality. For the first time, Nina Alexandrovna was struck by the fact that Alexei Afanasievich had wended his way back from that hostile Germany, lugging this gilded cot—tens of kilos of lovely metal, separately luxurious in its Gothic mesh, chain netting, and separate headboard and footboard that looked like chromatically tuned musical instruments—and for what? What dream had he clung to in his fierce, war-rattled mind when, already lame and shackled like a convict to his trophy, he had made his way frenziedly through half-destroyed train stations and loaded his goods on passing dusty plywood trucks? Had he been dragging his future royal rest from war across half of Europe or had he after all had some woman in mind and the continuation of his stock? Or had Alexei Afanasievich guessed even then, as he languished in the unhurried *peacetime* freight train, which jerked every half step like a fishing line, sitting at the feet of his disassembled bed, as if at the foot of his own future, that this German beauty he couldn't part with due to the senseless obstinacy that had overtaken him would become a worthy gallows for him—that this importunate thing was in fact his inevitable death, acquired, after all, in war? He probably felt that, no matter what, he had to bring death home—across the entire upside-down space littered with architectural devastations—drag it there and finally lie down in it, in the bed and in death, under the protection of his authentic, rear line, reliably closed walls. Actually, Nina Alexandrovna thought, every person hopes to die in his own bed, so what was surprising about that? Only Alexei Afanasievich had preferred to find and choose *for himself* what would become his last place on earth and the last thing he saw. Alexei Afanasievich's choice was so specific and willful that he didn't spare whatever remaining strength he had that hadn't been exhausted by the war or dragged out of him by the hospital in order, without God's help, with only crude luck pushing from behind (small change from what he'd paid for thirty victories over an agile and well-fed enemy), to drag the monster he'd taken such a liking to home to the Urals, never to be parted from it again.

Now, having cried her eyes out and soaked her handkerchief so thoroughly that it was slick, Nina Alexandrovna would have liked her husband to have given at least a faint sign of regret and guilt. After all, what had happened was worse and more hurtful than if she'd found Alexei Afanasievich with a lover—in their marital bed, whose height and vehement ringing, like the ringing of meadow grass full of grass-hoppers, Nina Alexandrovna couldn't forget on her own canvas cot. However, the paralyzed man, lying as before on the wet, wrinkled spot (where he evidently had slipped down, in some unknown way, along with all his lopsided bedding), was now so self-absorbed that his face, where the calm half had in the past fourteen years become much younger than the twisted half, seemed to be floating on the surface of deep water, the way they sometimes show it in the movies: waves, scrunching up and then smashing forth, rocking a drowned man's straw hat. Evidently, the attempt to hang himself had not been without effect. Pulling out from under her husband the long wet sheet and the reddish oilcloth, crumpled and burning like a mus-tard plaster, Nina Alexandrovna felt that his body had filled with fatigue and become much heavier and turned over without its for-mer apish agility, without the habit of *yielding*, a habit his lifeless limbs had somehow acquired over his years of illness. Picking the blanket up off the floor (and hearing in the front hall the whistling rustle of a jacket and a cautious bustle—probably Seryozha getting ready to leave), Nina Alexandrovna suddenly saw in the corner of the top sheet a light, half-empty swelling. Plunging her arm up to the elbow into the wide-open, shapeless bag, she pulled out into the light a tangled nest: shabby bathrobe belts; summer dresses sent long ago to the attic; tie strings and stretched elastics pulled from fitted sheets. The biggest was a battered gold polka-dot silk tie that stood out from the mass like a cobra among skinny worms. In horror, Nina Alexandrovna attempted to tie all this into a noose-like slip knot, winding the dangling ends around it (in the front hall the cramped shuffling continued, and clothes fell off a hanger as if in a dead faint, with a sigh and gentle clatter, to the floor). Suddenly—or so it only seemed, so fleeting was the ticklish touch—the paralyzed man's left hand, entwined with swollen veins that looked filled with air, stroked Nina Alexandrovna behind her ear, accidently brushing the sharp seed of her earring.

Nina Alexandrovna's thoughts immediately took a different turn. How weary he must be from fourteen years of his lying weight torturing his back, from the discomfort of unstrung bones as heavy as chains, from the moribund functioning of his stomach, where food was transformed into soil and languidly pushed through the twists and turns of his intestines—while in his chest, an oar was planted crosswise at each tight inhale. All this Nina Alexandrovna knew vaguely from her own self. All this had been *communicated* to her through the nonverbal connection that had arisen between her and her husband the moment Alexei Afanasievich fell on the balcony, on the grumbling cans, and his brain exploded. But this connection meant exactly nothing in the sense of their relationship. Even if there had been something like love between Nina Alexandrovna and her husband, could she really now claim that Alexei Afanasievich had been patient and fed her with his languishing flesh, his veteran's pension, which the state had been paying for nearly a quarter-century—and couldn't pay forever to a *man who couldn't die*. Alexei Afanasievich had the legitimate right to end his own suffering once and for all and to let Nina Alexandrovna find a way to feed herself. That's what all the lonely women did today, women impossible to look at the way they were, dressed in what was no longer worth a ruble, on the street selling swollen pickles in cloudy brine and Turkish underpants set out on newspapers and gathered under headlights. Nina Alexandrovna was willing to join these ranks of disabled traders, only she didn't know how. She'd been spoiled, after all; her husband had never left her without money. Touching herself behind the ear with her most impartial (middle) finger, she tried to remember the sensation, but stupidly fingering the sand of her hair, she just spread the vague warmth, transforming it into a venomous redness. Then she leaned over (incorrigibly believing in *good*) the already covered, swaddled Alexei Afanasievich, hoping to speak to him in the language of the floating electric figures that she feared from her vague memory about an article on ball lighting in *Science and Life*. But the brain inside his skull, which looked like a delicately glued-together archeological vessel, was mirror-smooth this time, so that looking into Alexei Afanasievich's eyes, Nina Alexandrovna imagined she saw on the fluffed pillow her own face with traces of her former avian beauty.

■ □ ■

Life burst in rudely: the door swung open as if from a blow flatwise to its full height, and Nina Alexandrovna shuddered. She thought Seryozha probably needed something in the closet—but it turned out to be Marina, not her son-in-law. She was wearing a twisted, ash-gray suit and holey slippers over black stockings, so that it was unclear which of the children had been fussing in the front hall all this time and clattering keys. "Mama, did she bring the money?" Marina asked impatiently, casting her usual quick glance at the paralyzed man, followed by another, closer one that seemed to press on the bridge of Alexei Afanasievich's nose—at the wrinkled root of his old-mannish face where today there lay a suspicious, oddly even shadow. "Yes, yes. I've already been to the market," Nina Alexandrovna said hastily and ingratiatingly, realizing she couldn't quite remember how much each purchase had cost and that she was going to have to account for her spending, collecting from her pockets the pitiful change and answering to her daughter for the unheard-of food prices, which had quietly inflated again. Nina Alexandrovna was insulted that Marina seemed not to believe her and deep down thought that her mother was buying *incorrectly*—saving up for lottery tickets for her own pleasure, possibly, to win canned goods or a piece of sausage. "What do you have there?" Marina suddenly asked, indicating with her eyes the chaotic bundle of rag herbage that Nina Alexandrovna was squeezing in her damp fist. "Oh, I was just sweeping up the floor," Nina Alexandrovna replied in an unnatural voice, putting her hand behind her back, a movement that immediately reminded her of the deltoid pain under her left shoulder blade. "Throw it out, for God's sake. Why doesn't anyone ever throw anything out here?" Frowning painfully and slowly disentangling the two-pronged belt lashing at her, Marina turned to walk away and only then, by accident, did Nina Alexandrovna see that the glass on Brezhnev's portrait, with its steely sheen, had cracked in the corner.

The explanation was not extensive. Marina was distracted and angry about something, and the money seemed to stick together in her clumsy counting fingers. For some reason, she was having a hard time eating. She seemed to keep biting her spoon, and the borscht in her bowl got cold and murky. Time and again, without a word,

Marina would go out in the hall, and then a worried Nina Alexandrovna, up to her elbows in a burbling sink of greasy, badly scraped dishes, would start to imagine that her daughter had gone to see the paralyzed man for some additional verification. She couldn't imagine what an indignant Marina would do if she found out about Alexei Afanasievich's attempt to reject his monthly 1,300 rubles. Most of all, Nina Alexandrovna was afraid Marina would beat her stepfather. Who or what could stop her? However, she did not hear steps heading toward the far room. Peeking cautiously from the kitchen, Nina Alexandrovna saw in the dilute gloom that her daughter wasn't going anywhere but was standing perfectly still, facing the darkest corner of the front hall, listening to the sounds of the front entrance, sounds that could have been drawn with a ruler, the blunt notes of someone's ascending boots that couldn't seem to get as far as their empty sixth-floor landing.

Late that evening, after feeding Alexei Afanasievich a pale steamed meat patty and rubbing down especially zealously his sweetly sour body with a soapy sponge that sputtered in his wet gray hair, Nina Alexandrovna put her husband not in his usual place but farther from the edge, leaving the blanket's selvage free. As she was coming in from the shower, all hot in her tight, chest-squeezing robe, Nina Alexandrovna noticed a dull strip of yellow light still under her daughter's door—the weak, uneven light sawed through the darkness—while a delicate tittering, like a bird's chirp, came from her room. Deciding her daughter was reading something funny before going to bed, Nina Alexandrovna herself smiled and fluffed her hot, damp hair a little. Alexei Afanasievich's body lay just as she'd left it; the tulle's large-checked pattern fell dark on his forehead. Cautiously perching on the bed's high footboard, Nina Alexandrovna wondered at its half-forgotten resilience and the superior quality of the luxurious metalwork. Trying not to disturb Alexei Afanasievich's sleep—not that this was sleep in the ordinary sense of the word—clumsily, holding onto the back of the bed so as not to fall on him, she arranged herself at his side. The oilcloth crackled under the cold sheet, making the bed alien, like a doctor's exam table; her husband's body was alien and a little sticky, too, sweetly fragrant from shampoo. In this unwarmed flesh there was little, very little life, just the heart jumping up hard under the skin, like rubbed hair, and it seemed to Nina Alexandrovna that his heart was no longer pushing nutrients through the tissues but was itself feeding on the old man's compressed organism, sucking at his half-empty muscles, like rotting, sprouted potatoes, through his circulatory system.

Nina Alexandrovna felt sad and good and so sorry for Alexei Afanasievich but simply could not warm up. Turning on her back, her feet not reaching the foot of the bed, where, like in communicating vessels, a weak silvery color rose and fell, she floated on that metallic cloud into an obscure and gentle past, into a thirty-three-year-old October snowfall that covered the streetlamps thickly, like white bread being crumbled into milk—and the precious two tickets to the last showing presented to the ticket taker turned out to be wet. She was twenty-six, and he was all of nineteen, but over a lifetime, that difference in years seemed insignificant. It was surprising, but Nina Alexandrovna could barely remember his face, only a blob, a blob scorched by an ethereal chill she now found pleasant rather than unbearable. He was unattractive and ungainly on the whole. His hair—a stiff reddish cap—felt like doll's hair, and in their complicated way his fingers, on which he carefully explained things to his interlocutors, resembled a small collection of chess figures.

She went to his apartment a total of four times—the seventeenth floor, where the gray snow fluttering out the windows was darker than the sky and the distant courtyard, which looked like it was covered in cigarette paper, where his old brown furniture seemed too heavy to be so high up, and where the wreckage of his closet gave off a sharp whiff of musty wool and mothballs. . . . There were lots of small dark moles that looked like wrinkled winter berries on billowy snow on his white, very delicate ribs; his bony feet, which got tangled in the folds of the sheet, were covered in a soft, reddish down. For both, they were their firsts, and what they had for now was cramped, painful, and harsh, with a bare trickle of pleasure at the very bottom, but what they failed to achieve was replaced by a sweetness that simultaneously filled their tensed hearts, which found a rhythm, and in the curtained daytime room something like a pink balloon breathed, moist and cloudy. Hastily, to the nasal alarm of the clock that had woken up in the next room (his parents arrived at six-thirty), he tore the crumpled sheet off the couch, flinging open the tight window vent to air the room out, while outside, oatmeal-like spots hopped around as if hastily pecked at. He took hundred-ruble discs of impossibly satiny blackness out of their glossy foreign sleeves and holding them, cleanly, on the edges, by his palms, placed them on the record player and then lowered the obedient needle to their spinning, sentimentally damp smooth surface. He was boastful, good, and haunted. After lovemaking he taught her to smoke, lighting a drooping cigarette and switching it directly to her lips; outside, he always removed her prickly rustic mitten so he could hold her hot hand. He'd let her listen on the dorm's cheap record player, which resembled nothing so much as a hot plate, to lightly scratched discs that sounded almost like the real thing but when the needle snagged would suddenly let out an arrow of sound, like a stocking with a run in it.

Surprisingly, Nina Alexandrovna remembered everything except for his slippery image; any detail from those weeks she kept separately and in exemplary order, and due to this *separateness*, their relationship seemed longer than it really was. Nina Alexandrovna would shut her eyes and see his parents: elderly, with identical brown eyes like four two-kopek coins. They had affectionate names for each other and their friends, as if they were all children. Her father had a disproportionately large, almost elephantine skull solidly covered in curly gray hair; his mother had a mustache, burr-stiff, and a lot of skin and corn-yellow amber hanging on her neck. Both of them were gynecologists well known in the city. It was their fame and specialty that left no secret to the relationship between the "young lady" and their younger son, and they made the "young lady" blush. In her own Severouralsk, where she had graduated from vocational school before going to the university, she'd had no idea that there were people like this: Jews who were suddenly fired and exiled, as if dying then and there, in their home-land, holding their own wake amid the chaos and discarded furniture moved from where it belonged and holding unneeded keys in its locks, like dangling cigarettes. Naturally, she shouldn't have come. She was a total stranger at the oval family table, where they ate laboriously on cracked dishes as dingy as a smoker's teeth, where the adults were still wearing all Soviet-era clothes, as clumsy as if lined with cardboard, and the children sparkled in foreign-made jeans outfits and fancy little sweaters—and he, crazed and tipsy, barely escaping the confinement of his talkative relatives, was anxious to see her home.

Afterward there had been one postcard from him, mailed from Moscow, and nothing more. Ever since, Nina Alexandrovna had disliked Jews and had always spoken of them with suspicion and dislike, but she never did learn to pick them out among the good people with whom her life thereafter brought her together. Marina was born in July, when it was hottest and the grass and tree leaves grew up big and holey, as if burned by cigarettes, and the yellow centers of the waterlilies on the pond by the district clinic were as rich as hard-boiled egg yolks. While looking after her crawling cotton bundle, Nina Alexandrovna tried to imagine a different, exotic heat, with palms, from the travelogue film club, with desert sands dissolving in an unreliable haze, like sugar in a glass of boiling water, and him in the city's full stony blaze of sun, with a shadow no bigger than a ball's on the slabs and a book under his arm. For a while, imagining him in connection with herself became a habit for Nina Alexandrovna, and she had an acute need to sense him *alive*, but the synchronous connection became more and more fantastic, his image wore out from overuse, and gradually Nina Alexandrovna began confusing her imagination with her dreams, in which he appeared like a plaster Young Pioneer, and colonnades and a gigantic three-tiered *Soviet* fountain burned in the sun like a giant chandelier, a fountain whose dust on the asphalt was hot and soft, like wet ashes. Here, on the marital bed, she also finished looking at the last dribs and drabs the soul had taken away: murk and snow, he came from Israel a very old and wrinkled man, and sat on a bench in some ghastly lane, and for some reason the tracks leading to him were as round as saucers of milk.

Originally, his redheadedness had come out in Marina's sparse baby hair, and there was something of him in the structure of her lionish little nose, which made Nina Alexandrovna imagine she'd had a boy. But gradually all this ironed out and his face gradually dropped from memory as well, and even the resentment, the burning resentment at *that* life yielded to simpler, plainer resentments: at the superintendent's wife, who gave the young mama the most torn sheets worn to a gray gauze; and at her own parents, who fell ill whenever Nina Alexandrovna asked them to take little Marina for a few days and who with the years turned into identical village kulaks with faces like bone-dry gingerbread men. She held no grudges against Alexei Afanasievich, though. In essence, he had never abandoned her, had never once left her without flowers on International Women's Day. Just as he had May 9th, Nina Alexandrovna had March 8th, which was observed religiously. Even if they were just cheap stems, pins in an emptyish newspaper cone, nonetheless Nina Alexandrovna felt set apart from the many women who were only given a tiny little tulip at work, out of petty cash, and it was so nice to unpack the cold newspaper cone full of thawing March air and arrange the little bouquet that loosened up in the heavy, cut-glass vase where she now kept lost buttons: the wobbly circles now almost filled the vase to the top.

Because Alexei Afanasievich was a man for whom Nina Alexandrovna could feel gratitude without having to invent anything about him, her husband suddenly seemed so valuable and unique that her eyes moistened and in the half-dark became like two deep inkwells, while the night's ink slowly dried on the walls, dark in the cracks on the floor, and stuck several heavy old tomes together on the shelf— and right then, outside, all the way down, the streetlamps went out. The umbral pointers that leaned the floating room slightly laterally were replaced as a reference point by the invisible alarm clock ticking off to the side. Tenderly, as only she could, Nina Alexandrovna stroked her husband's cold shoulder (as had often happened before, too, she imagined a nonexistent cord from a medallion or cross passing under her fingers), quietly slipped her feet into her cold slippers, which were damp from her shower, and trying not to run into anything, unfolded the tottering cot. Come morning, waking in a sweat, on the bare canvas with the loose sheet, Nina Alexandrovna told herself she'd manage somehow, and if today took more out of her than it did ten or twenty years ago, then that was what it was like for everyone, that meant those times had come, and despite the odd jerking in her tight chest, she had to get up and cook breakfast, and she would not let anyone lay a finger on Alexei Afanasievich, who was stretched out close to the wall—helpless, his arms pressed down, but who over his years of immobility had become neither an animal nor demented.

■ □ ■

Now Nina Alexandrovna kept a very close eye on what was going on around her. Inasmuch as she had to keep her husband's secret from absolutely everyone, she listened closely to steps in the apartment and didn't let them get close to the forbidden Red Corner without taking hasty measures and wrapping Alexei Afanasievich up to the chin in his blanket. Now no one could catch her unawares. Nina Alexandrovna knew exactly who was where in the apartment at each specific moment, and in the morning the first thing she did was ascertain people's presence, making herself heard under the long-occupied bathroom's swollen doors, which even on the outside were wet from the steam of the noisy water and which also let through the wet, almost hoarse shout of one of the children. Risking their irritation, she would look in on them in their unaired bedroom, always discovering one of them in the stuffiness—and sometimes getting a blank, unblinking gaze from her daughter, as if she were weighing all objects.

Intent though her surveillance was, Nina Alexandrovna felt cut off from the young family. She couldn't even fight their slovenliness properly. Sometimes her daughter and son-in-law's ignorant faces seemed like strangers', as if they'd retreated into the shadows; the necessity of watching them kept Nina Alexandrovna from worrying about their daily well-being as she once had. For some reason, only once, one late inclement evening, did she manage to catch them together. Her son-in-law seemed to be leaving on a business trip. Beside him on the front hall floor was a haphazardly packed—as if everything that should have been packed crosswise lay lengthwise—gym bag, and Seryozha, pulling on his laced rust-brown boots as if they were lion's paws, gave her a merry look, from which Nina Alexandrovna concluded that her son-in-law now had a new job because parking lot guards didn't go on business trips. Marina, who had just come in from the TV studio, was seeing her husband off, leaning against the wall, her hands hidden behind her back. Occasionally her immobile face would flutter like a butterfly pinned for an entomological collection. Her daughter was looking far from her best, and her eyes were flooded, so that Nina Alexandrovna nearly said something about seeing a doctor right in her son-in-law's presence. The expression in Marina's eyes was such, though, that Nina Alexandrovna hurried to her room, nearly losing a slipper as she did, so as not to listen to their conversation, which didn't happen, actually. There was just the constrained space of the front hall, the general skewedness of the gym bag dragging noisily across the floor, and Marina giving the lock a sharp turn. Since then, Nina Alexandrovna couldn't stop feeling that she and Marina were each jealously guarding their own territory, and neither had anything against putting locks on the doors to their own rooms, no matter the cost, so that when they left home they wouldn't leave their abandoned rears defenselessness.

Now a guarded Nina Alexandrovna felt a strange need to announce her appearance, and her own call or the dull tap of her puffy limbs seemed like too little (little Marina, when she came in from playing, wouldn't knock or ring but would slap the door with her dirty hand); Nina Alexandrovna felt as though she should throw something ahead of herself before entering—and in this one felt a vague reference to some folktale in which the character tosses various objects on his path so that loyal friends can follow this dotted line and find him. Here, it all felt backward. Her desire was not to sweep away the past but to explore the future along this dotted line. For the first time in her life, Nina Alexandrovna felt a need to sound out the unknowable tomorrow, a spectral tentacle of the mind that would tell her whether precisely what she feared and what Alexei Afanasievich, resisting being packed away, obviously continued to want had in fact happened up ahead: if you substituted movements for speech, his tensed resistance and his attempts to strain to the hilt what remained of his shackled strength reminded her of the bellowing of a mute.

Nina Alexandrovna didn't like losing anything. She sensed a void in her well-kept space if a bobby pin dropped or a coin rolled away (which was why she collected lots of little odds and ends around herself) and now felt more favorably inclined toward the willfulness of things. She pictured a vanished object, which later—she knew this—would certainly turn up, as having rolled ahead and arrived in the transparent box of *tomorrow's* apartment (an observer, if there were one, would have been amazed at the similarity between

Marina's *daydreams* and the glassy sketches of future days that arose in Nina Alexandrovna's mind—a similarity that better expressed their kinship than the approximate similarity of their facial features). Nina Alexandrovna's futile attempts to project into the future were reminiscent of her long-ago efforts to keep Marina's father real and alive and for the sake of that to be more than herself, and in just the same way, she could feel a wall in her forehead.

Apparently, the period of stagnation preserved in the Red Corner would not allow for forward movement, so everything had fallen back in place; now that was even more true. At night, the window sealed shut for the winter would crackle and tinkle as if holding back the press of some growing mass, as if the paralyzed immortality were flexing an invisible muscle. Nina Alexandrovna, who lately had been sleeping unusually alertly, as if lying all night at her own side, listened superstitiously to this crackling and quiet sucking in the cracks. Brezhnev, hanging oddly due to the fat crack in the glass, would wink and change like those playful effects that billboards use to catch your eye—several pictures of products and their smiling representatives fanning like a deck of cards all at once. Now in a state of constant emotional tension, Nina Alexandrovna guessed that what she was seeing was substantially a product of her imagination. Previously, she would scarcely have been upset at finding the tube of cheap lipstick she'd recently lost in the front hall behind her daughter's calloused sandals, which should have been boxed up for the winter. Now, picking the crushed remnants up off the floor, remnants that looked like a gnawed chicken bone, Nina Alexandrovna turned cold at the thought of the blow that had destroyed the small tube, which had obviously been crushed by the heel not of some household member but of some malignant fate that had been in their home.

Feeling sealed up in an autonomous little world that she would now have to protect even more zealously from outsiders, she sometimes felt an insurmountable urge to break free, to see people—at least to pay a visit to her nephew, who kept transferring money to her with the indifference of an ATM. Nina Alexandrovna didn't remember even half her nephew's debts, but the transfers kept coming—in precisely the same unround, *embarrassed* amounts in which her nephew had borrowed "without even any extra for a bottle," and there was something mechanical about this, as if a totally different person were paying for her nephew. Nina Alexandrovna would have liked to understand what had become of her nephew's sincerity when, while sipping the hot water she called tea that he hated so, he talked about his new wife, a good and long-suffering woman he'd found right in his lobby wearing just her nightgown and a man's sturdy jacket with a medal. He'd told her about Nina Alexandrovna, of course, and so shuttled like a honeybee between various people, carrying warm flower pollen. Trying to solve this puzzle, Nina Alexandrovna wondered whether her nephew had become a "new Russian." Knowing very little about that bizarre species of apparently synthetic people who had gold threads sewn into their faces and money inserted into their metabolism, incorporating it into their own biology through wine cellars and expensive restaurants, Nina Alexandrovna imagined the community of "new Russians" as the one place a person becomes inaccessible by joining, interacting with the world exclusively through ingested and secreted sums of money. If that were true, the precise figures of the transfer became understandable. Evidently there was a reverse logic to returning accumulated debts: the preciseness of the figure held a message and was no less important than the recipient's correctly indicated address. Nonetheless, it seemed to Nina Alexandrovna that even a "new Russian" could retain something human. More than once she'd imagined one of those long, shiny cars stopping in front of her, ideally inserted into the reflected landscape, and her smiling nephew wearing a slightly baggy raspberry jacket and a gold tiepin, climbing out of the door, its glass tinted like a television set.

■ □ ■

Nina Alexandrovna jealously watched Marina and Seryozha but even more jealously watched Alexei Afanasievich, who obviously didn't trust her anymore. Every so often, though, when she was busy with something, he would give her a look as if summoning his wife to come closer. The doctor, Evgenia Markovna (who herself had suddenly gone downhill, with an unfamiliar messiness to her bun of yellowing gray hair), noted an improvement in motor functions, which surprised her mightily. Shaking her dry little head, which had hardened from the temples up, and adjusting the errant tip of her stethoscope in her perforated ear, the doctor listened to the patient for a long time and then asked him to move his hand—and Alexei Afanasievich's hand took a surprisingly easy jump, which made it look very much like a mechanical prosthesis. Actually, this was no cause for surprise. The delicate substance of immortality, from which there settled so much of the very even, rather bright dust characteristic of this room alone, had become palpably stronger. Apparently, if this dust—a by-product containing perhaps a small percent of the basic substance—were sprinkled on the cockroaches whose husks lay around the chemically treated kitchen, they would immediately start skipping like drops of water across a red-hot skillet.

Alexei Afanasievich, who now slept much less than before, would not be parted from his Chinese inflatable spider, which jumped for him with a whistle and a kind of obscene smacking, its cloth feet quivering on the flight up, and flew at Nina Alexandrovna from the folds of the blanket, occasionally touching her leaning face with its fake fringe. The spider had become like a second heart for Alexei Afanasievich, connected to him by a mysterious link, apart from the tube; its convulsions never ceased, even when the toy hopped off the bed and dangled between heaven and earth, huffing on the dust. Although he couldn't see his fledgling (rarely observing from his pillow the leaps of its blurry body), Alexei Afanasievich continued to work the swollen paw, which the rubber pear, squeezed to the bottom, filled over and over again with a pleasant roundness—but occasionally jammed the badly strained mechanism. This persistent, steady work seemed to have taught Alexei Afanasievich to combine the twisted and normal halves of his face so that he ended up with almost one whole: a bystander wouldn't have noticed anything special other than an expression of distasteful sarcasm and a thread of saliva dried on his salty stubble like egg white.

Nina Alexandra managed to sneak an occasional peek, but Alexei Afanasievich was unusually hard to fool; the paralyzed man was probably picking up the simple impulses released by her consciousness much better than she was his electrical rebuses, one instant of darkness after another. Lately these impulses had been coalescing, like clouds, or lingering until they coalesced, losing their distinctness, into a solid shroud. Despite this overcast, Alexei Afanasievich could apparently tell quite well whether Nina Alexandrovna was dozing off or just pretending as she sat in her chair over the hole of a mitten she was knitting, outside his blurry field of vision. Clearly she was present, though, and holding her breath, whereas asleep she tended to snore. Very rarely, Nina Alexandrovna would sit so long (the yarn moldering in her damp hand) as to produce the hypnotic illusion that she had drifted off, and then her half-closed eyes, which looked like they'd been smeared with a clear oil, witnessed what her mind could scarcely believe. She didn't even try to figure out how the various ropes and strings, some of unknown origin, got into Alexei Afanasievich's bed. She simply observed what she could. First, raising his shoulder and making himself asymmetric, like during a vigorous walk with his cane, the veteran would slowly lay out the outlines of a noose on his swaddled body. Then, after a long buildup, he would give a sideways jerk, like when he used to take his characteristic, very very small step, and a fold would form on the blanket, and above it, if he was lucky, the rim of the main loop would rise up with a divine opening, into which he endeavored with slow persistence to insert the rope's end. The rope thrust out of the paralyzed man's hand, violating the laws of physics and looking as taut as a cobra lured into the air by a fakir's flute; the paralyzed man's attempts to get the rope to land in the hanging opening reminded Nina Alexandrovna of a spectral needle-threading. An incredible tension blurred both the rope and noose in the trembling air and brought up a scour of glistening sweat on the veteran's temple. Finally, his hand would fall to the bed and lie there for a while as if severed. Then Alexei Afanasievich would begin preparing for his lateral jerk all over again. And something almost imperceptible happened to him: as he started building up to this exertion, the gray-haired, disheveled muzhik began to resemble a woman in labor, emitting the occasional suppressed moan.

Upset, but trying her utmost not to give herself away, Nina Alexandrovna observed his desperate struggle. The paralyzed man's material world, which had been stripped of any detail and reduced to large, schematic objects, the only ones accessible to his manipulations, reminded her of the letters on a child's building blocks, or the top line on the eye chart; and the large font in which this destiny was written evoked her respect and a superstitious fear. Nina Alexandrovna sometimes thought of her Alexei Afanasievich as an overly ambitious pretender to the throne, a shadow general secretary of the Communist Party. The veteran's struggle with matter, which previously had been limited to the toy stuffed animals he conquered, had taken on an altogether new quality. Nina Alexandrovna couldn't imagine how the paralyzed man, who couldn't bring a spoonful of kasha to his open mouth, might wrench his own death from the world around him. There are many things even a healthy man has trouble doing for himself—a haircut, say, or a foot massage—let alone commit suicide! Nina Alexandrovna knew from her own experience that this type of self-servicing requires agility, strength, and the skill of a hunter chasing a wild beast. What was she saying? It took more, much more. To be both hunter and hunted in your one and only body, to battle yourself with a kitchen knife—this Nina Alexandrovna remembered well. She remembered the new knife, sharpened spotlessly clean, until the whetstone's slick was black—sticking into her ribs dully, like a finger, and even when she stripped to her bra, thinking her slippery blouse was the problem, it was still no use. You had to make some special movement, a little like the twist she knew how to make squeezing into an overcrowded bus and opening a jar simultaneously. It was too hard, though. Maybe it was something you had to learn to do. But how? Nina Alexandrovna knew better than anyone (maybe even better than her heroic husband) that it's easier to kill someone else than yourself. Suicide is a job for the *left hand,* and if you're not born a lefty, then you do it wrong way around. True, it was Alexei Afanasievich's left hand that could move, but what use was that? After all, he was spread-eagle on the ground—yes, on the ground, even though there were five stories and a cellar between the veteran and the earth. Since the dimensions of his flabby body had lost all physical meaning, you could think of him as Gulliver in the land of the Lilliputians, tied down by hundreds of thin strings, over which his fat rubber spider scurried, testing the rigging.

Now, watching Alexei Afanasievich through the keen diopters of her dozing trance, Nina Alexandrovna understood deep down that an unnatural death, be it murder or suicide, was all about physical objects. You couldn't do away with yourself without a tool. Virtually anything could be used to kill someone, after which it remained *here,* as innocent as ever and undiminished. Meanwhile, the everyday objects in this room (muffled by dispassionate philosophical dust) contained very little death; their shapes were too smooth, their corners too wooden; their harmless *dullness* could drive anyone to despair. At one time, Nina Alexandrovna had dreamed of special, expensive things, out of ordinary citizens' reach, a gun or a rifle, say, things that held death like a faucet does water; just press—and out it spurts. Truth be told, she, too, had tried the rope—and this was the last thing that hadn't worked for her. Maybe because she was four months pregnant and had been extremely sensitive and irritated not so much by smells (winter itself, all melting ulcers and icy bald patches, seemed to smell of the morgue) as by the least mess, which would not let her abide in the focused stillness she needed to calm down and stop her bitter thoughts from racing for just a while. She had been willing to pick up every speck and bring it to the communal kitchen's garbage can, which stank of rotten newspaper juices. She had endlessly put away and taken out her few possessions, trying to achieve an evenness and parallelness from the robe and cardigan lying on the bed—the evenness of a sausage. Standing on a stool now, with the noose, cold and sticky from soap, right under her chin, she saw below her a room so perfectly neat it looked like a scale model (her library books, pens, and note to her parents looked like they'd been drawn on the table), but far away on the floor there were some torn white threads that she was not going to get to in this life. Her legs were trembling minutely, the stool was trembling more and more, and her mouth, like a wound, kept filling up with saliva. After a while she winced and slipped out of the noose, which caught in back on her pinned-up hair. She got to her knees on the stool's tottering square and alit feeling as though she'd just stepped off a merry-go-round. Afterward, she washed the floors with the laundry detergent that was so hard to get and that foamed up in hot water. The noose, half stuck together from too much smeared-on soap, swung over-head like a flaccid, *post-party* balloon. It was with this hot, blubber-ing cleaning that her new life had begun, a life continuous to this very day. Nina Alexandrovna had never told anyone about her illegal and unsuccessful attempt. Least of all had she been prepared to tell Alexei Afanasievich, a man sufficiently stern that in his presence his spouse nearly forgot her own illicit act, the cigarette butts in the sau-cer, and how she had removed her silk blouse, which had stuck to the bloody spot under her heart, as if to commence lovemaking.

It was much harder for paralyzed Alexei Afanasievich now than it had been for Nina Alexandrovna during those incredibly lonely months when there had been no one to help her and no one in the world who might steady her wayward knife, the way a teacher grasps and aims an unsteady pen for a first-grader's hen scratchings, or to slap her on the back when, bent over with her weapon, she had coughed up her fear. The veteran was attempting the impossible. He was already a failed product of death, a defective good from whom death had taken a step back without dispensing with the continuity of life in his illuminated consciousness. The veteran had not reconciled himself to this and was now planning to *make death* by his own hand—to repeat the mirror image of what he had done to others with such ease. He was a cobbler without boots. The only human resource he had left was the grim patience of a prisoner multiplied by the endless years of his sentence: the ability to move toward his goal millimeter by millimeter and fashion any movement as if it were a clever detail for some homemade gadget. Death seemed to be lying in bed with him like his lawful wife, and the paralyzed man was studying every millimeter of this being through a mental loupe and transferring it to his own mind, which was still like a steel trap. Maybe his lack of success (Nina Alexandrovna had no idea how many attempts there had been or when this had started) could be explained by the very fact that the veteran had still not assembled the whole from its parts, had not pictured his own death in its entirety. The terrible grip of his mind left no doubt as to the ultimate outcome of his struggle, though. The moment Alexei Afanasievich *understood*, he would immediately succeed: he would cross the line between sleight-of-hand (which was all you could call the paralyzed one-handed tying of the noose) and the miracle of his *authentic* disappearance so easily and quickly that even he wouldn't notice.

Nina Alexandrovna didn't know whether this would happen in a day, a month, or ten years. When she tried to gaze into the future, it seemed impossible, a figment of her imagination. Even that winter, which had already made itself felt in the mornings in the stannic asphalt and the void of the puddle at the front door, which looked like a broken toilet, seemed just as implausible to Nina Alexandrovna as it might to a Papuan who had never seen snow. Nina Alexandrovna simply couldn't tell where the boundary lay where reality came to an abrupt halt. At some point, the future, which she had always used pictures from the past to *imagine*, ceased to communicate with this past. There was some disconnect or defect here, as there can be defects in glass—needles of moisture, like veins running through a perforated landscape. No matter how Nina Alexandrovna strained her inner vision, though, she had no sense of how long she had before she reached that spectral line. In essence, she, too, like her husband, was attempting the impossible. Whereas an ordinary person backs into the future with his unprotected back, keeping a more or less intelligible past in front of him, Nina Alexandrovna wanted to turn around and follow the guiding crystal ball—and plunge into the unknown face first.

She who had been compelled to shut herself up in the Red Corner more and more felt like seeing people, and right away. In going out to stores and the market, she told herself that it was this—the muffled, gyrating sounds of the overfull streets, the circle of little clay Chinamen sitting on their haunches beside a mountain of traders' baggage, the mirrored glass in the windows of dilapidated private homes, which were strange, the way sunglasses can be strange on old people's faces—that it was this that was *reality*, not a dream, that the objects here denoted nothing but themselves and did not predict her destiny. This alone would remain, she told herself, when Alexei Afanasievich was no longer on this earth. Somewhere among the new, *abstract* human breeds—especially often she came across bloated beauties in slim black coats, with lips like bonbons, and businesslike young men wearing jackets sticking out under leather jackets—the people near and dear to her, a mere handful, had gone missing, and now Nina Alexandrovna wanted to be convinced of the reality of their existence. One day, she thought she recognized the broad-shouldered man who spilled out in a businesslike way from the front seat and across the windows of a dirty Zhiguli that drove off immediately as her nephew—his purple ear, his bulging cap, his spattered trousers. But then the man lit up out of his fist, turned his repulsive, pockmarked, alien face toward the smiling Nina Alexandrovna, and moved toward her quite calmly. Reality had preserved a few islands of goodness after all. One day, next to a concrete wall behind which a Metro construction site was rattling and thumping away, Nina Alexandrovna saw a fine-looking man who from the back looked like her son-in-law Seryozha carefully supporting the elbow of his ungainly companion, who was wearing a flowered, rhinestoned scarf and a long coat and whose cautiously stepping feet reminded her of duck's feet; a block farther on a child in a red snowsuit chased chubby pigeons that were too lazy to fly and only ran, spreading their wings and tails just slightly, while the child was responsibly shepherded along by a gangly soldier who looked as flat as a domino in his greatcoat. Although touched, Nina Alexandrovna couldn't shake the feeling that only she and no one else was seeing this. The sun's odd light, the harsh light of the last autumn clarity before a wet snowfall, like an ax hacking away at a bared wooden carcass left over for the winter from the summer's splendor, had come from so far away, its source lay so many tremendous thousands of kilometers away, that the reality en route to demolition seemed insignificant, illuminated *from there* out of some pitying interest. The man on the street whose temple was beveled by the sun was also quite blind, his opinion was of no account, and his head spun from the presence of the abyss, and maybe from death's presence in each piece of substance, from the heightened background on winter's eve; strange though it seemed, only this background let the weary Nina Alexandrovna feel briefly like one of the many people in the fresh air, which was practically solid from the cold, so that there was even something crystalline about the little sun, which had sprouted icy needles.

■ □ ■

Election day opened as if to order: a splendid, wintry, golden Sunday, a long, quiet morning, a blush along the entire butt cheek of the sleeping apartment building; the windows of the prefab buildings—so faceless that it was almost impossible to imagine a human face looking out from them—were gently tinted a pearly white. Splendid snow-mica toward the top sprinkled over the unsuccessful, dwarfish relief sculpted by the various types of autumn snow from the unattractive material that had fallen to the ground; snow in the pose of a cat lay on the cornice of a very tall and bare school window that looked out on a playground where an empty basketball hoop was covered with a frosty sky, like a bulging iridescent film for blowing clusters of melancholy soap bubbles.

Starting around ten, the school with the polling place where Marina had been assigned as an observer shone in the sun and snow like a very bright, very clean diagram and was filled with the drone of voices. In the auditorium, a buffet table sponsored by the A Fund had been set up around four samovars, where four pretty servers wearing sarafans and kokoshniks were cheerfully selling fantastically cheap baked goods, yeast dough in sealed bags, and frozen pelmeni that looked like bruises. In the vestibule, everyone who had come to vote was met by the candidates' portraits in alphabetical order—the two main ones and three additional ones; these false targets, shot into the air by Apofeozov's headquarters, were as unprepossessing as good color printings allowed, absent gazes that looked past the voter, who, in turn, let his gaze fall on these sunken faces as he did on the sunken keys of the voting machine. On the other hand, Fyodor Ignatovich Krugal, who toward the end of the campaign had tried desperately to look younger, had insisted that his flyer run a ten-year-old photograph of him that had once hung in the plush lobby of the provincial dramatic theater—and doubtless someone had vaguely recognized this winning three-quarters pose, the curving jaw that looked like a pill in a paper nest, the grape cluster of Italian curls placed on what looked like a larger fruit, the jutting brow of an actor who played lead roles but in the theatrical troupe's second-string cast. Of all the candidates, Apofeozov alone was present *here and now*. The joy on his face was irrefutable proof that the birdie had only just flown from the photographer's camera.

The observers from Apofeozov headquarters—a prim gentleman who looked like a well-educated Hitler and whose jacket was a little too big for him and kept slipping off his right shoulder, and a slim brunette in a peach blouse who had red spots on her clavicle, which poked out of her low neckline like glasses' earpieces—were so amiable and even loving, it was as if they'd become man and wife for this Sunday. They wandered confidently among the voters, like salesclerks in an expensive shop, and readily came to the assistance of perplexed old women who kept being afraid of ruining the big white sheet of paper given them, where the candidates' names stood firmly and in order, while the empty boxes opposite their names kept slipping and getting mixed up; other timid voters, seeing such authoritative graciousness from the consultants, approached them with questions and even stood in line, their round, woolen backs gradually melting around the edges, as if covered in sweat from their zeal for listening to competent and pleasant voices. Marina knew she had the right and duty to stop this, but her soul, which seemed filled with pig iron, remained so fixed as to feel immovable. The cramped school desk (the voting organizers had set up a presidium table and a classic, dry-throated gray pitcher for the Apofeozov people) pressed painfully against her knees and in a way reminded her of the medieval stocks where a criminal was ensconced on a square for the crowd's enjoyment; it took Marina an incredible effort of will just to wiggle out of this instrument of torture and go to the bathroom. She, too, could have mingled and talked to people, but the voters who flooded past (turnout, as everyone noted, was unusually high) were an indistinguishable mass with a multitude of human hands carrying something, handing things to each other, manneredly removing their tight gloves, as if plucking flowers, and pulling an unusually dirty handkerchief out of their pocket like a page out of a book. In the homogenous crowd, Marina could not pick out *her* canvassers and recognized them only when they demonstrated their familiar trick of taking a flat object out of tight clothing and showed their passport; at that moment, as if just looking on, Marina saw the dank headquarters basement and the slow line trailing along the walls, where people, because they were now where someone else had just been, were like shapeless specters. The canvassers, too, probably recognized in the sleepy woman behind the desk the person who had given them the advance money in the basement; their looks, cast from the registration tables, were the *remembering* looks of traitors. One slight consolation was that nearly all her recruits showed up at the head of a decisively arranged handful of invitees: after being given their ballots, these communities of all ages crammed together into the cramped, curtained booths, which were like department store changing rooms, and occupied them for an amazingly long time, evoking concern among the salesclerk-consultants about the integrity of the goods—after which the delegation's head, somewhat tousled and rather disheveled, as if he really had stripped down to his underpants in the booth, led his people toward the ballot box.

Marina's partner was Lyudochka, of course, who showed up at the polling place wearing a miniskirt so tight it looked like it was about to split and didn't leave much room for her heavy legs, which were swathed in velvety Lycra. Apparently, she had taken an active dislike to the Apofeozov brunette, so she perched on a light stool and kept crossing and recrossing her legs, with the obvious intention of letting the brunette's provisional husband see the tightness and darkness, barely covered by the diagonally stretched fabric, and casting flickering looks over her open compact, making her foe's mustache quiver like a leaf stuck on her upper lip. Nonetheless, her rival did not yield to the provocation and, her high forehead patterned like an actual tree haughtily blazing, demonstratively took the arm of her headquarters better half—for which he was encouraged with doses of a smile. Lyudochka responded with a sullen grimace. This was outrageous, of course, and the local teachers registering voters gave Lyudochka the hairy eyeball—but Marina herself was in such a state that she couldn't inflict even that kind of indecent injury on her opponent.

She was surrounded by a strange, lifeless emptiness. Not that she hurt, but the cotton wool resting on her heart like a solid compress did. Ever since Klimov, caught in their marital bed embracing an unbuttoned pillow, covered in feathers, like a skunk in a henhouse, had finally been kicked out, Marina had felt bereft of ordinary human emotions. Each morning she woke up with the memory of how he'd woken up that time, without even looking at what had roused him (the chair piled with his clothing, which Marina had gently pushed over); his eyes opened immediately and looked up, as if they'd seen a snow-white angel on the ceiling lamp. Marina, whose heart was pounding as it had during their first declaration of love, had expected him to try to justify himself and cite fantastic circumstances that she herself could have dreamed up for him—but Klimov didn't even try to say anything and walked around in front of Marina shamelessly, wearing just his clingy swimsuit, which he adjusted by slipping his finger under the side elastic and shaking his leg, whereas Marina was embarrassed even to change into her robe and stand in front of him in her swimsuit, as black and rigid as a fly. This whistling Klimov was an utter stranger and even a different color. His body, always white in the sun, like a 10-watt frosted lightbulb, and afterward shedding its sticky skin like a new potato, down to the same defenseless whiteness, now had a crude tan that lay in scarlet and brown patches on his filled-out shoulders. In his new guise, bowlegged and tenacious, including his polished bald head with three identical yokes of eyebrows and mustache, something quite Asiatic came through, as if his unattractive girlfriend had made him change his nationality. Klimov didn't utter a word of objection to the demand to free up the veteran housing he had no right to; the things Marina had provided he kicked with cheerful indifference into his yawning gym bag, and after a while it became clear that all his pants and jeans had been stuffed into the very bottom of the lumpy packing, and if Klimov was to have something to wear when he left the building, he had to dump back out on the bed all his limp, unfresh rags, among which a bright red sweater Marina had once knit from very expensive English yarn stretched out like a victim pulled from rubble.

After Klimov's departure, everything seemed both exactly the way it had before and at the same time slightly unreal, as if Marina had rendered habitable an *invented* environment that someone had once described in words. If she was going somewhere, she felt as though she were taking a *narrated* route, and she would recognize *narrated* buildings and lanes that corresponded rather loosely to their communicated features—and sometimes the discrepancies multiplied so quickly that Marina's sense of direction evaporated and she could have gotten lost if it weren't for the strange paucity of things. The world around her was surprisingly empty. This corresponded to the devastation of late autumn, when something on the naked streets seems to get cleared away or borne off, but you can't figure out what, and the heart searches for what doesn't exist, and you see trees on which not a single leaf remains filled with the substance of emptiness, and their blackened branches don't have a single cell left not filled to bursting with empty, colorless space. All this time, Marina couldn't shake the *physical* sensation that nothing was worth anything now. Randomly wandering into high-end clothing stores, she could barely keep from laughing when she discovered tags on soft slippers with seven-figure prices that meant exactly nothing. Now Marina imagined the same kind of label on the back of each person's neck. When she watched Professor Shishkov scribbling and speckling the campaign's newspaper galleys with insertions, as if deriving the square root from each statement and turning the article into a system of mathematical calculations, the professor seemed to be distracted by his irritatingly stiff, neck-scraping label. When candidate Krugal, having first looked around to make sure there were no reporters, started luxuriously scratching his back against the door-jamb, as if dancing the lambada, not sparing his cashmere Hugo Boss jacket one bit, Marina had no doubt that the artist had a whole sheaf of that lacquered stuff dangling from his collar. No, Marina didn't really feel bad. She could smile and joke as if nothing were the matter—although her smile gave her away more than her usual, even serenity, her even voice, and her half-mast eyes. She really wasn't suffering particularly. Her head, which had been splitting the entire month previous from campaign cares, had stopped hurting. Marina even had her appetite back, or at least, at the headquarters dining table, she ate as much as the others, only for some reason all the food was tasteless and dense, like underbaked bread that Marina seasoned with her own sourish saliva. Sometimes she thought she might not be nearly as picky about food as ordinary people, and if she needed to weigh down her stomach with something, then she might as well gnaw on a wet, stringy branch, say, or bite off a crumbled corner of the crackly brown Khrushchev-era apartment building that all the candidates had promised to raze. Crazy thoughts like that amused Marina. She felt like a toothy predator from a Hollywood movie capable of devouring steel, stone, and concrete. In moments like these, the far from foolish Lyudochka, who for some time now had been jealously eyeing all her possible future bosses, would give her coworkers a look to turn their attention to Marina Borisovna and would twist her finger at her temple as if she were dialing a long telephone number.

■ □ ■

In fact, the true predator to loom up like Godzilla over District 18's primitive urban landscape was Valery Petrovich Apofeozov. One relatively beautiful, sun-yellow Sunday, a brigade of Turks who did not speak Russian unfurled his portrait many meters high on the side of a twelve-story apartment building that was not one of the best but that stood on a hill and was visible at that moment from nearly every point of the engraved district, which gleamed like a ruble. Unfurled over some outdated mosaic figures whose hands were lifting a satellite and whose legs seemed to be wearing brown, black, and nude stockings, the painfully vivid portrait of the people's leader billowed slightly, and from time to time folds stretched over it, making it seem as though the leader was chewing on a rusted balcony bit off the nearest wall and was just about to take a step forward to wade waist-deep through the smoking ruins like a swimmer through waves. At the same time, the viewer couldn't shake the distinct impression that everything here was here thanks to him. Given such intent and loving care, the district seemed to acquire a self-awareness and even a semblance of sovereignty. It was hard to believe in its daily diffusion and dissolution without visible borders in the soaked urban tracts, which in turn dissolved from the cloudy rain and the industrial waste that fed the soil and air, just as it was hard to believe in the flat areas, which were scarcely nature and were more like half-green economic wastelands where nature did not get the solitude it needed to weave its private secret even between three birch trunks. The voting district's residents, who had absolutely no choice about declining the printed campaign materials, knew, as any citizen does, the shape of their state, the outlines of their electoral district, which on maps looked like a woman's hand with short, bent fingers. More-over, the graphically legible lifeline, the role of which was performed by a dead little stream, turned out to be so long that in and of itself it inspired groundless but for this reason contagious optimism.

The optimism epidemic set off by Apofeozov's life-affirming per-sona took on truly fantastic forms. Several residents whose faces had become hollow-cheeked and gray from long years of poverty, like that cheap eviscerated fish they bought in frozen slabs from wholesale shops, suddenly yielded to the illusion that a car and bank account were possible in their lifetime, too. Under the influence of strange, iridescent fluids, unemployed Igor P., still a decent man in cracked glasses and clean clothing that looked like hospital pajamas they were so old, showed up one day in broad daylight at the super-market, chaotically collected in his cart a mountain of items that fell to the floor, pushed his load up to the checkout line, and instead of paying, demanded cash. A dreamy smile wandered across the assail-ant's intelligent face, and an ax-like item that looked to the cashier like her grandmother's meat grinder but subsequently turned out to be a six-barreled rifle of Afghani production started shaking in his hands. Security hustled over and had no problem taking the heavy object, which hadn't been fired in years, from the bluish hands of the former senior research associate, who immediately sank with relief—and this wasn't the only instance of an optimistic criminal. Some even tried to get rich by showing their victim a chicken bone wrapped in newspaper.

Apart from the get-rich-quick spirit that had stamped the golden autumn with a strange literalness and lent the foliage the paranoid gleam of a dream coming true, a more complex emotional phe-nomenon was felt in the district that could be defined as citizens' sudden belief in immortality. The situation *here and now* had taken on incredible acuity; moments now seemed to stop at the least whim, at the wave of a hand, and since you were alive this minute, then it was totally unnecessary for you ever to alter this satisfactory state of affairs. The inhabitants simply wanted someone to give voice to their condition, to assert authoritatively what they were each thinking privately. Unlikely to have established business contacts with the Apofeozov headquarters, more likely sensing in the atmosphere a seductive void that he could and should fill, a doctor of nontraditional medicine—the author of a rainbow of brochures and an honorary member of some incredibly long-named academies by the name of Kuznetsov, which, ironically enough for that industrial district, means "Smith"—came to District 18. Initially, the lettuce-green posters posted everywhere and carefully stuck to even very complicated surfaces, led the public to take Mr. Kuznetsov for yet another candidate, but they soon figured out what was what and flocked to the Progress Cinema, which for over three years had been rented out for shows and had stood encased in a multi-tiered scaffolding that made the building look like a Chinese pagoda—so much so that many of the district's inhabitants had supposed the cinema in the scaffolding was long gone. As it turned out, though, it wasn't. You had to enter through a covered wooden walkway splotched in ossified repairs that began far from the old front entrance and, under the uneven weight of many steps, had warped so badly that stagnant water oozed between the weak floorboards like doughnut filling. After sidestepping a damp area of sludgy water in your nonwaterproof footwear, you ended up in that very same lobby where you had once eaten ice cream before seeing *Irony of Fate*. In the dimness (the filthy windows glowed like blank frames from an old film), the gray columns still stood, like shadows, each as if between two mirrors coated by time, and walking up to one of them and not seeing your own reflection in the nearest one, you suddenly felt the emptiness of this architectural cave, even if the ruin was full of people who had bought their thirty-ruble tickets next to the old refreshment stand. The stand—apart from Dr. Kuznetsov's assistant, of whom all you could see were his quick white hands and low-bent bald spot—was decorated with a monster of a machine that had happened to survive and had three, spectrally gray cylinders for selling fruit juices, of which one was blacker than the others and of a color reminiscent of a burned-out lightbulb. The conversations between the people waiting impatiently for the performance to begin seemed to reverberate on the resonant ceiling, which had its own feminine voice and collected the sounds on an invisible lens; finally, a loose-jointed buzzer buzzed.

Everything in the theater was exactly as it had been during the days of Soviet cinema. The rows of flipped-up wooden chairs, like rows of wooden briefcases, were all mixed up: row five followed row eight and row fifteen was missing altogether. On the other hand, the metal rings of the green plush drapes, which had hardened with age, like canvases painted with stiff oils, clattered exactly as before, and the small yellowed screen was still in place, as if it had collected dust from all the film beams that had ever flickered above viewers' heads, beams that had once held popular artists—the objects of candidate Krugal's unjust envy—like cosmonauts in a spaceship flying at the speed of light. Dr. Kuznetsov always arrived ten to fifteen minutes late, forcing the seated hall to spend a long time looking at the coffee table prepared for the maestro and the spindly-legged chair that was too tall for him which, taken together—due to the fact that you could see through this rather contrived composition—reminded you of a magician's setup. Finally, when the most nervous were starting to think that Kuznetsov had been in the hall for a long time and would materialize any second from the cleverly set-up, supposedly empty set, the long-awaited maestro stepped on stage with his cozy, flannel-soft step. After blowing and spitting at the microphone, which hissed as if it were red hot, the professor told the audience in a slightly muffled voice that the human organism was meant to live for at least one hundred fifty years and that following up on his therapeutic lecture would not only help each person start down the path to longevity but also, through its particular sonic and symbolic components, produce a rejuvenating transfusion of energy not unlike the way his unenlightened colleagues in ordinary clinics performed a routine blood transfusion. Gradually, the warmed-up hall's discordant wooden creak fell into alignment, like galley oars gnashing or park swings swinging, straining to clear the bar; the gussied-up women, one in four of whom was a Kuznetsova, too, leaned in waves from right to left and left to right, insensibly rubbing soft shoulders and gazing at the maestro with many pairs of eyes deeply set in darkness; every so often, eyeglasses would flash lemur-like in the swaying rows.

The professor, who was so marvelous at adjusting his patients to the wooden-lattice milieu their bodies were inside, was unusually convincing because of his appearance as well. His large face was made up of parts that looked sanded, without any wrinkles whatsoever, and between these broad patches of youth lay winding darknesses that also looked sanded, darknesses that retained the professor's age, like soil in the cracks of a polished stone. From a distance, the caprice of these dark deposits made his face look like jasper. Even more convincing was the appearance on the stage of Kuznetsov's assistant, who, the maestro swore, had recently turned sixty. The youthful, languid blonde, sky-high tall, her ears sticking out of her limp locks, ears that in turn had silly gold earrings sticking out from them, like fishhooks, was not only long-lived but also a famous poetess. After she was announced, she strode nonchalantly downstage (the front rows distinctly heard the blonde's big feet scuffing against each other under the crushed evening gown, whose only adornments were a few crude rhinestones), brought a thin passport-sized book right up to her eyes, and began in a mournful, nasal singsong to recite a poem about dark passion and a glass of red wine, about the evening seas and a youth of antiquity with curls like tea rose petals whom the poetess reproached for cruelty and the loss of certain important keys described with a metalworker's precision. After pausing, like a little bird, to feed on the crumbs of applause skipping through the rows, the professor informed the quieted audience that the poems of his talented companion not only possessed great artistic merit but also, by virtue of the energy they contained, healed various illnesses, from women's ailments to neuroses, and suggested that sufferers send him anonymous notes to the stage.

Immediately, the now buzzing hall sprang to life, and more notes were sent to the stage than the professor could possibly get through by the performance's end. However, after sorting through the squares and scrolls of paper with his usual knack (the long-lived assistant meanwhile stood perfectly still like an impenetrable barrier on the path to any human thought about her therapeutic poetry), he handed out the most frequent diagnoses and took over supervising the reading entirely. He said that an elegy edged on the right by an elegant ornament to the rhyme and having as its subject a recent kiss in a lyric garden as unnatural as a flower shop helped the stomach; for high blood pressure, a ballad was read, a long one, like a multiplication table, in which two medieval kings, one handsome and the other ugly, multiplied endlessly in tessellated rhymed quatrains and deep secret mirrors—and what the languishing Kuznetsovas in the audience listened to for appendicitis was a treasure house, so easily was everything the long-lived assistant's pen touched transformed into emeralds and rubies. Even a common sparrow, which for some reason had flown into these poetic skies covered with a frightening moiré of clouds, became at the poetess's word a golden figurine and, one had to suppose, was immediately plunked into the common treasure chest.

No one understood why such vivid happiness spilled from the stage. The women who were offered something that was simultaneously a cure for illnesses and about love had the vague feeling that they were getting exactly what they wanted. Others had hysterics. A chubby, likeable woman on whose cheeks' tear tracks sparkled like tinsel nearly rushed the stage to sing. She was nabbed before she could and blanketed in polite murmuring by the professor's assistant, who materialized out of the dimness not all at once but one distinct contrasting part at a time, kind of like a movie. It cost the professor no small effort to bring the audience to relative order. He stood on tiptoe and waved his arms as if he were trying to hang an invisible towel on a high branch. Finally, after restoring quiet, Dr. Kuznetsov moved on to the most important part of his performance and reported on the essence of a personal discovery he had made. No, he uttered solemnly, strutting in front of the screen on one side and the audience on the other (moreover, the screen reflected him no less closely than the raised faces), there was no universal recipe for longevity. What people said today about breathing exercises and the necessity of drinking cold and warm water alternately was undoubtedly beneficial and would help each of us, and everyone sitting in that hall would get noticeably younger in the coming years. But in order to achieve the ideal correlation to one's true age (here the audience turned their gazes to the rosy, sixty-year-old blonde with cheeks like two jars of jam), an individualized health regimen was desirable, along with special blank verse composed for each person separately. Those who were prepared to take care of themselves comprehensively the professor invited to his personal consultations in such and such a room at the North Hotel. He also informed them that his estimable assistant's book would be available for sale in the lobby as they exited.

There was something inexpressibly seductive in the professor's performances. Because they took place in the Progress catacombs (the professor was exceptionally sensitive to his environment's emanations), the more mysterious cinematic effects were emphasized all the more distinctly—along with stage effects picked up, like an infection, from some variety show. Thus, individual lady patients imagined there was no Dr. Kuznetsov in the hall at all, there was just a depiction on the dusty screen that, like a flock of silly butterflies, could land on everything that fell into the film beam; others subconsciously saw in the healer an art scholar introducing before the viewing that same film about love in which they had always dreamed of playing the heroine, and now their dream was finally about to come true. The professor's work in the district could also be compared to the work of the early days of cable television, when the business's pioneers would run several American films a night; at the time it seemed as if real life, in watercolor due to the low quality of the pirated cassettes, was just about to begin here, too, that each person would be like Sharon Stone or Arnold Schwarzenegger, and if someone still had material problems, then they would be measured in the millions of dollars.

Now, in some unfathomable way, romantic hopes had returned to human hearts, which in District 18 were like fruits in a Garden of Eden. Candidate Apofeozov, having acquired a private house and a Mercedes by his talents, so praised by the press, was a genuine hero of the new era in which low-level managers and the unemployed, homemakers and the homeless had all of a sudden come to believe. Even though for all these ten years most residents hadn't been able to break away from the gloom of their miserable apartments, which had rusted like enamel basins, their family jalopies, and all the Soviet goods they'd acquired, which were now worthless and screamed their fantastic unreality from every corner and at every step— Apofeozov, endowed with an indestructible will for *actual reality*, became what every inhabitant of the district should have become had it not been for the illusory quagmire of the everyday, of habits, of outmoded professions. Only Apofeozov, whose tie pin cost so much as to become an almost magical object, could represent the district in the Duma; Apofeozov was loved the way people could love an American president running in District 18. Professor Kuznetsov's experiments (his female patients, after spending time with him in the hotel, returned covered in gooseflesh, as if they'd been rolled in semolina, and for a while would express themselves exclusively in verse) promised each person not only longevity and an extended youth but in essence the rescinding of their past life. Each could now start over, from childhood if they liked, which is what happened with many. Immediately several stores, including Athens Furs, were robbed with the help of cap guns—good-looking hunks of metal, caps that clicked loudly like smelly tiddlywinks—after which the

Athens window, decorated with marble copies of gods and heroes dressed in fur coats, started looking tediously like the Pushkin Museum of Fine Arts. Children's World, in turn, enjoyed brisk sales of metal and plastic toy guns, so that Nina Alexandrovna, wandering there as before in vague search of a Young Magician's Set that might distract the veteran from his magnetic rope play, was struck by how empty the department was, like frontline positions abandoned by a retreating army. Only tin soldiers, like spent cartridges, lolled on the shelves, which were cleared back to the wall. The sleek manager who was loitering for some reason behind a bare counter looked shell-shocked, and his smile, which automatically popped up whenever a customer got close enough, made no sense at all.

■ □ ■

Actually, no insanity could surprise Krugal's campaign headquarters: things happened here that made the performances at the outwardly invisible Progress Cinema seem like sweetness and light. Professor Shishkov's plan, which had seemed at first like the model of a brilliant economy of means, had become a black hole. The top estimate for the cost to ensure victory for his candidate had been left in the distant past. In the basement, whose walls, rubbed by the human mass's slow scuffling, had changed from latte to dirty pink, insane sums were handed out every day. Professor Shishkov lost weight and firmly avoided discussions of their prospects, and his gestures and expressions were like a Moebius strip. Twice, without telling anyone, Shishkov took the red-eye to Moscow and brought back sponsor cash obtained in exchange for secret promises. But even these fat packets, which in the beginning had looked like a *reserve*, were snapped up like ice cream bars during a hot spell, and the district residents kept coming. The slightest delay opening headquarters in the morning, and the outside metal door would start to boom under the pounding of fists, and individuals would squat at the windows—where you could barely see strips of slanted light, like the edges of sheets in half-open drawers—impatient: their inverted faces looked down, into the inverted little world of the headquarters basement, and for some reason these people seemed like giants, their hanging heads looking into a dollhouse standing defenseless before them.

Having lost control of the situation but not his mind, Professor Shishkov understood full well that if he stopped handing out money to canvassers, then everyone who hadn't received his legitimate share would vote against Krugal in the elections, merely out of a sense of outraged justice. So he kept it up, taking his medicine, seeking out funds, and just told his registrars to work as slowly as possible. Each of them invented his own red tape, which made it look as though the disciplined headquarters workers had suddenly fallen ill. They truly didn't know what to do with themselves under the impatient stares of the pressing people in the middle of their workspace, which was now alienated and in a way undermined by the demand to slow things down. As a result, the registrars, working as if under someone's hypnotic loupe, in its powerful magnifying jelly, became deathly afraid of making grammatical errors in the logbooks. One impressionable worker had a newly opened pack of fifty-ruble bills go missing, and one woman ground her twisted chair into its extreme position, as if shifting a system of levers, and proceeded to faint.

Some, unable to withstand the pressure from the soggy line that kept coming in from the street—pressure that mounted, pistonlike—would sit for hours in the headquarters' back room, but even from there they could hear the line, which no one was waiting on but which, obeying its inherent direction, would automatically take a small step every ten minutes—like dozens of shovels driving higgledy-piggledy into a blunt heap of immovable earth. Sharp-witted Lyudochka was the first to notice that the expression "standing in line" was a misnomer because in fact no one was standing: no sooner did people line up single file than they immediately got the impulse to forge ahead, as if the line could become humanity's long-sought means for passing through walls. Even in the absence of a registrar, the body of the line, pressed forward and cut off at the tail (those who had joined last and who had gone off on errands comprised a kind of extensible cloud impregnated with a very fine frozen rain) continued to *function*: dozens of feet shifted, scuffed, and kicked at bags, and some adjusted their fogged-up glasses on the shoulders of those standing in front of them. In order to stand and also rest a little, they had to step to the side and find a spot by the wall; there, shirking the common efforts and rubbing their somber coats against the dirty pink, unusually corrosive chalk, there were always individualists hanging around with their noses in books. How they were able to read under the bare, low-wattage bulbs, which rather than spread light seemed to suck it up and collect it from the whole corridor, a thimbleful for each, was anyone's guess, as was why the district's inhabitants kept streaming into headquarters for their pathetic fifty rubles with a doggedness worthy of some better application. Most likely, they were driven here by a sense of fairness that demanded the equal distribution of free stuff, just for the signing.

Some applicants, in no way discouraged by the delay getting to the dispensing tables, came several times each. The line's stamp on them did not come down just to yesterday's and the day before's traces of corridor chalk but was expressed in the particular ways of habitués. Doubtless they had taken a fancy to the quaint playground opposite headquarters for their drinking, a playground that vaguely resembled a circus ring with props for small trained animals. In the evenings, the workers would sit for a while after closing and then emerge into the dark courtyard, where a thick layer of wet leaves lay like tea at the bottom of a teapot, and they would notice on the playground an untoward, residual presence: stooping figures whose stirrings the eye picked up against the small plaster statue of a Young Pioneer that had been shoved into a bush. Their volumes collided neatly, and sometimes their out-of-control shouts sent a maddened cat flying across the lawn like a sudden missile. Marina, who had not been singled out by any specific assignment but who had come to a feel an almost maternal responsibility for the staff's well-being, understood full well that if the residents of the surrounding pensioner apartment buildings had still not complained to the newspapers or the police, it was only because they themselves, to a man, had taken canvasser money and had hopes for even more. After the workers separated and ran off to wherever, and the professor's old heap, having fallen into a sneezed puddle, turned onto the avenue, Marina, overcoming her chemically complex fear of men and the dark, attempted to get closer to the picnic herself to ascertain whether it did or didn't have anything to do with their headquarters. In reality, she only managed to take three or four hesitant steps over the slick leaves in that direction. If anything could be seen more clearly from that compromise distance, then it was the abandoned Pioneer hero with his smashed tie and scary little face, like plaster dough. Several times on the playground she saw a mellow fire sputtering in the drizzle; in its little red cloud you could see pink hands in thick gloves occasionally tossing cardboard scraps on the fire—but even in this dim light Marina was able to identify the faces of two or three half-basement acquaintances, which for some reason seemed very old-mannish and shimmered with a fleeting heat, like cracked coals. Ever since then, this inevitable discovery had weighed on Marina with a presentiment of disaster.

Marina's intuition told her that the local populace's persistence was a legitimate part of the general campaign madness. Evidently, the romantic determination to get rich inspired by Apofeozov's person wouldn't let the voters pass up even the very small chance his nominal opponent's headquarters offered. It was also likely that the bonus promised to canvassers in the event of Krugal's victory—even though it was a known and modest quantity—was in some way linked in their bewitched minds to all the fantastic promises that that unrecognized artist had made in his two low-budget videos. Despite the fact that an inspired Krugal, appearing on the backdrop of a streaming state flag, spoke about local improvements, in particular about the now notorious natural gas scheme for the private sector, the viewer got the feeling he was talking about some small town in Latin America; whereas when Fyodor Ignatovich, shot on a backdrop of the district's real scrap heaps and characteristic semi-ruins, which were oriented, like anthills, from north to south, replaced the deplorable landscapes with computer pictures with the wave of an illusionist's hand, the voter's native clay soil slipped out from under his feet altogether. Perhaps because the sun in the pictures was unusually intense, lending the white architectural mirages' surfaces the vividness of film screens, the resident had the vague feeling that they meant to relocate him to Rio de Janeiro; he probably imagined that his post-election bonus would simultaneously be a share in those fairytale tropical hotels that this large-browed man in the light, loose trench coat with all kinds of compartments and big buttons like electric outlets was somehow going to build in place of their potholes and damp hovels.

Although she'd written the scripts for both videos, even Marina couldn't figure out why on paper the district sounded *fictional*—despite the fact that she now felt a strange tenderness for District 18, as if it were her little homeland whose presence so close to hand she hadn't had so much as an inkling of before the elections. Previously, her life had always extended from home to the right—toward downtown, where with each intersection everything got fancier and cleaner, where a third-rate town was gradually replaced by a second-rate one. But now she had turned left, toward the poor, muddled place that Marina in the last four months had come to know better than in all the years before, when the district sloping to the horizon had been just a boring view out her window. Now that the traitor Klimov had left her altogether for his Asian girlfriend, Marina discovered that she was more at ease in her district than anywhere else. She liked to say hello on the street to people she half knew. She was surprisingly mollified by the landscape's slope and its pallid colors, the prone poses of every part of the undulating relief, the black wooden dampness of the weather-beaten fences, and the old-people scent of damp nettles full of water, rot, and strong, rubbery spiderwebs. All this was *real*—unlike the situation in the "right" part of town, which Marina had for too long depicted as the place for her life going forward, without Klimov, but now, finding herself in this new life, she couldn't convince herself of the reality of those streets, which moved a little too fast, like sped-up film.

Here, in District 18, even shaded by the waist-length portrait of her waterproof foe, everything coincided gratifyingly with the rhythm of leisurely steps and unhurried thoughts; everything here was *pedestrian*, and the remains of the leaflets about hiring canvassers, which had disintegrated in the wet and lingered the way a butterfly leaves patterned dust, nothing but a fluffy scrap of letters, evoked waves of nostalgia. Obviously, no one had read these old papers—pasted up in the dark and as if spoiled by the light of the many passing days—in quite a while. Not only that, it was gratifying to observe a tall blonde in a worn green coat and black bell-bottoms, which looked like two whale's tails, trying to read, with a childlike curiosity, the chilled notice half stuck into a fence's cracks. At the sight of this simplehearted child tall enough for basketball licking a melting ice cream bar with her milky tongue, Marina felt that life had a sentimental value independent of Klimov's presence or the invented Communist Party membership that no longer warmed or inspired her in any way. Her paralyzed stepfather, papered over with skin that was already thinned and run through with frozen veins, resided in the ocean-bottom depths of old age's oblivion. For him, all the objects in his room, including the Brezhnev portrait Marina had stolen from the university's Theory and Practice of the Press department, were nothing more than *his* memories. These *long-ago* things, covered with the finest layer of dust, made thirsty by her mother's endless housecleaning, remained in place with the help of the same magnetism as did the weak smell of the burned match from which her stepfather probably had been intending to smoke when a small vessel in his head burst with a roar. It would be simply blasphemous to rouse this half-dead body to participation in life, even if it was an invented life and bore no relation to reality. It was wrong to taunt the old man with the television, which made the paralyzed man's neck tense on its taut roots, where what looked like an old scar, like a dirty silk cord, appeared. The alternate reality, in which Marina really did join the Party because she properly wanted to be among responsible and progressive people, probably had come out fairly convincingly for her, but deep down Marina always guessed that it wasn't she but her stepfather who by some incomprehensible force was maintaining his autonomous little world around him, and this force, this magnetic field, was no illusion. Now Marina just wanted to leave her stepfather in peace and save herself, her strength and blood, for feeding the spectral Klimov, whom she couldn't forget anyway. The district Marina was used to considering her own, though it was driving her quietly mad, nonetheless did allow her to breathe. Sometimes she imagined it as a discrete small town where she could know all the inhabitants by face and name, buy food in the same little shops, graciously exchange greetings with the salesclerks, and see newly arrived strangers laid out before her—the way they confidently tromped through the streets and used the newsstands and public transport, thinking they didn't differ in any way from the locals, while their *differences* became a free show for everyone. This idyll (which betrayed Marina's secret inclination to construct self-contained, illusory worlds) was so speculative that it demanded no improvement from District 18 whatsoever. Marina found even the little river's trampled banks, blotted with thick, sudsy garbage, beautiful. Blue stove smoke floating through the soft drizzle and smelling like wet wool was more romantic than banal gas burners, and the face, as bare as a mushroom, of the old woman gathering logs with her black canvas glove symbolized the reassuring mortality of all living things, which were under no obligation to overrule peaceful natural law.

For Marina, a loss in the elections now would be tantamount to being driven out of her own home. She could view an Apofeozov occupation only as a personal insult and a major calamity. So she patiently bore the trials of the campaign's last few weeks and carried out Professor Shishkov's instructions more conscientiously than anyone else. In order to work as slowly as possible, Marina counted silently, maniacally counting to as high a number as possible without losing track, even when she was recording an applicant's passport information. If the other registrars drooped more and more under the yoke of delay, even laying their heads on their tables, then Marina was like an indefatigable windup doll with a clockwork mechanism. In response to any impatient canvasser's trick, she would calmly shift to a tough division problem that demanded her full concentration. Sometimes the windup would last for as many as several difficult-to-pronounce thousands, and the higher the count went, the harder it became to balance the imagined number column and simultane-ously manipulate the registration materials spread out below. Often, Marina would drop what she'd been carrying right in front of the people languishing in line. For minutes at a time, it seemed that if she worked not slowly but, on the contrary, incredibly fast, she could be rid of, exhaust, the wearisome uncertainty and come to the end—whatever that meant—ahead of time.

■ □ ■

Nonetheless, the alarm bells that penetrated Marina's days of exhaus-tion were not just her fraught nerves dancing. One fine day she dis-covered that the line, which had been a phenomenon that renewed itself daily, had become a permanent entity. This happened when one of the basement unfortunates who flashed by, easily identified by his canvas raincoat—possibly army, possibly a fisherman's, evidently his one garment for all seasons and all life's occasions—suddenly appeared in front of her table. Taking the filthy document, like half a smoked chicken, from the autochthon's big hand, Marina noticed behind his thumb's healthy haunch a tiny, painstakingly drawn number. Thus it had come to pass that the line had become something like a citizen organization and had spontaneously inherited the power of lines that had once drilled through unnourishing socialism, like roots drilled into poor soil.

The line had given rise to its own activists. A few dyed ladies kept permanent guard at the basement door. One, taking new arrivals by the arm with the professionalism of a lab nurse, wrote a number on their palm, while the other recorded the line-standers in a tattered notebook that looked like a twisted, unfastened umbrella. She discovered the painter who, not coughing softly now but hacking and screeching like a rooster getting its throat slit, wouldn't leave the courtyard, which was already sprinkled with groats and glassy broken ice. His job was to escort out imposters who had stood in line since morning but didn't have their ink mark from yesterday, half-eaten by sweat, on their hand—which the painter did by grabbing the retracted arms, like big balky fish caught on a spinning rod, and stomping on dropped caps with his heavy army boots. He also stayed at his post when the soap opera was on television and the courtyard turned into a quickly whitening frame, where in people's wake their icy footprints disappeared as well on the increasingly pixilated, also disappearing ground, and the thin cornices were like hourglasses spilling a fine white flour. All the rest of the time, the painter engaged in commerce: he placed on the steps, under the overhang, not his own paintings, in the pathologo-anatomical genre, but bundles of decorated clay bells and little hollow ceramic birds that hooted instead of whistling, and offered them to potential customers—a painful reminder for Marina of the departed Klimov. Evidently, having slashed prices to sell, the painter was asking fifty rubles for each piece of craftsmanship—and making no sales whatsoever. When people made their way out of the dim hell with their hard-earned fifty rubles, they had no desire to trade their share of justice right there, at the door, for hollow rubbish and instead hurried to the nearest store, where they were awaited by full sealed containers whose muteness promised a depth of sensation, a clarity of conversation, an infinite multiplication of essences, and an iridescent layering of ordinary objects.

Most dangerous of all, though, was that the community brigade was in the charge of the energetic Klumba, whose head was crowned by a new mink hat as hairy as a coconut and on whose feet gleamed new boots with fashionably turned-up toes, in which Klumba braked cautiously as she stepped, as if she were constantly going downhill. The pensioner ladies around her, already wearing their dark red and navy winter coats edged in molting dog or cat fur, treated their basement elder respectfully and with a certain trepidation. No sooner did Klumba appear and begin talking to the group than they all crept away from the apartment entryways, which looked like wooden outhouses, to catch every word—although they listened as if they were always expecting bad news from her.

In charge at the headquarters entrance and personally driving off the local lush, who was nearly blind he was so bloated but who knew how to extract empty bottles from any human assemblage, Klumba squeezed through sideways, arousing agitation and a sympathetic murmur, into the registrars' room—to yell at them. Surfacing in front of the tables with her hat askew and her raspberry red lipstick smeared from ear to ear, Klumba began denouncing the red tape in bouts of speech that resembled texts by Mayakovsky in their rhymes and meter. All work came to a standstill. The registrars, taught by experience, quietly carried the money to the portable safe, and the agitation behind Klumba's back rolled to the corridor and reverberated there in a metallic echo, like when a semitruck stops short. Finally pulling out of the living human crampedness the practical bag Marina knew so well, Klumba demanded whoever was in charge of handing out the *subsidies* so they could coordinate measures.

A couple of times, unable to reach Shishkov, who had gone missing from time and space, Marina herself attempted to play a supervisory role. Klumba recognized her, but in stages. At first a suspicion dawned in her awareness and in her symmetric eyes burning on either side of her nose that instead of a supervisor they were foisting on her something she knew well that had nothing to do with supervisors, and as soon as she remembered who in fact this tightly belted Young Communist with the pinecone hairdo was, she would immediately expose the deception. Then, provocatively following Marina into the headquarters' back room, immediately clearing out the alarmed staff, who abandoned their unsweetened tea-drinking, Klumba softened a little, and her speech, still labored, as if by a stammer, an involuntarily galloping rhyming (a side effect of visiting the North Hotel), became increasingly confiding. She accepted boiling water and a steeping teabag in one of the relatively clean mugs and took from her bag a securely bound file, and out of the file—stapled sets of documents: raggedly torn-out notebook pages covered in large, old people's handwriting; statements addressed to Krugal enumerating medals, illnesses, and hardships; yellowed certificates attested to by old seals as pale as traces from glasses; diplomas falling apart at the folds into two richly soiled pieces; and archival excerpts as frail and flat as ironed rags. Occasionally even small photographs fell out of paper clips, in ones and twos. Time had stiffened the paper so that it curved like an uncut fingernail. Watching closely to see that nothing got lost or mixed up in Marina's hands, Klumba pulled out the principal summary document: a list of District 18 residents, non-able-bodied invalids and veterans of war and labor who needed subsidies more than anyone but who for health reasons couldn't stand in a line or even go outside. Their basement leader suggested home visits made by the community, which was prepared to work selflessly simply for the right to get them and their family members their subsidy without having to stand in line.

As proof that the list of the needy was no amateurish compilation but complete and objective, Klumba reminded her that she was authorized by the philanthropic A Fund, to which she had been invited, as an experienced social worker, back at the campaign's start. It was according to these lists, which had been corrected more than once, that the fund had distributed large food baskets—and now that groundwork could be used a second time and to no less benefit. Having finally recognized Marina as someone who knew full well what a helpless ill man was, Klumba found Alexei Afanasievich's number on the list with her chiseled index finger: opposite it, in the margins, which were speckled with bushes of notes and symbols, there was a checkmark and a plus sign. Indeed, Marina did recall waking up on her one day off in the past few weeks to harsh, police-like voices in the front hall. Jumping up, she saw her mother, alone, clumsily turning the locks and fumbling with a fancy bundle where on the background of vivid Aeroflot blue a polished Apofeozov headed into the bright future. Found in the gift was an entire set of literature, including Apofeozov's program printed on coated paper, a general plan for the revamping of the district (where the sketches of modern structures, which, just like in shop windows, reflected fleapits ready for the bulldozer, suddenly coincided with Nina Alexandrovna's notions of her unfilled days to come), as well as a biography of the candidate illustrated with photos from his family archive. In the first, a baby as naked as a jaybird, milky white and rather listless, reached for a blurry toy; then came a sullen schoolboy gazing intently at the ghost of his own nose; and then, as older, weary, and male-looking relatives of Apofeozov were replaced by a new population organized and cultivated by him personally, the family's First Lady began playing a bigger and bigger role in the camera's space, like a lady elephant in a submarine, and expressing through fixed poses her extreme delicacy—while her hands, constantly clutching the sleeves of some household member, were like the brutal clawed feet of an eagle hen. Highlighted in the same brochure by every possible typographical means were photos of Apofeozov with major politicians; moreover, the handshake, if there was one, made it look as though Apofeozov were grasping the lever of some mechanism or, at worst, a slot machine. The violation of election law by unbidden benefactors was blatant, and the very next day, while handing Shishkov the press release she'd written the night before, Marina reported the incident. But the professor looked the other way. Massaging his pale eye sockets, which shuddered under his fingers, he waved at Marina and left blindly, running into the white doorjamb as he went. Actually, proving a violation was almost impossible. The exact same kinds of literature, only without the cans of meat and condensed milk and sausage, were delivered to every voter; they poked out of the brutally violated mailboxes and lay scattered underfoot in residents' lobbies, their pages enriched by prints from various soles. Like it or not, Marina ended up using the Apofeozov gifts, whose sad gastric scent made it clear that they were about to expire. What stung most was that her mother didn't throw her opponent's junk literature immediately in the garbage but quietly kept it and secretly examined the family chronicle, paying special attention to the big-assed doll stretching her little hand into the blurry foreground, as if it were her own future, where her well-deserved prize awaited her.

The charity lists Klumba brought included 236 people entered into the computer and another 10 written in by hand. Accepting the perilous papers, Marina promised to consult on them, evasively citing her instructions and making it clear that the headquarters' resources in the sense of *subsidies* was extremely limited; their diplomatic talks, in which her visitor was immune to hints, like the impersonal wall behind her that was yellowed from rank whitewash, dragged the tea-drinking out for a good hour and a half. Watching Klumba dip her vanilla wafers into her cloudy tea until they were a rich velvet, Marina's grated nerves felt that even this fierce public activist, who looked like she'd stepped out of a political cartoon, embodied the human enigma. Why did she, so fastidious during her state visits to the sick and elderly and obviously not wanting to have anything to do with their mean and musty daily life, defend their interests so passionately in the outside world, thereby identifying with them—the object of a metaphysical hatred she neither could nor tried to conceal? Even before, it had occurred to Marina more than once that Klumba was behaving like a crazed Chichikov, buying up dead souls not for a mortgage but for the sake of perpetual ownership of a host of dead people; by sharing her constrained property with death, thereby violating its legal rights, one could acquire yet another surrogate of immortality—and evidently it was something of this sort that Klumba had in mind in privatizing District 18's moribund population. All the illnesses and infirmities of Klumba's charges were now at her disposal. She needed only certain mechanisms to leverage this working capital intelligently—and the Apofeozov philanthropic fund and Professor Shishkov's scheme, which Klumba was so calmly turning on its head, were of equal use here. And evidently she could do even more: the power bestowed by the summary indisposition of 250 voters was a good deal more than what an armed brigade of the same numbers could offer. Only what was to be done about her hatred for the very source of her moral enrichment—a hatred all the stronger because it wasn't human in general but specifically a *woman's*, that is, tangled up with one variety of the sense of beauty? Could Klumba, having taken in so much physical pain by proxy and worked to make that pain as real as possible for everyone, have been left unscathed by the transmission?

For all her self-confidence, she didn't look like all that perfect and indifferent an automaton. Evidently (and here Marina wasn't far from the truth), Klumba's contempt for her pensioners and invalids was a defense against the immediacy of the pain and impoverishment that reached their benefactors in digested form—which meant that Klumba was left with the remainder, the toxic waste from the production of her own power. Had she belonged to the category of politicians who derive moral capital from the collective image of the suffering citizen, from ideal dead souls previously cleansed of everything worldly, she might not have done too badly. But in order to engage in this privileged business, you had to have both money and power *already*, and Klumba came from the lower depths. She'd gained her mite of power by primitive prospecting, out of the dirty ground; she'd had to sniff the stink of suffering, see the rabbity eyes and drool of fat, mentally disabled teenagers, see a lot of musty old flesh, stumps of worn-down old fingers, white glaucoma eyes, and stale human poop on unswept floors. One could only admire Klumba's doggedness, her ability to curb her own feelings. Close up, across the table, Marina saw that the benefits rep did not in fact look younger. Quite the opposite. Purple, blue, and pink veins had swollen all over her, as if the woman had been filled with different colored inks like a ballpoint pen, and nasty tobacco-ish shadows had collected under her eyes, speaking to some hidden malady. It might well have been that Klumba (Marina didn't know this) had in fact been given some mysterious ability, had some talent for experiencing a stranger's infirmity herself, a talent that manifested itself crudely in her misfortune. Under other circumstances, Klumba (whose real name was Vera Valerievna Belokon, née Repina) might have become an exceptional diagnostician or, just as good, an indispensable nurse—not an ill woman but, thanks to her curbed and properly applied gift, quite a healthy woman with a sharp eye and rigorous hands capable of soothing inflammation and making firm dressings as pretty as a crochet doily. Evidently, this woman's path was the path of mercy, and her life should have been spent in a chlorinated hospital for the poor. Now, Klumba's path and its passionate *depiction* on the philanthropic stage had been distorted; her indomitable activity was a theater where she portrayed herself as best she could, and the list of invalids was the play Klumba passed out to the entire cast. Understandably, no power could force her to admit that she was doing something inauthentic; Klumba trampled the falsity of her efforts in a crushing passion that made her close-set eyes sink deep and glitter there like oily, spoiled egg whites.

Definitely: up close, face-to-face, she was a pathetic sight; with eyes like that, Marina even thought, Klumba should wear dark glasses.

The moment Klumba got up and moved away, though, she again looked, at a distance, like a full-bodied, thirty-year-old woman with pink blazing in her cheeks and the unconscious happiness of moving, of breathing the cocktail of oxygen and snow, of sneaking a peek at her new boots wrapped around her leg so marvelously by a braided leather lace. Marina couldn't figure out what caused this effect. District 18's very air was now probably obliterating time's devastation as it refracted, so that from far away even the pompous Khrushchev-era hulks with their 1950s resort design, which had turned to slime and rot, looked nice and new, elegant even; their precarious position at the edge of a snow-covered cliff—under which a dark, accident-fed sewer, a badly frozen puddle, lay, like a spot under a mouse—was as picturesque as a fairytale illustration. If you could somehow just not get close to anything, see everything from far away and nothing up close, then life in District 18 would be better for everyone. From that astronomical distance at which the district was illuminated and made visible (the distance from the Earth to the Sun these days was about 0.9884 astronomical units, or 147,864,640 kilometers), everything here must have looked like a little paradise beaded with buildings and gently coated with precious human breath. A protective arm seemed to sweep over the district, as if this land were the imprint of an enormous and benevolent hand that had drawn itself on the patterned surface, the way children outline their hands on paper. Marina caught herself thinking she was getting soft.

She had quietly doled out Klumba's canvasser money long ago, the very first time—Klumba, her unexpected husband, her twenty-year-old son, and her in-laws. The entire family in the passport photos

Klumba presented were like characters out of some Soviet black-and-white movie about a vanguard factory. As for the philanthropic lists, Marina wouldn't take any action; basically, she couldn't breathe a word of them. She shuddered to think what Professor Shishkov would say or do if he suddenly found out, if only from Lyudochka, about her conversations with the persistent Klumba, in which she, Marina, had nonetheless conceded, almost promised, to find the necessary funds for her invalids after all. Spending twelve thousand of headquarters' money, putting it in the hands of the self-appointed activists who had besieged the half basement, was tantamount to stealing—worse even. Moreover, there hadn't been sums like that in the safe, sums you could quietly pilfer, for a long time. Each morning, when they showed up for work and walked past the early birds who'd marked off the location, the way a group at an entrance marks the location of a funeral, the campaign workers didn't know whether money would be brought that day, and if it wasn't, then whether they could make yesterday's leftovers stretch to the end of the workday. No one had any idea whether they would be able to survive as long as necessary without a scandal while hemorrhaging money, as if they were giving it out drop by drop to the accursed Apofeozov, or whether their efforts would be in vain after all and the sight of the battened-down half basement and the fury of the deceived people left in line on the street would give the lucky vampire a decisive advantage just before the election.

The conscious slowdown under the line's terrible, physically palpable pressure was not lost on anyone. After closing up, the registrars shuddered, and the women climbed out from behind their tables like tortured insects from half-open matchboxes. Those who could still move and think would gather with set jaws and leaden occiputs to count the remaining money. The discovery that they'd managed to spend even four hundred less than the day before would evoke weak smiles of relief and hope: people were prepared to continue the red tape torture, to wind time around their bodies as if it were a taut, ringed boa constrictor. Meanwhile, Apofeozov's people, on the contrary, were speeding up, stepping up the organizational pressure. Charter buses pulled up to the polling places, which were already open for early voting, almost like clockwork, and out of the buses, squinting, came entire labor collectives, among whom were many women all dressed up and carrying little white-blue-red flags. Others, for beauty's sake, were underdressed: their knees in thin Lycra were bright pink over their tall boots, and their gauze scarves, tucked into their coats, looked glassy and faded in the snowy wind. Occasionally, five vehicles would pull up near the polling place simultaneously and discharge very specific young citizens—wearing fur-trimmed leather and short haircuts that exposed the baby-like softness of their small but hard skulls, like snowballs kneaded by strong fingers. Everyone, including the specific ones, followed the lead of knowledgeable managers who showed up out of nowhere and were so discreet that, while having faces, seemed not to have profiles at all; the arrivals proceeded in organized fashion to the ballot boxes. The only time the polling place was closed for some reason for the latest Apofeozov tour bus, they demonstrated a few times on the TV news: an indignant voter, shaking his cropped nap, explained on inked fingers about his civic duty, and the camera lingered on an official door with a naïve "Principal" plaque shut tight to democracy. Everyone understood that the votes cast early had in one way or another not been free; however, in the election campaign, as in any business, big money fed on those who had less—so

Professor Shishkov found himself trapped, basically having played into Apofeozov's hand. The 250 invalids and old people who never left home and were incapable of shuffling to their own polling places (and were hardly able to refute what, in fact, the 50 rubles received "for charity" obliged them to do), were like full hands of utterly useless cards that Shishkov was forced to accept by the foolish logic of the events he himself had set in motion. It was very important not to yield to Klumba's pressure, especially since Shishkov's fury, had he learned of the charity lists, might prove truly terrible. Despite his emphatic calm of the last few days, his long face quivered as if he were being thwarted, and once Marina caught the utterly self-possessed professor suddenly, with incredible force, rip an emaciated plant out of a pot—and the escaped root, which looked like a rat's tail, sprinkled the professor all over with fine, caseous soil.

Clearly, Marina did not have the right to publicly divulge the true state of affairs. On the rare occasions she did get out in the fresh air to smoke (other than her, only Lyudochka dared such a bold move as throwing her wind-dappled rabbit-fur jacket over her shoulders and making small talk with the frozen-stiff painter), Marina caught the expectant looks from the friendly group, which stepped back specially to get an unconstrained look at her from a safe distance. In any case, Marina took the compromising lists verified by Kukharsky's familiar signature, which looked like a curly lamb, from headquarters, out of harm's way. At home, she hid the papers in an awful old leather bag sewn from scraps that looked like a creation of Dr. Frankenstein's, a bag she'd been tempted to buy by the naturalness of the material; she'd hoped that the shapeless monster, to which she would never entrust even the smallest denomination of currency, would digest everything she didn't want to remember during her tense daily labors and especially at night, when her pillow became as heavy as a dead body and sleep just wouldn't saturate her impervious brain, where a clear, still, empty, and anesthetized dozing buzzed and buzzed and buzzed.

■ □ ■

Winter, which for a long time had resembled an old newspaper listing the last few summer and autumn events, finally took firm hold. Venturing forth into the splendid light frost from the stifling air of her domestic immortality, Nina Alexandrovna saw in the distance, amid the well-covered vacant lots, intricate, soapy-looking cloverleaves; on the horizon, in a dark blue strip, as if in the shadow of the vast, crisp, sparkling day, she could make out a light railroad bridge, micaceous like a dragonfly wing—and under it, clearly discernible in the spiky vegetative nap, the perfectly ethereal snow-covered river stretching out as if counter to the laws of physics. Nina Alexandrovna couldn't believe it was already November and everything in her family was as before. Actually, she'd stopped trying to thwart Alexei Afanasievich's *left-handed* exercises, tacitly agreeing that she had no right to stop him and prolong his royal decomposition in a gilded sleeper coach, his body's daily torments, and the even bitterer torments of his irreconcilable spirit, which saw not the slightest sense in extending this recumbent existence. Now, if Nina Alexandrovna suddenly noticed the familiar flower of the undone rigging on the blanket, rather than rush forward, she averted her eyes. His persistent efforts to hang himself were no longer something to be hidden; it was all in the open now, the very slow fussing with ropes no longer required solitude or secrecy; husband and wife had tacitly admitted the possibility of death and its legitimate proximity. After this chaste barrier fell between the Kharitonov spouses, death for Nina Alexandrovna and Alexei Afanasievich became something much less shameful than their clumsy nighttime lovemaking, no hint of which had been permitted during the sensible daytime hours. In an odd way, this changed them both, since seemingly nothing in the relationship between the elderly spouses, one of whom was also a nonverbal, nonmoving doll, could change.

Once this had happened, Nina Alexandrovna could help Alexei Afanasievich when he was drenched from exertion with the old-man sweat, cloudy like moonshine, that burned his sheets. It would have taken Nina Alexandrovna, who was divinely nimble and light compared with the paralyzed man as she hovered over him in the apartment's rectangular heavens, mere minutes to reproduce on the blanket the well-studied bowel of death, to make all the pulls and turns and offer her spouse the ready-made noose, like the hole from a world-size bagel. But Nina Alexandrovna understood that she, as a woman, had to make sure she didn't touch *that* with her hands, that no matter how much beyond his strength it was for him to do that terribly slow, winding work, Alexei Afanasievich would never allow her to do anything improper. Basically, Nina Alexandrovna still didn't dare speak with the paralyzed man about his attempts to contrive death's universal monogram. Although Alexei Afanasievich couldn't shut her mouth with a pneumatic palm fat with pumped-up air as he once had, she well sensed the inappropriateness of any discussion—and no outside listener, had he snuck up from the dark hallway, would have caught anything at all suspicious in the comments of the wife reporting as she tended to him about the weather, burned pancakes, and the doctor's imminent arrival.

Meanwhile, her spirits fortified, Nina Alexandrovna soon became convinced that the paralyzed man, who was coming very close to a result, could never cross the invisible line. Not because Alexei Afanasievich lacked decisiveness or the frenzied soldier's obstinacy: it was just that a rubber wall kept bouncing him back. Rather than contemplate the nature of this mystical boundary, Nina Alexandrovna decided to trust in fate: simply not to want anything for herself and to accept the possibility of any turn of family events. One fine quiet night, when the lines of the glowing landscape softened for the first time under a cloak of new snow and its reliefs began to smile under the streetlamps' sparking light, Nina Alexandrovna suddenly realized she didn't have to fear death. No more did she cut off the bed the results of Alexei Afanasievich's labors; each subsequent knot, as intricate as a small animal's brain, took up minimal space on the bed lattice, but now the reflecting gold of the lattice branches barely peeked through the tangled fringe. The wonderful trophy bed had come to look like a hothouse for cucumbers. Raggedy plaits bestrewed it, and standing out like a tubular flower was the same gilded tie—she had no idea whose—as well as a few cords of quite obscure origin, unusually filthy and stringy, smelling for some reason of sweetish ash and giving the impression of *last year's* dried stems. The hothouse had not borne fruit, though. The hollow-bodied fruits (in essence, the loops, shapeless and devoid of content, were embodied nothingness) did not germinate or grow. Only a couple of times, while straightening Alexei Afanasievich's beaten-down pillows for him, did Nina Alexandrovna find behind them pathetic seed buds, tiny and stuck together, like failed cucumbers, which resembled, in turn, collapsed balloons with a curved nipple at the tip. Evidently, Alexei Afanasievich was putting the rigging not so much on himself as on his own death, but the beast would not be caught, although it was undoubtedly clawing at and consuming his soul. To judge from the opening in the loops she found, death was the size of a field mouse.

For the visit from Evgenia Markovna, the doctor, all this unattractive activity was curtained off by the caked navy blanket that had once covered the marital bed: in the depths of its permanent folds, like the powder left over in a pharmaceutical pack, a *new* blue remained, better preserved than in memory. Unaware of the paralyzed man's successes with death macramé, cautiously, not trusting her own words, the doctor gave a positive prognosis, specifically: the toes on Alexei Afanasievich's left foot had started to move, the red webbing had stretched between them, like on a duck, and the battered big toe wagged back and forth, like a lever being tested by a mechanic. As to the fingers on his working hand, they were no longer mitten-like but moved independently, and this movement had made them surprisingly long, and their tendons apparently functioned all the way up to his elbow. One day Nina Alexandrovna caught her husband with his index finger firmly aimed at the ceiling—and this *decisive* gesture was strikingly different from his usual wayward movements. At first she tried to figure out what Alexei Afanasievich was trying to say or, maybe, ask for, but then she realized that for the paralyzed man what was important was the vertical, plain and simple—a finger-length vertical, negligible compared to his mighty size, yet a victory over the *incorporeality* of his recumbent body, a ten-centimeter measure of his real existence, a successful attempt to skewer nonexistence.

The understanding that the range of possibilities was increasing, that the options for the future were growing farther and farther apart, made Nina Alexandrovna feel strangely empty and free to act. Now it was not out of the question that Alexei Afanasievich, after so many years of immobility, might by some miracle get back on his feet and forget about his attempts to hang himself; it might also be that thanks to his astonishing improvements he might actually carry out his plan. Also likely was that nothing in his usual life would change and the stagnation sealed up in that room, a stagnation sprinkled with a white sleeping powder, would retain its unique qualities and the dead would remain alive here forever. Never before had Nina Alexandrovna had such a broad range of options. Her movement from past to future had always followed the sole possible line, as if through a schematic tunnel where the inhabited cubicle "today" shifted continuously into the waiting "tomorrow:" if something altered the direction of this curve, then that "something" (Alexei Afanasievich's stroke, the introduction of free prices, the ruble's fall) immediately found itself in the past, and the more unexpected the turn, the stiffer that shift. Now Nina Alexandrovna's fate had slipped off that line like beads off a thread. Suddenly, she found herself in the middle of a big white patch without guidelines; the future no longer stood up ahead in the form of an unfilled shop window, and there was no point peering into it. From here, from the vantage of her new freedom, Nina Alexandrovna was surprised to note that it was the suicide attempt that had given the impetus to Alexei Afanasievich's recovery. That attempt had yielded an effect that medicines could not have achieved. The more furious the veteran's efforts to hang himself on one of his hardened, odd-smelling cords, the more actively his organism's restoration proceeded. His left leg had already started quietly to bend, and the veteran's knee poked up out of its horizontal nonexistence like a calloused tree root out of the earth; a crooked yawn had suddenly begun coming over Alexei Afanasievich, too, nearly ripping his half-dead facial muscles, and his face seemed to express the torments of Tantalus trying to take a bite out of some invisible fruit. Having lain all those years at death's side, a few millimeters from its sovereign boundary, Alexei Afanasievich, in his attempt to breach this final gap, had been thrown back into life by death, had bounced back from its unreached line, like a ball from a wall, and now his efforts were yielding an inversely proportional result.

Amazingly enough, Alexei Afanasievich's death and recovery posed identical practical problems for Nina Alexandrovna, including moving furniture, which now was divided into lifeless stationary objects and objects that due to the crowding kept having to be dragged around to turn the room into its nighttime version with the cot. Nina Alexandrovna tried to gauge the best way to pull and drag apart the awkward furniture jam that had formed over the years beside the paralyzed man's bed in light of his capabilities and convenience of care; she also wished she could replace the wallpaper, which was greasy from age and was pulling away from the walls in puffy yellowed folds. One day she stopped by the nearby hardware store, which had once smelled like a shed and toxic new pressed-wood furniture; nowadays the fragrant store was filled with fantastic, graceful plumbing fixtures that looked like cases for marvelous musical instruments, and Nina Alexandrovna thought she could sew an evening gown out of the wallpaper there if it hadn't been paper.

The main thing, though, was employment. Nina Alexandrovna thought she might work as an aide in an old folks' home. After fourteen years of caring for a paralyzed man, she didn't have a drop of squeamishness for old people's turbid organisms or the musty mushroom smell of their gnarled excretions. In their dilapidated corporality, old people seemed closer to nature than young people were, and therefore purer. Merely imagining replacing Alexei Afanasievich with some other "granddad" was just as hard as it was impossible to imagine another daughter replacing Marina, some stranger who wore red lipstick and drank fruit kefir in the kitchen. Be that as it may, Nina Alexandrovna knew she could handle the work. Right now she was physically stronger than she'd been at twenty-five and thirty. Her hands—now twice as thick and flabby on their backs but covered with a rough, chitinous armor—dragged and flipped over something that would have been unthinkable for her even to have attempted in her student years. Of course, Nina Alexandrovna's own health had been badly rattled. The feeling of a fist under her shoulder blade would linger for hours, and even gripping a knife as she cut vegetables she could feel it in the back of her head, where a solid air bubble throbbed right under the bone. The combination of physical strength and the unreliable fine mechanics poorly installed in her crude muscular mechanism made Nina Alexandrovna acutely aware of her own transience and each moment's insecurity. Sometimes she felt as though she could barely think. Whatever she drilled her gaze into became an insurmountable obstacle to thought, and if she succumbed to temptation and *physically* moved the impediment out of the way, then she couldn't stop herself from cleaning, as if demonstrating to herself how much simpler and more natural it was to move things than to mentally picture them having lately become free-flowing.

She did need to worry about the future, after all, and prepare for it in some real way. The only person Nina Alexandrovna could go to for advice and help was her now sober nephew. When Nina Alexandrovna finally realized that her son-in-law Seryozha was gone and wasn't coming back to their suddenly very quiet apartment

(Marina's shuffling steps, which Nina Alexandrovna continued to listen to closely, did not fill the silence, which prickled from the fine ticking of the clock), she decided, no matter what, to seek out the sole male relative capable of heading up the family at a critical time. Having no idea how to go about this properly, or whether the information bureau was still functioning, Nina Alexandrovna decided to start by inquiring at her nephew's old apartment, where she had gone regularly before his new spouse came on the scene. There was a time when she would drag bags of rotten garbage out of that den and defrost the aging refrigerator, which suffered from incontinence and barely endured its huge wet ice blocks for the sake of one frozen bag of faded hake; then Nina Alexandrovna would wash the impossible floors down to their pale, etched out spots and in the bathtub wash the gray sheets, which had started to ferment like mash. Now things in her nephew's apartment were very different, of course, and so as not to embarrass herself in front of her newly rich relative, Nina Alexandrovna prepared for her visit. She pulled out of the closet a half-forgotten, minutely moth-eaten bouclé suit, which was now so snug that her figure looked like a sheep's carcass; she searched for her fake Czech pearl beads, which had peeled like an old manicure (Alexei Afanasievich had never understood her tender attachment to all these baubles, which for her were like cheap caramels, her favorite candies, were for her sweet tooth—anything but symbols of wealthy diamonds, which were unattainable and therefore *unreal*). Finally, after finding that her old evening bag was too small for the rough, deposit-laden daytime city, Nina Alexandrovna borrowed Marina's leather bag, which was hanging idle—perhaps too young for her, but decorative and obviously recently purchased. Bags like this, made of pieces exquisitely selected according to the radial laws of avian plumage, hung in the best shops in the clothing section of the wholesale market, where the customers were fashionistas with money; this one, practically unused, with its comfortable broad strap, had a design that reminded her of a grouse. You could even see the wing's curve. Removing some loose papers that scattered staples behind them, papers that had been stuffed inside so the bag wouldn't lose its shape, Nina Alexandrovna first shoved the papers into the trash can, where they stood straight up, and then, frightened that someone might still need the unintelligible lists speckled with coded comments, she shook the limp chicken innards off the pages and laid them out to dry on the kitchen windowsill.

■ □ ■

Thus prepared, and knowing that Marina would be kept late at work, Nina Alexandrovna decided that the next day she would pay her visit, a weather forecast promising twenty below notwithstanding. That night, as thick ice feathers froze on the apartment windows, she dreamed of a strange, lackluster beach, a sea consisting of several long bands of silver, and above the sea, ash-gray cumulus clouds in which the sun was merely indicated, like the capital city on a map. Flat waves ran onto shore and ironed out the fine sand, and this sand—this sand held *everything*, both the matter of the world pulverized into atoms and the sleeping woman who kept sifting the colorful, dusty flour between her fingers but couldn't find a single stone or shard or any remnants whatsoever of the *reality* that had drained into this watery sandy pit. In the morning, Nina Alexandrovna awoke with no memory of her dream and for some reason with wet eyes and her hair matted at the temples. She didn't remember her dream until she was outside, when she saw the neon luminescence of the drifting gray snow on a sidewalk made desolate by the freezing temperature. In her dream, finely shredded foam glowed on the sluggish water that poured onto the endless sloping sand like a pancake onto a skillet—and now the lackluster landscape, singed at its white corners, was solidly covered with a volatile silver glow: people turned around and exhaled a white flame, and reflecting scraps sped after the bus that had trundled off right under Nina Alexandrovna's nose from the congested, pointlessly stamping stop. Lining up modestly at the edge of the crowd, which kept sending frosty representatives into the thoroughfare, Nina Alexandrovna observed through her stuck eyelashes a subtle luminescent streaming on the road, which was scraped to the bare asphalt and covered in white wrinkles. Sand was sprinkling from barely noticeable rivulets of disintegrated matter, and the impersonal cold penetrated Nina Alexandrovna's light coat like pitiless radiation, making her defenseless spine ache as if it had been lowered onto the last *living* thread, exactly as in her dream. At first, Nina Alexandrovna thought that if her family survived this era—which for others had stopped short at 1990, apparently—then the logical outcome would, of course, be war.

While the heavy bus, which kept dropping on its ass, was hauling Nina Alexandrovna and the rest of its squeezed passenger load to the Vagonzavod stop, the frost abated somewhat—and continued to abate, creating the intermittent impression of the air subsiding dramatically, like a melting snowdrift. Feeling her body's center of gravity drop, Nina Alexandrovna gingerly descended, as if climbing down a tree, over the bumpy paths, in the direction of some two-story stuccoed barracks that stood quite a bit below road level. At this point, the residential area was even lower than the humped sidewalks, which were as narrow as small berms: the lower-floor windows sealed with insulating tape looked up touchingly, and in front of them, as if in deep holes, the modest front gardens were white with smooth, untouched snow, which seemed to touch the branches, as if the bare twigs had latched on and pulled invisible threads from a fine white fabric. Right there—a stone's throw over the fence—Nina Alexandrovna saw in the branches of a ruddy, deformed apple tree a trough made of a shipping crate with the remnants of a mailing address, and in that trough, two perfectly identical little titmice pecking at some frozen bread, and to hear it you'd think a wall clock was striking the hour on the tree.

Far past the barracks, the standard-issue apartment buildings began on bare vacant land, without any courtyards, connected by a system of paths as intricate as a billiards game, converging and diverging at irregular angles. After well and truly wandering, Nina Alexandrovna suddenly found herself in front of the right entrance with the same slab underfoot, wobbling on the diagonal, only now the entrance was cut off from the world by a brown steel door. The only things on its entire surface were crudely cut holes through which she could see the steel aperture of an enormous lock. Distraught, Nina Alexandrovna stepped back to look for the familiar windows, although the tenth floor left her with no hope of drawing anyone's attention. After lifting her swaying head *incorrectly*, instantly making the pain squawk, she saw that at a certain height both the building and its receding windows clearly lost their connection to the ground, passing through a centimeter of invisibility to become unreal, as if made of some very flimsy material. While Nina Alexandrovna was coming back down beneath the clouds and blinking back a harsh tear, a blurry, round-shouldered person applied himself, like a spider, to the impregnable doors and gnashed an invisible key as if sawing through metal—but by the time Nina Alexandrovna, still not done blinking, reached the treacherously tottery slab, the door lock, which was the size of a bench plane, had come crashing down and the brown steel was once again shut tight. For a while she could hear the man ascending and slapping the banister and humming some repulsive march.

But she was in luck. About a minute and a half later, the steel clanged again, and out the door, carrying a tidy garbage can packed with newspaper, came a neighbor Nina Alexandrovna recognized—a positive-minded woman with a very serious, *judgmental* face who in Nina Alexandrovna's memory had never spoken ten words but who sometimes had knocked on her nephew's wall so that crumbs sprinkled down under the wallpaper and the cheap clock that hadn't been drunk away skipped a beat and stopped. Holding the squealing door for Nina Alexandrovna, the neighbor drilled an intense look into her—but at the last moment her look shifted so that the woman ended up greeting not Nina Alexandrovna but the twiggy bushes poking up out of the snowdrift. As she ascended in the shuddering elevator, whose buttons had turned into black ulcers long ago, Nina Alexandrovna thought that the neighbor simply didn't know how to get along with people without erecting a wall between herself and them. But a nasty presentiment dogged her; next to a radiator where she had once found a treasure—a drunken woman in a man's jacket with a medal "For Courageous Labor"—there now sat a healthy kitty spotted like a cow: its round little head tilted back, it had chewed off a piece of bloody innards that had stuck to the tile, and the spot made around the kitty's meal was stamped with partial boot prints.

The apartment door had been replaced, naturally. Instead of the old leatherette wretchedness, which had occasionally dropped rusted-through wallpaper nails, like rotten teeth, there was sturdy insulation covered in figured lath and equipped with a clean, purple peephole the size of a good shot glass. Nina Alexandrovna pressed the sugar-white bell and heard way back in the apartment a musical intro like when a magic box opens in movie fairytales. Nothing followed, though. After listening to its melodious summons a good fifteen times, Nina Alexandrovna suddenly had the feeling that someone was standing behind her. Turning around, she saw a pale creature approximately Marina's age. The creature's pinched face reminded her of an autumn puddle frozen over with icy splinters. Her bloodless emaciation didn't connect with her huge pregnant belly, where her shaggy rabbit-fur coat—with brown spots exactly like that kitty, which now seemed to have gone missing—wouldn't close. "Who are you looking for?" the pregnant woman, evidently the apartment's owner, asked in a vibrating little voice. Her keys played nervously in her hand and under Nina Alexandrovna's gaze were hastily put back in her pocket. Calmly, trying not to scare off the mistrustful creature (suppressing a strange desire to pat her coat, that soft childish fur, the cheap, crunchy fell), Nina Alexandrovna explained about her nephew and gave his name. "I don't know anything. I bought the apartment through an agency," the pregnant woman said quickly, mixing the keys in her pocket with some kind of soft trash; her blunt little boots, which looked orthopedic due to the slenderness of her legs contrasted to the size of her belly, took tentative steps right and left.

Not knowing what to say to that, Nina Alexandrovna smiled reassuringly and held out her hand to touch the pregnant woman, who nearly fell down shying away and backing into the scratched-up wall. Her coat flapped open comically, like chicken wings: evidently, she'd been squeezing her fists in her jangling pockets. Nina Alexandrovna's heart suddenly melted. She thought about how incredibly comic she herself would have looked to a stranger when she was pregnant and tried to hang herself—like a cuckoo stuck in a cuckoo clock. "Don't you smile. I really did buy the apartment," the woman said challengingly, shaking out her hem. "Later they told me why it was so cheap. A man was hacked to death with an ax here." "What man? What ax?" Nina Alexandrovna said gently, amazed at her pregnant fantasies and with no intention of budging. "I'm telling you, this is my nephew's former apartment, and he's definitely alive. I received a money order from him a few days ago." At that moment, the mooring elevator groaned. The neighbor, holding the emptied bucket with its stuck-on snow-sole away from her body, slipped past, and her angrily pursed lips looked like neat sutures made with gray thread. "Gulya Kerimovna!" Nina Alexandrovna called out to the neighbor, suddenly remembering her name, as if someone had whispered it in her ear. But the neighbor (who had in very timely fashion brought in realtors to draw up and backdate a power of attorney for selling the apartment and who now kept the dollars she'd earned in one of her four—she didn't remember exactly which one—well-worn armchairs) didn't even turn around; hiding behind her cornflower blue back, she turned her keys in the locks as if she were drilling into her own door and trying to pass right through it. It really did seem to Nina Alexandrovna that the neighbor, rather than enter the half-cracked door, passed through the wood and steel: after turning into a surprisingly slender and undulating silhouette, she broke up into dynamic blue spots that quickly vanished from the wood's surface the way the fog of human breath vanishes from a mirror's. Nina Alexandrovna suddenly thought she'd been given a graphic illustration of how to forget someone: as if he'd gone through a wall and what lingered for a few seconds in your eyes was like a Chinese hieroglyph drawn with a quick brush.

"Fine. Let's go. I'll show you," the apartment's owner said decisively, moving Nina Alexandrovna away from the nice new door. Together they entered the half-empty front hall, which seemed to Nina Alexandrovna nothing like it was before—because the light turned on not where she expected but on the other side. However, a long bare cord and moldering socket still hung from the ceiling, and Nina Alexandrovna instantly remembered how the heat of the overheated bulb, after it had gone out, felt on her forehead and raised hand if you stamped abruptly or dropped a heavy bag on the floor. There were surprisingly few things in either the hall or the room, which was oddly drafty the way only spaces in abandoned buildings through which you can see the ashberry trees and garbage in the rear courtyard can be. The new life seemed haphazardly laid out on top of the remains of the old, not destroying it, but not using it either. To the left of the front door, Nina Alexandrovna saw the familiar peeling coatrack with a single, shriveled glove on the shelf posed like a dead sparrow; to the right, a new, almost identical one had been nailed up and on it hung a very few pieces of women's clothing—all of it with big buttons and soft shoulder pads sticking out like empty camel humps. "Now you can see for yourself, the blood hasn't been completely washed off here," the pregnant woman said, clumsily turning herself out of her coat and loading it onto *her* half. Right then Nina Alexandrovna sensed the unreality of what was happening.

On the floor of the front hall, bare as before, with clayey tracks worn across the old floor cloths, lay the one and only rug (right then Nina Alexandrovna couldn't come up with another definition) the size of a grave's flower bed. The rug's placement was *off*—not in front of the door, as one would expect, but slightly to one side—and not quite to the wall; on it for reliability—to press down harder on what was hidden beneath it and might somehow pop out—stood all the worn footwear there was here, plus a cart with a splattered bag. Dropping heavily first to one knee, then the other (her belly, stretched in checked fabric, looked like it was about to fall out, like a ball from a basketball net), the pregnant woman cast aside her ridiculous barricade and turned back the rug. The sense of unreality immediately vanished. Nina Alexandrovna could only wonder how she hadn't immediately remembered about that spot—now nothing but dark red cracks between the faded planks. About four years before (no, I'm sorry, a good six!) her nephew, needing to earn a little extra on May Day, contracted to paint some structure the Communists were planning to take out on the square to hurt Yeltsin. For some reason, her nephew brought home an entire can of revolutionary oil paint and tripped, as often happened with him, on level ground, spilling the contents. Fortunately, that day Nina Alexandrovna had dropped by to clean: the thick paint tongue spilled on the floor hadn't dried yet—it had just darkened and set a little—and Nina Alexandrovna scraped up the soft paint with a heavily greased knife, wiping the collected clods on stuck-together newspapers, while her guilty-looking nephew (she recalled especially vividly his shaking forelock with yellow dry weeds of gray hair) fussed with gasoline, which left swaths on the rust-brown floor that looked like damp, swollen cheese. After telling the pregnant woman the whole story, Nina Alexandrovna saw with relief a new interest on her elongated little face and, simultane-ously, pink dots of a delighted strawberry color. "Well, would you like me to prove to you that I've been in this apartment?" A newly dawned-upon Nina Alexandrovna, supporting the heavy woman by her elbow, which was swaying like a testicle, led her to the toilet, where, as in the old days, the old basin, red with rust, was making a furious noise.

Due to some awkward gradation of the niche, the painted ply-wood behind the basin, which concealed the wastewater pipe, which was making very strange sounds, stood out a good ten centimeters from the wall. Slipping her hand into the tight crack—there, inside, just like in someone's mouth, first breathing cold air, then plowing up a deep warmth—Nina Alexandrovna immediately felt a slippery glass neck, shifted it aside, and pulled it out into the light: a bottle of Stolichnaya covered with yellow slime, like a newborn babe. "Oh my!" the apartment's owner said, clutching her flat cheeks. "Give me a rag," Nina Alexandrovna demanded, and taking a silly scrap of lin-gerie with a little mother-of-pearl button, wiped off the slime along with the label, which over the years had turned into foul-smelling curdled milk. It was still filled with vodka, though. One day, hav-ing found her nephew in a state of drunken bewilderment, intent on putting on his watch, which kept slipping away like a lizard, Nina Alexandrovna decided that the unopened bottle, which her nephew *didn't see* on the absurd table, cluttered as it was with so much dingy glass, was one too many that evening. Subconsciously, she was sure her nephew and his wife had long since found and partaken of their half-liter—but today the momentary inspiration, which was con-nected somehow to the apartment's echoing, thoroughly visible space, which sounded like a radio tuned to an empty frequency, suggested to Nina Alexandrovna that the Stolichnaya was still behind the tank.

"This isn't mine. I don't drink vodka," the frightened pregnant woman said in her own defense as she stepped back into the hall and allowed Nina Alexandrovna to carry out the virtually immortal product. Reassuring the woman, who obviously felt she'd been caught at something unseemly, Nina Alexandrovna told her in plain words what had happened. For some reason, she thought that the story of an alcoholic who gave up drinking and became one of the new rich would encourage the apartment's owner, who obviously was planning to give birth without a husband. Intuition whispered to Nina Alexandrovna that the child's father was a drinker—and the overall blue cast to the pregnant woman's face and her overall resemblance to the most delicate and delicate-skinned toadstool on a dandelion stalk spoke to the fact that vodka was a familiar family misfortune many generations deep. In the kitchen, where the bottle naturally brought them, Nina Alexandrovna noted the well-scrubbed cleanliness—the luxury of poverty, when the happiness achieved is not the presence of things but the absence of that repulsive quality with which ungodly relatives surround a person. Now she understood that for the sake of purchasing an apartment in wild Vagonzavod, which left off in ravines and onto sad, snow-swept fields only slightly lighter than the sky, the woman was prepared to stretch herself very thin indeed. Actually, in the kitchen, next to the cracked teacups and the warped cutting boards, which looked like parts of a broken trough, there was a lovely stainless steel sink—new, like the door and bell. Evidently, the woman believed in a *normal* future and was buying it one piece at a time. To the pregnant woman, those expensive things, which were in striking contrast to the poverty of the one-room habitation with its faded wallpaper made nearly of ordinary paper, may well have seemed eternal.

"You should take that. I don't need it," the apartment's owner said almost hostilely when she saw Nina Alexandrovna put the bottle on the table. She, of course, had no intention of drinking it. Only now did she notice that on the bottom, disturbed after so many years of warmth and immobility, a fluffy, stirred-up sediment looked like the slippery film left after the water drains from a washing machine. Right then she thought of Marina's story about knock-off vodka. This Stolichnaya, purchased long before that incident, nonetheless seemed dangerous, especially in proximity to the growing new life, which amazingly, like an apple on a withered branch, was ripening in that feeble body, which had focused all its feelings and blood-stream inward and so was utterly defenseless. Pointing out the sus-picious growth to the pregnant woman, Nina Alexandrovna used the opener lying on the table to pull out the nastily banged-in cork, which had hardened like a fingernail. Dumping the contents down the drain proved not so simple. The vodka seemed to get stuck in the bottle's neck, and she had to shake it in blops, turning away from the warm spirits' copious and fleshly stink—and even a brisk cold stream couldn't immediately wash away the alcoholic mirages that appeared in the polished sink. At last the bottle was emptied, rinsed modestly clean, and sent wet into the garbage pail. Refusing coffee (yet another of the apartment owner's precious objects—an imported white electric kettle with a visor—gurgled and clicked off, as if saluting, while the owner cut a dry and greasy cake that crum-bled like burned paper), Nina Alexandrovna hurried to leave. As she was drawn through the cracked door—by either the distant winter street or the steamed darkness—she noticed that the latch had been knocked off and was dangling freely. There were black notches on the doorjamb as well, as if hacked by some mad woodcutter who'd mistaken it for a tree. "I haven't had time to do repairs everywhere," the owner said in justification, lopsidedly handing Nina Alexandrovna her coat. The visitor cautiously climbed into the winding sleeves, afraid of striking the child she'd felt for a second in its bubble—as if her hand were filled not with flesh but with a tense watery stream, as if there, in that heavy, crooked vessel, a magic fluid on the verge of becoming a human being was sloshing around. "I'm going to install a telephone very soon!" the pregnant woman said, now in the doorway, and Nina Alexandrovna, knowing full well that being happy for a *stranger* was practically stealing, nonetheless melted at the sight of the now warm little face and crinkly smile.

On the bus, Nina Alexandrovna smiled and raised her eyebrows in amazement at the thought of the odd misconception, which, thank God, she had managed to dispel. Even the thought that she had found out nothing about her nephew didn't spoil her mood. Nodding like a roan, the bus dragged itself from rise to rise, and the way back felt long. Nina Alexandrovna scratched the little bit of thawing ice, as thin as the foil on a can of coffee, off the window and gazed at the snow-crusted fields, fields blindingly clean and lying in crude folds, like frozen sheets taken off a winter clothesline. Tomorrow was pension day again, and Nina Alexandrovna decided that after she'd waited for Klumba, she'd take a detour on her way to the market via the train station, where the City Information Bureau had once operated so efficiently. She hadn't had occasion to be away from home for so long in quite a while, but today she'd taken an entire journey; despite her worry about Alexei Afanasievich, who hadn't been fed his dinner on time, Nina Alexandrovna felt restored.

Getting off at her stop, she started walking, in no hurry, readjusting her paper-light bag, which kept slipping off her shoulder, making her movements not quite natural, slightly on the theatrical side. What was that she'd been thinking about war this morning, in this very spot? What foolishness! Silver dots swarmed peacefully in the gray air, and the white, delicately drawn trees were so still, they looked like glass lamps that had been turned off. Constrained by unnatural snowdrifts that yardmen and snowplows had already pushed off the pavement, drifts as angular as furniture under sheets, the pedestrians hurried along single file and peeled off into the various stores; their faces, ruddy from the freezing temperature, were like different varieties of apples.

From a distance, all the people looked blurred and slightly translucent to Nina Alexandrovna; as a person got closer, he firmed up, acquired a flush to his cheeks, a fur coat, sometimes even a beard, at the same time losing a captivating haze, as if he'd emerged from the fog of his own soul. This odd effect was observed at a distance of about ten paces and came about in two indistinct stages—a right and a left—like someone taking clothing off or putting it on; Nina Alexandrovna, who had always seen this but only now realized it, thought that perhaps a human soul really could be seen at a distance—this was the gentle miracle of myopia—so all people were better far away than up close. At the end of her day's trajectory of freedom, she lingered by a newspaper kiosk to check out the magazine covers and the young beauties dressed in what were either evening gowns or lacy lingerie; she was drawn by the sudden discovery that the *depictions* were blurring in her mediocre eyes not at all the way live people did. They lacked some kind of watermark certifying a creature's authenticity. Inadvertently, Nina Alexandrovna's gaze

slipped down from the beauties to a level array of unfamiliar newspapers. There, amid unfamiliar spikes and dips of very large and very
small type, she was struck by a single word printed in powerful letters and so spaced out that they had to be mentally squeezed like an
accordion—but they spread out again, emitting a low, stripy sound.
"WAR"—and an undulating, radioactive chill ran down Nina Alexandrovna's spine.

Naturally, "WAR" had nothing to do with this outside time where
the shops shone as before and jingling red streetcars bunched up
at a stoplight (only the souls seem to move closer). This was about
inside time, for which there was now a vague but secretly anticipated
endpoint. Nina Alexandrovna stood in the small, packed line for a
newspaper, the coins in her freezing fingers sticking together like
fruit drops. After taking her capriciously folded copy from the low
window, she tried to step aside with her paper; she couldn't wait to
open up to the horrifying page. To make sure not to bother anyone,
Nina Alexandrovna climbed the long, unnatural snowdrift pushed
all along the thoroughfare, a snowdrift the half-toppled poplars
poked out of like widely spaced teeth from a jaw. As soon as she
tried to unfold the unusually thin newspaper, the wind slammed into
the page, from the outside first and then the inside. The turbulent
street air just wouldn't let her turn the newspaper all the way back,
allowing her to read it only firmly folded in fourths—nonetheless,
Nina got the general drift of what the top headline had been saying.
"WAR in Television: Crude Takeover at Studio A" announced the
headline under the banner, and next to it was a grainy, as if heavily peppered photo where broad-shouldered figures in some kind of
uniform berets were dragging a bearded fat man out of an armchair:
his tie, dark and askew on his protruding belly, made him look like

a gutted fish. Below that was a more modest headline: "Triumph of the Victors." Next to that, a slightly more decipherable photograph depicted something like a demonstration: in the front row, a shriveled old woman with a face like a grasshopper's and an old fellow with medals spread wide across his chest and wearing ugly felt boots that were firmly trampling the snow had unfurled a banner which, in a handsome designer font—better than the one used in the newspaper—said: "Krugal! Give us our money!" "Mr. Krugal's election campaign was run on the voters' money," the article began, but before Nina Alexandrovna could get to Krugal's pilfering of some philanthropic fund, she turned over the quarter-folded paper to find a photo of a woman wearing Marina's knit cap. The woman, emerging from some blurry underground, had her arm raised to ward off the photographer and the arsenal of microphones thrust at her: the large-scale palm, thrown out in a helpless kind of farewell gesture, repeated with amazing precision the outline and angle of the innumerable maps of the electoral district that had been pasted up on all the neighborhood fences, garages, and posts and were now frayed as if from a cultural deficit. Nina Alexandrovna could try to fool herself all she liked, but she had knit that motley cap the color of buckwheat groats herself, and the woman blocking off the reporters with a childish gesture was Marina, who was somehow mixed up in this scandal. Inside time had definitely been annihilated from without, and the reason for this went well beyond any conceivable family circumstances.

■ □ ■

While Nina Alexandrovna was standing on that snowdrift, fighting the wind-gasping newspaper, while Alexei Afanasievich, having constructed a rather crooked noose from his most successful cord, was trying on death like a hat (at the same point in inside time, a nuclear warhead had reached its target and swelled and burst, and a city had flown off the face of the earth like a tattered wrapper)—at that very same time, Marina was nervously loitering in the corridor of Studio A, where the faint narcotic smell of the teargas used the night before had yet to air out. The studio had broadcast a bloc of ads as if nothing had happened (in inside time the nuclear explosion, which glowed like a quickly growing, outrageously transparent disc, very much like the ad for dishwashing liquid in which a finger touches a greasy plate, cleaning it all the way to the edges), but any outsider who found himself in the corridor would immediately have noted the traces of disorder. The doors to all the editorial offices were flung wide, and frantic employees were sitting inside like animals in a zoo where the cages had suddenly been opened. Some were cautiously making their way to freedom, actually, and Kostik the computer wizard, who had recently become the anchor on the morning show "Hi, Everybody!" was pacing near the waiting room, sniffing predatorily, touching the slanting sideburns he'd let grow (for his image) with the tips of his fingers, as if to make them stick better. Small windows had been opened to air out the teargas, and drafts were dragging cold, inflated papers around, restless papers, like paper boats released on a pond. Studio A had been ravaged and turned inside out; for some reason, prehistoric mannequins had been put on display in the corridor: women's torsos swathed in pink and nude stocking fabric that had shredded and laddered. The towheaded security guard posted by the waiting room kept shooting sideways glances at the mannequins, especially the most extensible one, a kind of woman-cloud, which for some reason had been set on a polished dowel.

Marina had been wandering around for two hours. She needed Professor Shishkov like crazy. Everyone said several hellos to Marina, but the forced tone of their greetings attested to the fact that she was just as much an occupier as the guy in the baggy camo with the ugly flushed face, white and pink, like a radish, who just yesterday had showered the employees with an oily, smothering stream from a gas canister. Each time she passed the makeup room—which was open like all the studio's spaces—where two girls in dollish robes sat at a worktable heaped with makeup and cotton balls, Marina felt a hostile curiosity emanating from there. Even the mirror opposite the door wouldn't accept her reflection; something seemed to get stuck there, and instead of Marina, an intense streak crossed it, like static on a screen. The whole scene in the studio corridor would have looked like it had been staged for a made-for-television movie if the truth hadn't seeped through the *semblance*. No one there today was looking through the full-length windows that were much too big for the office cells and that, due to their cold size, always made up a substantial portion of the editorial reality. There were always smokers smoking along the corridor windows, staring at the sloping industrial landscape, which resembled a sorting station comprised of various structures, and anyone thinking at his computer would dissolve creatively in the raven skies outlined by the old frames, but today not a soul had a thought to going out; the employees were afraid to leave the studio even mentally and kept away from the windows, the way people keep away from the edge of a roof or a construction site. Everyone was united by a concealed alarm. Everyone was sitting and wandering as if tagged—and when the swift figure of Professor Shishkov moved away from the elevators, bouncing slightly, it was immediately obvious that this man was not entangled, like the others, in that sticky web of anticipation of God knew what, that quite to the contrary, he didn't have ten minutes to spare. "Sergei Sergeich!" Marina rushed to intercept him but only pinched the dry fabric of the professorial sleeve. Breaking free of her fingers, like a huge strong insect abruptly smelling of some crude perfume, simply ablaze with this cologne smell, the professor muttered, "Later, later," and flew toward the waiting room doors, where he disappeared, nearly snagging his jacket wing. Trying to slip in behind him, Marina encountered the official gaze of Lyudochka, who was sitting in the secretary's place as if she'd always sat there. "There's been no decision on your matter, Marina Borisovna," Lyudochka said in a gentle voice, glancing sideways at her own hands, where a fresh, golden-caramel manicure was additionally decorated with a large new ring in a setting of diamond chips: the precious lump, which obviously wouldn't fit into any glove, played on her long ring finger in a multitude of sharp reflecting sparks. "Fine. I'll wait," Marina said dully, and she sat down on a stiff office chair, pushing it out of line a little.

Truth be told, she hadn't thought events would develop so swiftly. Left behind was the trying "deceleration" of the last campaign days: when, last Saturday, at precisely noon, the registrars, half-alive, propping each other up, rose from their tables and the line let up a roar as if it were a stadium. The full extent of the remaining money was a paltry 410 rubles. You could say they'd cut it close. At least two more hours passed before the line, grumbling and retaining its legitimate numbered order, under the group's watchful eye, left the basement nearly single file. Marina should have paid attention to the phenomenon at the time—because the *order* worked out over the many days of them stamping on the snow, certified by the sweaty, by now almost venomous chemical number on their left hands, represented nearly a greater value to the voters than the fifty-ruble note they'd already drunk up, since it was their sole means of fighting *injustice*— but she, happy that things hadn't reached the point of scandal, hadn't paid attention. What had she actually been thinking about at the elections as she sat there like a second-grader who'd been held back, at her cruelly cramped desk, dying to pee and covering her official notebook with identical Greek profiles, like paper clips? Secretly, for herself, she'd been hoping that Klimov, who was still registered in the district but had never voted in his life, now, changed, would show up to perform his civic duty—and this innocent meeting of strangers, like former schoolmates, this new look *from afar* would be the start of something unknown, something free of what had happened so recently in their failed family. Time and again, Marina mistook long-limbed men of about the right height for Klimov. Once, this turned out to be an elderly Tatar with a greasy shaved head that looked like a pile of pancakes, who responded to her look by baring yellow teeth abraded like a horse's hoof. Despite her fear of men, which resided deep inside her, Marina was so eager for a change that she thought she could fall in love with anyone who wasn't Klimov. In that concealed nervous agitation she'd been experiencing since early morning, she was ready to scream, she was so impatient to see her husband, and in exactly the same way she was ready to start something with anyone who paid her the slightest attention. In this regard, though, Lyudochka had the most success. Few were the voters of the opposite sex who remained indifferent to her flourishes on the chair, where she would cross and recross her legs as if she were deftly rowing with a stiff oar in a winding current—so that ultimately even Apofeozov's assistant, the well-mannered Hitler, couldn't take it and slipped away.

Marina held out hope up until the polling place's closing, and in the last twenty minutes, which were utterly dead—the schoolteachers, in the total absence of voters, stood up from their papers ahead of time and performed third-grade gym class—she imagined she saw Klimov, or Klimov's ghost, in a terrible hurry, galloping straight across the virgin snow, leaving dark blue boot-deep tracks. All hope was lost when they locked the school's front doors and turned off the light in the lobby, where the glossy candidates aged as evening fell. The commission chair, who was also the school's principal, a young man, much younger than his math and botany teachers, but a mournful and mournfully sleek little man, gave the signal to begin, and the contents of the ballot box gushed out on the prepared table, contents that lay on the bottom in a layer as solid as halva and took effort to knock out. The closeness with which Marina followed the ballot counting led to her remembering almost nothing afterward. All she did remember was some ballots being inexplicably dirty and worn and the Apofeozov brunette nervously pacing behind the vote counters' backs and sinking her teeth into the soft flesh of a ruddy, dripping pear. The sorting of ballots that took place on the table with the participation of many hands and webby shadows set off a slow calculation in Marina's brain: several times she distinctly shuddered at her own voice counting out loud, but each time it turned out to be the voice of one of the teachers quietly exchanging croaks with the director, who had blurred like a sad blot at the far end of the table. They started tallying the results. Marina was shaken. Apofeozov's victory by a margin of nineteen votes was so curious and disgraceful that among today's Sunday public it seemed they could simply exclude those nineteen extra citizens who hadn't fit their crosses and checks in the right box.

The brunette, however, had smiled with her beady little teeth too soon and had accepted in vain the congratulations of the principal, who held her dry little hand in both of his with such a tender look, it was as if most of all he would have liked to put this dear little thing in his gaping pocket. There was more of the same at the other polling places. Throughout this lovely, idyllic day, with its golden crust of snow, the odds had fluctuated in the air. Serving as a barometer had been the exhausted Krugal. Early that morning he'd arrived in his hulking 1978 BMW at Professor Shishkov's now quiet, amber sunlight filled office. Strangely resembling a colorized black-and-white photograph, with floods of pink on his soft gray cheeks, the candidate had perched like an orphan in the professor's waiting room, sucking down the innumerable cups of coffee served by the frightened secretary. The professor turned up a little later, fully pumped with medicines, to discover Fyodor Ignatovich on the edge of his monumental couch, where the candidate was sitting sideways, looking like a bent cigarette stuck to a protruding lip. Evidently, the failed actor, who had never won anything in his life and now dreamed of victory with all the powers of his bantam soul, had acquired a hypersensitivity to the atmosphere in which the likelihoods of various election outcomes not only swayed but rocked. From time to time, Krugal smiled agitatedly, massaging his heart, but a minute later he would sink and turn pale. Tousled, a blind spot on his glowing brow, Krugal walked and ran in zigzags around the crowded furniture, occasionally turning into Shishkov's wide-open office—where the professor, who seemed starched by medicines but who had grasped something, regarded his partner closely, the way an antique portrait painted in dark oils might regard a visitor. Probably, some secret part of Krugal was unconsciously registering the most minute events, which were constantly altering the correlation of forces. His blood seemed to have extra beads running through it, like the beads in those clever toys you can rock to the very top of a twisted pyramid—and you could tell from the candidate how his success was being wrecked, success practically guaranteed by the rousing of some big drunken family or a water main breaking, as a result of which Sovetskaya Street was awash in smoking, watery grease and dozens of women who hadn't finished their washing had decided against going to vote. The patient secretary, who had left her two boys at home unsupervised inventing TNT, had been run ragged looking after Krugal; through the window she could see the Executive Committee building dial, which looked like a bicycle wheel, though sometimes her eyes saw a gray rainbow of invisible spokes turning, nonetheless she could still register the main events of the day. At twelve-fifteen, Krugal's spirits improved, and he even ate the hot pelmeni brought up from the cafeteria downstairs—after bringing his plate to a state of total chaos and piggery in the first minutes of his movable feast, a characteristic Krugal trait. At three, he went back to wandering and going missing, turning into other people's offices, which were countless in this building. He was discovered nearly in the attic sitting on a stool splotched with either maintenance paint or pigeon droppings. Krugal, who hadn't smoked since he was a kid, was greedily smothering himself with some nasty cigarette he'd bummed off someone and sneezing so that he sounded like a nasty rag being torn up. They brought him back, shook him off, and sat him back down on the couch. At about five, a ravenous appetite awoke in him. At five-thirty, something else happened, and Krugal's features shuddered and suddenly became as plain as a Roman numeral. Forty minutes later, he seemed to wake up and looked at the secretary with a moist, human gaze. "So that's how it is. I have nothing more to say," he said unusually distinctly, but what this referred to was a mystery. Finally, at 6:08, not waiting for the polling places to close, Krugal became blissfully bored and yawned, gulping down the waiting room's rather stuffy air, and a minute later was sleeping, restlessly, in the cozy depth of the couch, his smashed cheek sticking to the brown leather armrest. Right then, Professor Shishkov, who had taken no part in anything all day, emerged from his office and stood over his creation, thoughtfully rocking on his feet, touching cheap, crude-smelling brandy to his penicillin-ish lips.

Actually, Krugal's victory in the overall elections was just as shaky as Apofeozov's in Marina's one district. The two candidates were as close as a man and his reflection in a mirror, and the decision as to which was real came down to a highly relative voting advantage. The three additional individuals in this Sunday's spectacle had not vindicated Apofeozov's hopes and had barely made a showing, garnering an insignificant percentage overall—and the one woman, a famous former athlete with a square, masculine haircut and sweet dimples on her chubby, angelic cheeks, had not had a single ballot cast for her, which was unprecedented. On Monday afternoon there were two press conferences and a live broadcast: in front of reporters, Krugal had the approximate look of the classic rabbit the magician pulls out of a hat, while Professor Shishkov, representing the chosen deputy as his proxy, spoke briefly, standing for just a moment, his voice flat and wooden and his entire gaunt body leaning on his spread fingers, which were trembling very slightly. The reporters, whose recorders wheezed ever so softly in front of the professor, letting their tape wind, asked boring, politically correct questions. Only the anchor for *Political News*—a veteran of regional TV, a still very lively and vivid lady with inappropriately delighted round eyes and a hairdo like a gold crow's nest—was able to rouse Krugal by reminding him of some story from their shared theatrical youth spent in the town of Upper Ketlym. After this, the deputy kicked away chairs and wires to make for the TV anchor's hand, at which he brandished his Roman nose—and all this was filmed by the dispassionate camera being carted around the studio like a motorcycle by a round-shouldered cameraman.

At the same time, other, much better attended press conferences were being held. At the Palace Hotel's business center, which was regularly used for filming presentations by the A Fund, a monkey house of photographers was going crazy, scurrying across the floors practically on their bare knuckles in search of an impressive shot, filling the air with continuous clicking and minty dissolving spots; the several TV companies were doing a respectable job as well, including one from the capital, red lights shining above their cameras' viewfinders. His thoroughbred face quite bloated—a heavy thought was written on his forehead, as if with a finger on velvet—Apofeozov hunched menacingly over the tailed microphones and his gray, bloodshot eyes with the sealing-wax bags tracked back and forth. To his right and left were his nephews, now called consultants, one wearing a pearl-white tie, the other a sky-blue. They were intently passing documents to each other behind their uncle's back, tattering the pages more and more so that eventually they turned into a tall stack of compromising material in which the nephews rummaged intently, digging in them with identical Parkers, as if they were plucking commas out of the printed text. The old, preelection financial scandal retreated into the shadows; what the losing candidate said promised Krugal every possible trial and made the failed actor out to be an utter swindler, practically a second Sergei Mavrodi. The chairman of the local Union of Deceived Contributors, a short man with gray peppered through his red hair and a shiny face almost the same color red from freckles, was in the hall at the ready, and he reacted instantly, reading out an anti-Krugal statement pulled from his antediluvian briefcase, choking on a few words—after which the very fresh, airy, extremely well-preserved and well-read page was added to the paper trash the nephews were already stuffing by the handfuls into the shiny briefcases open at their feet. All this time, in the next room, waiters—prim youths with birdlike profiles and dressed such as poor Krugal could only dream—were setting up a buffet: the most delicate salads in crisp baskets; expensive smoked meats, pale and laced with fat; amber petals of dry-smoked sausage; and all the red caviar sandwiches you could want—although they were a little soggy by the time they were bitten into by the mingling, droning, well-disposed press. Those correspondents who had already had time before this for plain mineral water with Professor Shishkov sized up the losing candidate's refreshments: for some reason they were especially hungry and tried to glean something from all the emptied platters, if only one last stuck-on, well-fingered delicacy—and the bottles cooed like doves as Absolut was poured into tilted glasses. Even the deceived contributors' leader, known for his principled refusal to take part in buffets and banquets, gave the noble fish assortment its due, since in the past he'd been an avid and successful fisherman; someone noticed the activist, holding on his knee the misaligned flaps of his plywood and leatherette box, neatly burying an opened but tightly closed bottle deep among his papers. In the end, a good five TV channels ran the necessary commentary on Apofeozov in the news. As for Studio A, where the shaken but not broken Kukharsky still sat, they ran all the footage, including the private scenes where the fat-nosed Apofeozov clan, imitating a tea ad, drank amber tea at a cozy round table covered in a white table-cloth spread tight as a drum and barely big enough for the multivalent family, so that some, crowded in, were only able to put an elbow on the common territory and participate in the shots with a slice of a smile—while the politician's seven-year-old granddaughter, heaving her little chest, tightly swathed in silk, like a grown-up, played the piano, her hands meandering over the keys like little bowlegged turtles. All this was very touching—but the episodes shot on the fly near Professor Shishkov's campaign basement aroused much greater interest among TV viewers.

■ □ ■

Marina slept through Monday, which the observers had been given off. The news of the victory, which she received over the phone from Shishkov personally, filled her weary mind with blissful lead. On Tuesday morning, unable to get through to the professor, who was either out of the service zone or had turned off his mobile, she set off for headquarters, feeling a need and a duty to go to work—expecting to enter into her new activity and new life from there. As she approached the basement, but still across the icy street where rickety tin streetcars were going in both directions, she could tell that the courtyard in front of headquarters was full of people, who had spilled over into the adjoining courtyards. All the snowdrifts looked like coastal cliffs in bird nesting areas, occupied by the slanting figures of line-standers, who were not paying each other the slightest attention but seemed to be searching for the same thing in the flickering of white dots that from a distance formed a powerful white swell and altered the perspective; adding to the picture, above the courtyard, twittering mobs of sparrows soared up, switching positions, and dropped, as if a net had been tossed into the cloudy sky, while the black hearts of the trees, bared due to their total lack of leaves and visible now in their interweaving of vessels, were ravens.

There really was no way to avoid the canvassers—who were even standing in the sandbox—as she passed through the courtyard. The old windows of the five-story buildings whose inhabitants—to a man apparently—were also registered for the bonus were taking part in the event the way lists and posters hanging on walls take part in a meeting. A low-slung woman in a round-shouldered mouton coat overtook the delayed Marina, whom no one had recognized yet; moving at a forced run, as if kicking an elusive piece of ice in front of her, the woman headed for the basement, and Marina, picking up her pace, hurried after her. Out of the corner of her eye, Marina noticed that the people in the courtyard weren't just standing there. The separate groups of people waiting were standing in some subtle order, and if someone stepped away from his trampled spot, he made sure to point this out to his neighbors, with a businesslike nod—while some even left a lumpy bundle on the ground with their pancake-shaped tracks, like on a taken chair. Meanwhile, the woman had already pushed through to the basement stairs. Standing on tiptoe, she was obsequiously dictating something to a woman from the group—Marina recognized her by her round steel glasses, in which an angry blind fire always burned in one or the other lens. The woman was recording the conveyed information in a notebook, which she lifted above the petitioner's upturned mushroom nose—and only now did Marina notice that the group's notebooks were exactly the same as the ones the registrars always used:

with black leatherette covers and embossing that always reminded Marina of the silk lining of some beloved coat from long ago. Finally, the activist finished writing, and the woman, hastily pulling off her knit mitten, which was as big as a bast sandal, held out her surprisingly tiny white hand; the activist licked her indelible pencil on her striped tongue and began drawing on the extended palm—as neatly and efficiently as if she were slicing bread. Then she commandingly waved her hand, and the woman wandered off in the indicated direction, time and again holding out her hand with the freshly drawn number to the surrounding canvassers, who showed her their palms in turn and waved her on—to where the last in line poked up on the snowdrifts, smoking match-sized cigarettes.

"Hello," Marina said politely, trying to maneuver around the group and feeling in her pocket for the crude, burr-edged key to the half basement. "Oh! Well, finally! You've shown up!" the activist exclaimed, and the glare in her glasses passed from left to right and right to left. "We waited for you all day yesterday. At least someone could have come!" "We had the day off after the election," Marina tried to explain, her frozen face smiling. Now she saw that the group was almost completely blocking the basement door. Naturally, the painter was here, over the last month having acclimated to the cold, like a northern deer. His cheap cigarette was smoking corrosively, like a soldering iron, and instead of his black leather he was flaunting a grimy beige sheepskin coat with a waist like the perimeter of a packing case, torn in spots and patched with tape, which made the artist glint at unexpected moments. For some reason, Klumba was absent, which Marina took as a good sign. However, her place had obviously been taken by a short, solid gentleman with a surprisingly ruddy face that looked like white plumbing stained by rusty water.

This man obviously enjoyed some authority, but he was sluggish. His fur boots, which were stamping only the very edge of the soft new snow, looked like they'd been outlined on paper with a dull pencil, and his shaggy cap, tall and airily covered in snow, reminded her of a dandelion. "Excuse me, may I get through?" Marina raised her voice, but it came out more plaintive than angry. "Just a minute," the activist said in a police tone and grabbed Marina firmly by the arm. "When're you gettin' uth our money?" a creature with what looked like a dirty sock on his narrow head and a mouth as toothless as a pocket suddenly popped up and coughed out in a hoarse lisp. Marina recognized the lucky bottle collector, who even now was dragging behind him a cloth sack with his slow-churning glass loot. "Just a minute," the activist repeated, upping her sternness, and she dragged Marina, who tripped, away from the basement. "We all congratulate our candidate Krugal on his victory in the election," she said officially and with a proper smile that slightly skewed her glasses, which flashed like ambulance lights. "We would like to hear from you, as a supervisor, when the payments to our voters are going to begin. Right here"—the activist meaningfully shook the almost completely filled notebook—"right here we have the order for payments registered in the order of the actual line. Not only that"—here the activist confidingly lowered her voice and winked her visible left eye, which looked like a slimy onion in a rotted brown skin— "we've registered another 420 in the district for advance payment. Those people never got the money they were supposed to due to your workers' poor work, and it's not their fault, and they need to be compensated for moral damages. There is also the matter of invalids, whom Krugal ignored, preferring to distribute charity to healthy citizens, and he rejected the public's proposal—" "Just a minute!"

Marina interrupted, feeling some semiliquid ball-shaped weight dipping and seeking balance in her head like in a Johnny-jump-up. "Right now I have nothing to tell you. I have to make a call." "This bureaucracy and red tape of yours again!" the activist said indignantly, and her face, netted with purple veins, started to look like a hot beet simmering in borscht. "You're the one holding me up!" Marina suddenly blurted out an idiotic phrase from some satirical newspaper that was unexpectedly effective. The group stepped aside, letting her get to the steel doors, which were covered in colorful, 3-D obscenities: someone had been hard at work on Monday.

After slamming the psychedelic folk art masterpiece behind her, Marina felt as though she was being smothered in the pink and brown corridor, where the fragmentary wooden row of numbered chairs reminded her of a dinosaur's skeletal remains. Another five or six people turned out to be hiding in the basement. In the back room, Marina discovered a gathering of pale shadows reluctantly drinking yellow tea brewed from leaves already used three or four times. They were thrilled to see her. They jumped up, offered several pulled-back chairs at once, and also poured her a full, tarry mug of the collective beverage, barely warm, so that sugar didn't dissolve in it but just hung suspended, like a teary cloud, picking up the sweepings. The first thing Marina did, though, after getting out of her coat, which dropped wet snowy husks on piled up bags, was to pick up the phone. As usual, the antediluvian equipment with a receiver like a two-kilo dumbbell honked like a formidable, almost automotive horn, but no matter how many times Marina dialed the professor's iambically rhythmic number, the result was the same. "The subscriber is temporarily unavailable. . . . Please call later. . . ." an impersonally polite, ignorant voice repeated, as if a train station were talking, and the other numbers she knew gave her

hopeless busy signals. Right then, several arms and legs started banging on the outside door at once, probably rubbing the chalk graffiti to
thin patches, and the steel rumble seemed to rattle the black spider
webs growing in every corner of the basement like armpit hair. Marina
shuddered. The registrars set their knocking mugs aside at once and
looked at her with frightened round eyes that held identical points of
light. But right then, out of the blue, the professor's office called back.
"I can't tell you anything definite," the professor's not unkind secretary
said hoarsely, and from her whistling, intermittent snuffles, Marina
guessed she was blowing her nose in her hankie. "He promised to
come by before twelve, so try calling back."

Now they could only wait until twelve. The people who'd been
pounding on the door had probably given up and left. The registrars,
with heavy, *upturned* faces, as if to keep their features from spilling
like wet compressed sand from a mold, had wandered away from
the common table to lounge around the basement. Some pulled
tattered, glossy-covered books from their bags. Observing them,
Marina saw that the women were still caught up in *delaying*, which
possibly wasn't just a trace or habit that would pass but a kind of
fibrous fabric that had been implanted in their being. It was as if their
circulatory and nervous systems had been stretched out by *red tape*
and were now much longer and more tangled, that now these poor
ladies, who hadn't been paid their November salary either, were
inwardly imagining more or less the same thing the wild painter
from the group had been trying to depict on his nacreous canvases:
a twisted, convoluted organism with remarkable superfluities sending blood and nerve impulses wandering through labyrinths.

To keep busy, Marina removed the registration notebooks, now
imbued with a languid chill and disconcertingly heavier, from the

safe. After separating the bonus lists from the lists of payments made, she took to the calculator. Half of its buttons were stiff or stuck, so that it would suddenly spit out long figures. Marina got caught up in the work while resolutely battling this defect and tried not to listen to the people in line bombarding the fatigued steel over and over again. Actually, the attackers now tired fairly quickly, and their infrequent blows sounded like they were wrapped in cotton wool. The figures, rechecked many times, kept mounting in a column that got fatter and fatter. No matter how the frightened Marina tried to fool herself (unconsciously resorting to delay and rummaging through the foul-smelling notebooks), she couldn't keep the sums from mounting. Apparently, the numbers were multiplying on their own, like fruit flies or something, and the preliminary results that Marina entered onto the stained piece of paper that came to hand were like fly eggs from which new generations of unpaid rubles were going to hatch.

After taking a short break before the terrible final result (the registrars brought Marina a steaming slush of instant coffee, made by washing out an old Nescafé jar, and a sandwich with a piece of herring in it that looked more like a comb than human food), Marina noticed that the headquarters' rooms had cooled off. Each of the women had pulled on her coat and tried to fold herself into a strange, cumbersome pose for autonomous heat generation—nonetheless they were freezing, like the large stacks of unlit firewood piled up here and there. The radiator, which Marina checked to make sure, was barely warming its own dust and obviously not coping with the battering wind outside, which carried loose, drifting snow into the window shafts, making it seem as though curtains were fluttering on the windows from the street side. Nonetheless, they could see the contributors up top, through the white heaving: their dark mass occasionally crouched, becoming even darker, and a crooked stick poking out of the milk would occasionally scrape insolently at the window gratings. Suddenly, someone—Marina thought it was the artist, who flickered in a gap in the wind for a second—threw a stiff, collapsed object into the shaft; stealing up to the window, Marina saw that it was a dead cat. Its wadded fur looked stuck to its flat body, and its gelatinous eye, covered with a white film like cold fat, glared at the half-basement's occupants. After pulling the stiff curtain to hide the repulsive missile—without the slightest confidence that another wouldn't follow it—Marina nonetheless forced herself to return to her figures, which she feared much more than all the live and dead animals in the world. Five minutes later she had the final result—an outright mockery of the headquarters' daily campaign thrift and the pathetic hundreds of rubles they'd managed to scrimp. Leaning on her shaky elbow, which she'd moved to one side so the registrars wouldn't accidently see the terrible sum, Marina asked herself whether Professor Shishkov understood the magnitude of his obligations. Something told her that the professor's brain was refusing to multiply the canvasser money sucked out of the district by a factor of 2.4 because he definitely had nowhere to put his hands on a million and a half rubles. She trembled just imagining the spontaneous voter fury that would greet a default.

■ □ ■

Outside, meanwhile, the news spread that the main supervisor, the one with the Jewish nose and dyed collar, had gone into the basement. The amorphous mass, fat from its long idleness, slowly went into motion. The line formed. People showed their neighbors their left palms and stood single file, breathing on each other's damp collars; some ran along the sections, calling out their number—the way the people being evacuated at train stations must have raced along in search of their family, torn away from them in the crush. Some little girl, to look at her, wearing a scanty little checked coat, clumsily wrapped up, as if wound around her head was not a scarf but an entire dress, was sniveling and trying to climb a frozen slide—but the higher she got, the less courage she had left to tear her gaze from the slippery rungs and look around. From high up, a large, glossy raven that had raised a human rumpus from its withered branch could see black scraps resembling the pecked remains of innards getting ready to reassemble into a black body, which was getting bigger—and the body coming to life as if it had been sprinkled with magic water. The line, more terrifying than any army, was stamping in the snow, and almost everywhere the trampled snow looked like a book with a yellow spine from which all or part of half the pages had been ripped out. Apparently, this was the moment District 18's residents lost their faith in personal immortality. The example of the loser Apofeozov no longer meant anything, and the women, who were still wearing starkly flared peach and green coats for the weather from the month before last, had grown old overnight. Their faces, thickly powdered by the cold, had hardened, and their hair, escaping from their flirty mink berets, had become thin, disheveled locks.

Nonetheless, people who no longer felt they had any grounds for resisting reality suddenly felt something like it in the space between their own souls. What united them now was more important than each of them individually. Everyone felt this *immortal* connection, formalized in the line, as the sole force that the district's inhabitants could now contrast to their own fate—which meant no one was trying to creep forward or cut out inattentive neighbors. For each of them, the person ahead had become like a big brother, and the person behind like a little sister. The deceived contributors' agitated marshal watched through a cold, wind-beaten eye as an austere young lady in black felted braids reminiscent of the Medusa Gorgon conscientiously stepped back to let in a cultured old woman in a brown cap that looked as if it had been sewn from a stuffed bear, while two scary-faced worker types, whose numbers didn't quite fit, in their case looking like the kinds of numbers that get put on the soles of shoes being turned over for repair, were waving to a comrade hurrying toward them, a low-level boss to look at him, who was carrying his own belly plus a worn briefcase as substantial as an accordion. The contributors' marshal recalled quite a few lines like this—gloomy demonstrations in defense of Sergei Mavrodi, who was as curly haired as the baby Lenin in the little October star pin—and recalled people registering one foggy September dawn at a firmly shut MMM center, and recalled especially clearly, for some reason, the stone banks of Park Pond, which attracted sharp floating slivers, papers, and other trash like a magnet. The swirling magnetized glints and trash stupidly signaled a suicide who had lost other people's serious money on MMM's pyramid schemes and who was pulled out alive nonetheless and subsequently shown to reporters. The failed suicide's hair remained wet, as if it had caught some watery infection, and the eyes in his gristly, eyebrowless face turned as gold as a bream. A lot happened in those informal communities called lines: meeting daily, sharing misfortunes, people became like family; some, a little younger, even got legally married, and brides, throwing back their white veils, which stuck from the wind, hurled liquidy rotten tomatoes at financial structures' brazen windows. Life, though,

which dragged all Russian riders without exception through the potholes, very quickly wiped out the lines' ties. People stopped phoning
one another, and when they happened to meet on the street, they
reminisced tearfully about the *good times* and swore somehow to
arrange a get-together of old comrades and drink a bottle of vodka
near the dark blue fir in front of city hall, as usual.

Right then the deceived contributors' marshal (a very lonely man
who had nothing left from the battle and his loyal fellow fighters but
piles of paper infested by pale roaches) observed a phenomenon
that did and did not resemble what he had seen before. This line
in the bizarre courtyard, at the door to the pathetic half basement,
was in some way *more powerful* than all the lines before. Something
suggested to the marshal that these people were not going to disen-
gage so easily. Given that this was a matter of very small sums—a
little more than a ridiculous hundred canvasser rubles apiece—what
stood out was the very principle of the line as a form of popular
self-organization uniquely combining hierarchy and equality without distinction as to the sex, age, or status of its human units. An
attack of insane pride that was his, the marshal's, secret trait and
would suddenly come over him either in his cramped office cubicle,
or in his bachelor kitchen of exactly the same size and proportions,
amid crooked, half-eaten pots, began to bubble up in his chest of
many buttons—and the marshal's heart took a leap, like a white egg
boiling in simmering water. Meanwhile, virtually all the deceived
contributors had sorted themselves out by number. After an abrupt
wiggle, like a looped hose wiggling under the pressure of released
water (someone nearly fell, and whooshing grain poured from
ripped-open drifts), the line's awkwardly lying loops *began to move.* It
didn't progress by a single person, yet it moved, its multitude of feet

emitting a soft, hoarse snort, like some persistent, self-aware energy pumping steadily onward through the human gut.

A microbus from downtown that had meanwhile pulled up to the tensely droning courtyard got stuck, like a boat in tall reeds, and barely honked its way through the human labyrinth, which yielded only reluctantly. Klumba—and it was she, determined, with a vivid blush that looked pasted on—was the first to jump awkwardly to the snow, and her freshly wound curls, which her slipping cap could barely contain, jumped as well. She was handed from the microbus a heavy, lightly battered roll of Whatman paper. Some half-buttoned-up reporters climbed out of the microbus after Klumba, bending and struggling with all their equipment. With the help of the artist, who'd run up, Klumba unfastened the springy roll, which popped open wide, and pulling out sheets, began showing the slightly disoriented line what she'd prepared. "We demand the election results be rescinded!" "Krugal! Give us our money!" "Our children want to eat!" "Down with the thief Deputy Krugal!" Klumba lifted all this as high above her head as she could. Her gloves, red like cockscombs, poked out humorously from her bared arms. Immediately, ten takers thrust their hands out from the line, dropping their steel watches in their sleeves, and the fat TV guy, wagging his granite jeans butt, climbed over the drifts to choose potential subjects. He especially liked a broad-shouldered old guy with a purple nose in the shape of a frozen potato and a clear, hundred-proof gaze, who looked a little like a Soviet film actor—not very steady on his feet but with medals under his camo quilted coat that were soiled but quite telegenic. Other candidates were found as well to represent District 18's insulted populace. Lined up on the snowdrifts, like the proud defenders of some snowy small town, they held the wind-battered

Whatman-paper slogans up by the corners (two couldn't cope and changed places, sensing some vague trick in the order of the words on the paper), while reporters bustled below like an assault brigade. Someone ran toward Klumba with his pickerel-narrow cloth back, sweeping loops of cable over the worn, tobacco-fertilized snow, and nearby the artist assiduously tested the megaphone, which whistled and honked, occasionally bursting out with howling vibrations that made the sparrows launch from the bushes like splashing brooms of brown water. "Okay, cut, good work," the fat TV guy ordered efficiently, rolling a gnawed match in his little crimson star of a mouth. "Now fifteen minutes of commentary. Where's that Krugal team?" "Over there, downstairs, sitting around, phoning," the activist in twinkling glasses reported. "They've been shut up for an hour and a half and still haven't finished." "Can we smoke them out? Anybody tried knocking?" the TV guy inquired, leaning his expansive body over the gloomy depression. "As if we hadn't," the activist said, offended, gesturing at the smeared door.

At that very moment, the heavy black telephone in the cold half basement started ringing like an entire streetcar. The registrars leaped up, as if they'd been half-asleep, and Marina dropped her coat and chair and grabbed the receiver. "Marina Borisovna? I'm connecting you to Shishkov." The good secretary's voice sounded like it was coming through a miniature radio. "Thank you, yes, I'm listening," Marina said hurriedly, stepping on something soft. "He just arrived and he's a basket of nerves," the mistress of the professor's office informed her, bringing her quiet voice closer, immediately after which mechanical scales started playing at length in the receiver. "Yes! Marina? Where are you?" Shishkov, seemingly terrified by something and sounding as distant as a cosmonaut, interrupted the sweet, didactic music. Trying to speak distinctly and choosing the simplest words, Marina described the situation outside the former headquarters. A staticky patch rustled and itched in the receiver, kind of like a little Shishkov angry at his end of the phone line, an electric bumblebee being prodded by a straw. She really didn't like it that Shishkov didn't interrupt her once. The receiver was itchy and thoroughly inflamed; a bumblebee, like a fat, dangerous larva, had coiled around a shaky straw, and Marina's palm was sweating so profusely, the receiver was getting slick. "You see, the canvassers are expecting us to start paying their bonus right away," she rushed to finish her report. "I don't know what to tell them. At least three hundred people have gathered, and we workers have been waiting for two hours for we don't know what, virtual prisoners." "So wait," the professor was suddenly close, having achieved his natural magnitude, as if he'd taken a seat and crossed his legs in the next room. "And what have you been doing, if I may ask?" "I've tallied how much we owe the canvassers," Marina replied in a cheerless voice, feeling the professor somewhere behind her. "Something has to be done. After all, getting hold of such an inconceivable sum . . ." "You think it does?" the professor said archly. "How's that?" Marina became distraught, looking through this crazy conversation at her registrars, whose puffy faces, smeared with yellow light, were furrowed with attention, as if they were all about to sneeze at once. Right then, feeling a pit under her heart, Marina realized that if she cited the exact figure to the professor, something between them would snap irrevocably. "Well? Where did you go?" a sarcastic Shishkov called to her. "You're not planning to *beat* these debts of yours out of me, are you, Marina Borisovna?" "I . . . What are you . . . I simply meant . . ." Marina imagined then and there, this very minute, the professor about to put his big cold palm on her open neck, on her bare vertebrae rubbed raw by her loose chain. "All right, let's forget that." The professor was once again collected and purposeful. "Marina Borisovna, I seem to remember you wanted to work in television, is that right? Come here tomorrow around ten and we'll resolve all urgent matters. The lease on the headquarters space ran out the day before yesterday. Collect the keys from the workers and return them to my secretary."

The slippery, squeaky receiver seemed to hang itself up, and the telephone now looked at Marina lifelessly, like a sheep's head placed on a table. She would have to lead her people out. At this point, Marina suddenly felt like the true daughter of her medal-bearing stepfather, as if the music of a military brass band carried on the wind had stumbled on some false note. A while was spent gathering up. The registrars opened the flimsy desk drawers, rattling the junk inside, wrapped their worn shoes in newspaper like sandwiches, and hastily rinsed out litter bins under the only faucet, which spewed out more putrid air than fizzy, rusty water. Finally, the column of six was ready to head out. Marina's purse was made heavy by the crudely clanking keys, and the most nervous of the women, the one who had once fainted when a bundle of bills went missing from under her elbow, was holding a pot with a multistage aloe, the trusting green fledgling's octopus tentacles swaying against her raised shoulder.

As soon as Marina pulled on the door, which emitted a steel shriek, the crowd's husky and for some reason partly equine presence and the day's blinding air hit her simultaneously. The human feet toward which she ascended over the rough, warped stairs took a small step back, weaving into a wreath. When Marina got to the top and stepped into the human circle, those birdies that always fly out from a photographer's camera flew right into her face with a menacing whoosh, a click, and a mechanical screech. Bending under this splash attack (a sharp wing slid flat across her cheek, and another creature, as weightless as a tuft of dry weeds, tangled its claws in her tousled hair), Marina screened herself from the reporters with a thrown-up palm, as she'd once seen in some magazine about celebrities. "When is your organization going to settle with the canvassers?" "Was the voter deception planned in advance?" "Were you able to reach Deputy Krugal over the phone?" The questions, shouted out in different voices, were accompanied by furry, spongy microphones, and the biggest camera, the size of a wall clock, kept sending out an egg-shaped, hiccupping cuckoo on a spring, like on that kiddie show, *Kinder Surprise*. "There definitely isn't going to be any money today. Beyond that, I don't know," Marina said in a raspy, muffled voice into the nearest microphone, feeling an emptiness behind her, which meant that in the confusion the women had been able to mix in with the deceived voters, who stood like an accordion, as if lined up for a group photo. "What do you think about a possible recount of the election results?" the pride and joy of ARM-TV, a well-groomed boy with marvelous, seemingly oil-infused lashes and the beautiful hands of a born pickpocket, shouldered his way through the crowd. "The elections are over," Marina replied firmly to her vague former acquaintance, catching out of the corner of her ear the canvassers behind the press trying to chant a garbled slogan and failing at syncing their voices—so the slogan, bogged down in extra syllables, just wouldn't get rolling. "That's it. Cut!" a fat director of unspecified studio affiliation yelled, energetically waving his puffy hand. The director was dressed, as usual, in a short quilted jacket that made him look like a cluster of dark blue balloons, and judging from the gnawed match in his mouth, he was, as usual, trying to quit smoking. The press thinned out immediately. Marina looked around and saw a narrow escape route next to the gray wall, right under the balconies, which looked mostly like hanging doghouses. No one tried to stop her, and she hurried off, stumbling on rusty sewer pipes tied with wires and frightening the broad-bottomed kitties perched there, obvious relatives of the one lolling in the window shaft, its rotten teeth bared; Marina couldn't shake the impression that the painter, following her with a heavy, seemingly blind gaze, had pulled a smirking knife from his sleeve.

■ □ ■

In his large, insipidly lit office, Professor Shishkov, having spoken with his staff, walked up to the window. Downstairs, on the institution's front steps, which were covered with ant-like chains of tiny footprints, a small picket line holding a white placard aloft was still stamping its feet. These dogged people had no intention of leaving. From time to time, the guards attempted to drive the protestors at least from the front steps, but all that did was draw attention from every floor to this display of scarecrows in front of the bastion of big and midsize business. The professor thought (although a certain chill prevented him from wholly believing this) that the canvasser problem would play itself out in a week, ten days at most. Once again, as had happened that morning, half an hour before his call to sweet Marina Borisovna, the professor had thought lyrically that in principle, for the sake of repaying the debt, he might sell his newly built summer house under the grandfather birch with the shaggy saddle and powerful mane, where it was so glorious to eat the summer's first crisp, prickly cucumber straight from the garden, and beyond the garden a rounded little lake shimmered as if filled above the brim so that you were afraid to touch it and disturb the delicate, glowing film—and in soft, rainy weather it was simply marvelous to read on the whispering veranda, peering through the gauze of warm rain at the nearby woods, which looked like a bright shadow.

Refreshed by this noble thought, as if he really had taken a break at his Losinko home, the professor nonetheless got back to business. Sitting in his office was the man he was going to be working with: solid, powerful, and short-legged, with a boyish chestnut bang cut straight along a deep forehead crease, the new director of Studio A, grunting, had scooped up a handful of the professor's special crackers, and after crushing them with his wonderful sugar-lump teeth, he ran his green silk tie over his slathered and crumb-strewn jaw. Sitting beside him was a tall woman with an ideal, Diana-like figure but a bulldoggish face whose exceedingly smart but makeup-wearied eyes looked as if they'd been drawn on in corrosive powder and who barely blinked. The woman, wearing an identical-looking, broad-shouldered, masculine jacket (the skirt, sewn from a length of the same fabric, wasn't worth mentioning), was sitting with her irreproachable legs precisely placed and was sipping pale jasmine tea, repeatedly pushing the string from the elegant teabag label aside with her pinky. The director had recommended her to Shishkov as his deputy. Although this pair's things (a pile of grubby, off-brand sports bags that looked a little like pigs, some in the trunk of the professor's car, some heaped up in the office) had obviously been packed separately, the nature of their relationship left no doubt. Still, observing the way they were exchanging barked comments and quick, feral glances (the director, shooting quick glances, could calm himself by smoothing his tie and knocking specks of dust off his round shoulder), the professor agreed that together they made a suitable and strong team. This woman in the masculine jacket with lapels like shark's flippers was just what was needed. Everything her demotic eyes—which were the color of cabbage soup and had a languid drop of yellow grease in them—saw she accepted with the imperturbability of a mirror, but she was apparently made of unbreakable stuff. From time to time the candidate for the position, abruptly lifting her pinky, said a few words in an even voice—and her comments, which were modest but accurate editorial corrections to the text of the conversation, attested to her calm, innate cynicism and total lack of complex ideas on simple subjects. The professor saw that the passion of this precious protégé differed most advantageously from sweet Marina Borisovna's, for whom he had previously experienced a pleasant fatherly feeling. Now, though, he had begun to worry about her aggressive alarm, this gift of hers for reviving moribund problems and constantly trying to represent workers or simply citizens who were irrelevant to his future plans. At this moment the professor, while not letting on, was quite pleased with his new acquisition, which had arrived from Krasnokurinsk with bowls and skillets whose outlines were well noted in one piece of the gypsy luggage. In particular, the appearance of an alternate candidate had lifted from Shishkov the dear-to-his-heart but nonetheless burdensome responsibility he felt for the charming Marina, who had lost her grip on reality and gotten mixed up with a crazy voters group—and this made the professor feel younger, as he did every time he slipped the leash of a beloved being. He saw that these two on his Italian couch got along excellently and in their feral language may well have been expressing the philosophy of the revived Studio A significantly more accurately than the professor himself had in his proper but cagey instructions.

Shishkov was also pleased with the way fateful events had unfolded that morning. Even though his hairy gray knees had been shaking in his trousers as if from applied cold and his left temple had been throbbing, the professor felt like Napoleon Bonaparte. The night before, his main investor (whose image even in the imagination of Shishkov, who had been admitted to see the body, was unreal, more like a fog that had gathered on the far side of good and evil) had acquired a controlling share in the Apofeozov television studio. The holder of the missing shares had refused to sell his politically profitable property for a very long time, but in view of the election results he immediately agreed. The investor, having invested a necessarily fair but nonetheless quite considerable sum (it was amusing to think he might start paying out money on the basis of the registrars' notebooks, with their pages like tattered cabbage leaves), immediately held a shareholders' meeting consisting of himself, and ordered Kukharsky fired, appointing in his place the Krasnokurinsk poet whose skinny chapbooks, bound by binder rings and decorated with magniloquent complimentary inscriptions, were lying in the investor's desk.

This historic order in hand, the professor and the poet, who had skipped breakfast to come in earlier, had headed for Studio A—and rightly picked up twenty or so young studs in camo from a friendly security firm along the way. The resistance offered by Kukharsky's security was perfunctory. For a little while, those men, who differed from those attacking only in the more peaty shade of their jackets and pants, secured several successive doors with their skidding bodies—but after one good jarring blow they leaped back like a popped cork and ran ahead of the enemy through the corridors, continuing to skid in their boots, which seemed to have grown heavier, as if they'd scooped up fear, and scaring the employees, who poked their heads out of their work spaces with the confusion of targets at shooting practice. The final skirmish in front of Kukharsky's office was short and sweet. The attackers twisted the demoralized defenders' arms and dealt with them exactly as they would folding camping furniture, also breaking a lightweight chair that got mixed up in the melee—and the highly cultured professor caught himself thinking how pleasantly exciting he found the sight of a bloodied face with a nose that looked like a used teabag in a saucer, the oofing and umphing of the brawlers, and the direct missile of an army boot knocking the stuffing out of a china cabinet whose heavenly smile over its own remains elicited a muffled groan from someone in the crowd.

Clearly, the use of teargas was now superfluous. All those nut job directors and reporters had probably acted on the mercenaries' nerves and were cackling like geese after the victors. In the directors' anteroom they had attacked the fighters, dropping burning cigarette butts and pointy women's shoes on them in the parterre. Before proceeding to Kukharsky's office, the reporters got sprinkled: the crisscrossing streams that filled the air of the dressing room with a herring-fat dust rainbow made the employees stagger back and goggle. To the hawking and screeching of a half-strangled birdman (one person grabbed his burned throat and fell backward onto his panicked comrades, and another fell to all fours and disgorged his viscous breakfast and juice on the trampled carpet), the professor's mercenaries burst into the holy of holies. Sensing a certain membranous rustle under his skull and trying not to inhale the offensive, sickly sweet perfume, the professor followed.

Kukharsky, tiny behind his horseshoe desk, had his cheek pressed to the telephone receiver, as if he suddenly had a toothache—though there was obviously no one at the other end. The professor, covered on his flanks, neatly approached the desk and placed a copy of the order in front of Kukharsky. Grinning from ear to ear, so that his beard looked like a wool sock stretched while being put on, Kukharsky picked up the paper with his hairy fingers and gently ripped it into two ethereal ribbons. Then he repeated the diminishing procedure many times while snarling and looking up into the professor's eyes until not even tiny pinches were left of the order and lofty signature. After letting him complete this tough, painstaking labor, the professor took another out of the file, like a saint who had accepted martyrdom, an even whiter copy, and suddenly—by instinct—gave his mercenaries a commander's circular signal kind of like a compass. Immediately, the men rushed around the director's desk and tried to extract Kukharsky from his quilted leather armchair—but ended up just rolling him around, his legs pulled up and his red maw cackling and looking like a split watermelon. For the first time since the raid began, the professor was distraught—especially as surviving employees, their faces now covered with weepy wet handkerchiefs, began to appear, one after another, in the office's half-open doorway. Someone wrapped up like the invisible man in an entire terry towel (it was Kostik, stone-cold and lightning quick on the uptake, who subsequently earned his living selling photographs to both print media and the Internet) was shooting the sensation of the day, diving behind backs, his point-and-shoot buzzing like a model airplane— and the professor instantly understood that to an onlooker what was happening looked nothing like what it did to his agitated soul.

Right then someone came forward who had until then held back: the Krasnokurinsk poet, physically hungry and pale but full of a primitive might. Pushing aside the sweaty fighters, who reeked of canvas and whose necks looked like they'd been rubbed with red pepper, the new director personally rolled up his sleeves. He made an abrupt tank maneuver with the heavy armchair and deposited the fleeing Kukharsky in the corner. Then, having oriented the seat smack-dab in the middle of the office and desk, he climbed, wagging his butt, into the chair's stoutly creaking depth and stretched out his perfectly parallel arms and clenched fists in front of him. Now the newly appointed director gave his subordinates a blank stare, as if he had seized and pulled the levers of studio administration, and under the visor of his jutting brow, his eyes were like air bubbles stuck to a sunken board. Everyone quieted down instantly at the sight of this phenomenon, which imperturbably allowed itself to examine the former director with a direct challenge to all the studio's accumulated administrative experience. Because the pretender had placed himself smack-dab in the middle of the main space, he looked like a convincing, *pivotal* person, and all of a sudden it seemed to the employees that a third, omniscient eye was swelling under his short, straight bangs, like a soap bubble slightly larger than the ones under his eyebrows.

The unseated Kukharsky—distinctly superfluous to the side of the midline that the new director had almost physically set out across the desk and the thick of the people crowding in—smiled crookedly and shrugged, his entire body catching the magpie gaze of the now absent camera like a ray of saving sun. Actually, all he had to do was leave and come back. But he couldn't get out, having just overcome an obstacle in the form of a solidly ensconced rival who had no intention of abandoning his newly won position. Dragging out the first few badly fastened files he came across from under the pretender's elbow (the pretender paid no attention, merely pressing his short

198 \ **The Man Who Couldn't Die**

legs harder into the desk crosspiece), Kukharsky tried to squeeze through. This wild climax lasted a few minutes. Kukharsky climbed, smirking and muttering something as if into his own ear, crawled and stood on tiptoe. His forehead was sprinkled with beads of moisture, and the loose papers pressed under his elbows quietly slipped down his belly. The *midline* that the employees now saw even on the wall, apparently, barely let the former director through and distorted his solid figure like a funhouse mirror. Observing this villainous scene, some people began to realize that in the eyes of the pretender— the only *geometrically regular*, properly seated creature—even they would look like fluid dispositions and that for all the seriousness of the newly arrived ogre (the keenest of them guessed that the collective would never see a hint of a smile on this three-eyed face), he saw the seized studio as one big house of mirrors created for his directorial pleasure. Finally, the tormented Kukharsky, nearly straddling the tall back of the unshakeable armchair (which the pretender, all puffed up with his sweeping force, leaned all the way back at the last moment), found himself on the other side; the papers in his grip immediately lost whatever cohesion they had left and spread out on the floor with a silent sigh. "You may pick them up," the triumphant professor said sarcastically, drumming his white, as if chalk-rubbed, unmusical fingers on the solid directorial desktop. In response, the beet-red Kukharsky flung the empty manila folders on the papers and shaking his head like a bull, pulled his hopelessly ruined jacket down as if it were a shoulder bag. "You're not going to get away with this so easily," he said in a reedy voice squeezed at the top, and his shaking hands threw his jacket lapels back over his tattered shirt, providing a glimpse of the hairy fold of his belly and his surprisingly small navel, as downcast as a faded rose. "You'll answer for this in court!" The employees parted for the outcast like funeral mourners. For a while, they could hear Kukharsky walking away, a scuff of lime down his back, over the black scuffs left by his security detail's boots, skidding on the light parquet floor, and shouting tragic threats into space. Not idle threats.

Actually, ninety minutes after his victorious seizure of the studio, the professor understood full well that Apofeozov's lawyers were already preparing their lawsuits and cursing excitedly. For instance, they could seize on the formal circumstance that the official period defined by law between a shareholders' announcement and its implementation (which consisted, basically, in the investor signing previously prepared documents) had not passed. No matter what headaches his opponent tried to cause for Shishkov and his team, though, the basic facts were now irreversible. The new director, who had not had dinner and was now scarfing down a huge sandwich brought by the secretary, holding down the ham with his index finger, had only to solve a few small technical problems. "Let's say I'm prepared to look into the question of an apartment for your assistant," the professor began warily as he sat down with his visitors. "A modest, one-room apartment, naturally, and not downtown, well, you get the idea. In return, though, I would like a favor in the form of . . . How can I put it?" the professor faltered, feeling a pleasant sentimental warmth in his chest. "A certain young someone helped me greatly during the campaign but lately has become rather . . . unmanageable. I would like to make modest arrangements for her further fate. Her name is Marina Borisovna, and she's a fine television journalist. Here's what happened with Marina Borisovna. Basically . . ."

■ □ ■

The pleasure Professor Shishkov derived from his own beneficence was not so important as to distract him from his top priorities, however. After being summoned to the studio for ten and not having first caught sight of the professor until noon or so, Marina sat there in the poorly tidied, nauseating waiting room examining either the glowing Lyudochka, who was rehearsing new smiles into her compact, or the large china shard with the surviving handle that had fallen under the secretary's desk. People she did and didn't know zipped by her, as did the focused, utterly unstoppable professor, who, like a deranged theorem, was made up of only acute angles. The hubbub's epicenter was the director's office, where, when the door opened, she observed the new boss's static figure within, like a picture in a flip-book. The more modest office across the way, which Marina in her naïve old dreams had seen as hers, had still not acquired an owner or status, but a tall woman wearing a hideous jacket with shoulders lined like house slippers kept looming up there. The woman's legs were indeed quite fine. When she walked into the waiting room, playing up this beauty, Lyudochka would rise from her secretary's chair as if randomly and they would vie for the best walk, traipsing back and forth over the crunching china crumbs. No fewer than four hours passed before Lyudochka, hearing the intercom's expectorating mumble, laid on another smile, and snapping it into her gleaming compact, like a coupon in an elegant wallet, headed off with her notebook to answer her boss's summons. Returning shortly thereafter (without the notebook and with a pink cocktail spill on her clothes), she announced in a delicate official voice, "Marina Borisovna, the director is busy today, unfortunately. He'll see you tomorrow at twelve-thirty."

Marina was so weary from her hours of sitting on the edge of a chair and from her exhausting idleness amid the feverish activity of

Studio A's new masters that she barely dragged herself home and, ignoring her mother, who was following her around with an enormous tattered newspaper in her dangling hand, fell lifeless on her bed. As she plunged into a droning doze, she remembered that tomorrow was the twentieth—pension day—and instead of the usual pleasant anticipation for which Klumba was forgiven the fact of her existence, Marina felt a spiritual heartburn. What the joy from getting that money—those large, starched hundreds that allowed them to eke out another month of life—had turned into was spoiled, drunkenly astray, and inexpressively vile. As she drifted off, Marina knew she hated the twentieth. Somehow this boded nothing good for her at the studio tomorrow.

That night, Marina's sleep was heavy and troubled. She kept butting heads with the pillow and couldn't seem to get warm in her bed, whose deep pockets had accumulated enough damp and snowy cold, you could scratch it off. Unlike Marina, Nina Alexandrovna smiled in her sleep, and on her lips lay a spot of light of unknown origin. What was so good that she was thinking about it as she fell asleep? What was it—more important than the newspaper with those horrid photos printed not with ink but with street filth, more important even than the state in which Marina had come home from work yesterday, frightening Nina Alexandrovna with her complete unresponsiveness and total personal absence? What on earth was she dreaming? Something strange, piquant, and springlike: the thawing earth, felt-like from last year's grass, tiny little flowers that didn't yet look real, touchingly white like toes in the holes of an old sock. As she washed up in front of the bathroom mirror, which Marina had splashed with dirty water and toothpaste, as usual, Nina Alexandrovna tried to *remember*. Something stepped closer and closer, more and more confidently, promising to decipher her happiness.

Lit by the morning sun, Alexei Afanasievich lay under his Chinese blanket, which was a little short for him, and his left, wide-open eye was perfectly transparent and as if pricked, like light green glass. Looking at her husband, Nina Alexandrovna noticed that the sun today was unusual, the way it can be in airplanes: harsh, slightly iridescent, *perpetual*. This astronomical light, which seemed not to know cloud cover, allowed her to see something stretched over the veteran: the light haze of nonbeing, probably consisting of that light dust of immortality against which brushes and rags were powerless. After her usual morning routine with Alexei Afanasievich, Nina Alexandrovna noticed that the haze, while retaining the dissipating trace of her labor, was slowly changing outline, so that any ruptures in the oh-so-delicate whiteness oddly lost their human meaning. The little workshop on the headboard, between the two gold, sun-stung balls, was ready for his morning labors: a few long strings freed from bast and rid of pesky nubbins lay on the pillow to the left and right of the veteran's head—and Nina Alexandrovna, having removed these preparations during the washing-up, restored his rag bench to order. Alexei Afanasievich was in no hurry, though. It was surprising, but today he was silent the whole time. Even the turning from side to side and the cotton wool touching his thoroughly baked bedsores, which always aroused a guttural protest in the paralyzed man, today passed without a murmur. Perhaps the puzzling celebration in her soul had something to do with it, but Alexei Afanasievich emerged from Nina Alexandrovna's hand particularly well-groomed and handsome. The wide-toothed comb had laid his transparent gray hair out hair to hair, and his scraped cheeks were like sugared honey.

She couldn't imagine that the paralyzed man had any interest in his appearance. Lying in the same place for so long excluded any ability he might have to see himself from the *outside*. Today, though, Alexei Afanasievich seemed to have some sense of his good looks and was pleased; his raised index finger, which made the veteran thumb-size but a man nonetheless, touched the invisible vertical like a taut string. This quiet bass vibration, echoed somewhere very high up, must have been the spectral sound to which Alexei Afanasievich listened so intently. Suddenly Nina Alexandrovna realized how to decipher her dream.

She was amazed at how she'd failed to remember and understand. That long-ago spring, back before they'd built buildings on the damp, dragonfly lot, had blurred in memory. She and Alexei Afanasievich were either out for a walk or coming back from the movies. Nina Alexandrovna overtook the veteran, who was working his splattered cane hard, like a lever, and began quickly climbing the warmed slope, plucking coltsfoot flowers, golden, like uniform buttons on gray army cloth. Of course, she was flirting, gathering this silly eggy bouquet, but she'd never expected Alexei Afanasievich to suddenly climb up after her, noisily poking his cane in the not-yet-dried bushes and leaving flagrant, plowed up tracks on the soft epithelia of a recent rivulet. When he stopped in front of Nina Alexandrovna with a streak of mud on his wet temple holding one defective flower, yellowed like a cheap cigarette and badly crushed, which he held out to her with an expression of pained displeasure, Nina Alexandrovna took serious fright and hurried to descend to the path, carefully holding up her husband, who was slipping in his muddied shoes over the mats of last year's grass. At the time, shamed, her nose yellow, Nina Alexandrovna had taken the addition to her bouquet as an earned reproach. In exactly the same way, her husband sometimes would hand her the salt shaker forgotten on the dinner table or a knitting needle picked up from the floor. Now she suddenly guessed that Alexei Afanasievich, having crudely taken her on his trophy bed, was in the light of day shy, like a youth, and didn't know the right way to approach the timid Nina Alexandrovna, who had always been in such a hurry to *put him off* through some kind of service: he never recovered the grave simplicity with which he had once taken her hand along with the watch that had come undone and nearly fallen on the floor and suggested that she move in with him.

Which meant he *had* once had that simplicity. Alexei Afanasievich was authentic because his consciousness had preserved the true significance of every episode and minor incident when he had scorned Nina Alexandrovna for forgetfulness—but he couldn't just go up to her and hand her what she had *forgotten*, just as he never had known how to derive symbols from everyday objects. That was why the myopic flower added to the sticky bouquet, which smelled like a chicken, meant exactly nothing other than the abandoned Alexei Afanasievich's clumsy attempt to bring back his runaway wife. In all the decades of their life together, the Kharitonovs had never reminisced about anything together. They hadn't accrued any symbolic property in common, such as any love, however brief, immediately tries to acquire. But Alexei Afanasievich had no need to capitalize on his emotions. Fully self-aware, he possessed not the symbols of things but the originals. The grim business of reconnaissance, when a man in camouflage disappearing locally to the dull tremor of a burning missile is required *not to be*, so that even a fascist's weak brain signals can't detect the enemy nearby—that business doubtless assumed a loss of authenticity. By rejecting his full self, the man ceased to be aware of what death was or even when he had been *picked out*. He merely had a better sense of his oneness with the fighting mass of his fellow countrymen. Unlike many of his heroic comrades who recklessly entrusted themselves to nonbeing, Alexei Afanasievich had refused to let go of the thread of his own existence and so had survived. Everything he did, including his quiet work with nooses and his insane lunge at a cunning submachine gun, a lunge his command knew about, took place in the clear awareness and full memory of his school's apple orchard and his waiting wife. Holding on to this *altogether* was nearly impossible, but Alexei Afanasievich furiously refused to let go. After this, all the veteran ceremonies where *his* war had become widely accessible symbols were utterly beside the point for Alexei Afanasievich, which was why he didn't need any of the *literature* that Nina Alexandrovna waited for so long and so hopelessly from her husband, not understanding that it was the absence of symbolism that signified the authenticity of his emotions. Alexei Afanasievich authenticated himself by his mere presence, and that was more than enough.

Yes, it was all perfectly clear to her now—and highlighted even more clearly than ever was the fact that Alexei Afanasievich's suicide would lead to the loss of much more than simply a man's life. Not because the emotion would be gone, but because it would be as if there had never been any. That different time—that ideal *stagnation*, when a natural ending was impossible by definition—had become a trap, and Alexei Afanasievich could now go only by betraying his wife with his death, which he had taken, like a woman, into his cold bed. Because Alexei Afanasievich *himself* preferred the other's eternal company, Nina Alexandrovna, who now spent her time in the kitchen scraping dishes under the hot faucet, which smelled like a foul mouth, suffered such attacks of jealousy that the fist under her shoulder blade was a joke by comparison. More than anything in the world, Nina Alexandrovna would have liked right now to see her rival face-to-face and see whether she was that pretty. She didn't realize just how blasphemous and dangerous her thoughts were; her hot wet hand wiped away her cloudy tears, which had scummed over as if with chlorine, and she wiped her hand on the dish towel for a long time, as if searching for pockets in it. Had Nina Alexandrovna been offered the chance to die that minute and see the fateful hooded lady and reclaim her husband, who had been summoning that lady for so long and at such incredible effort, Nina Alexandrovna would have agreed. She was so upset, she had even forgotten about the pension. She had completely lost sight of the fact that she needed to throw the blue blanket over the rope workshop before Klumba's arrival.

Meanwhile, a disheveled Klumba, who was now quite prepared to play her benevolent and salutary role in the Kharitonov family's history, approached the veteran's residence even more quickly than usual.

■ □ ■

That day, the city, lit from a distance at an unusual and harsh angle, looked like an assemblage of improbable staircases, twisted ledges, and stepped pyramids, and because all that was left of the streets and buildings in this parallel time was a fan of ruins and caked ashes breathing radiation, if you looked closely through the soapy, frosty air, they created a striking yet defenseless dramatic effect. Everything seemed slightly inauthentic. Because they had already ceased to be the day's top news story, the deceived voters' scattered picket lines looked like clusters of arrivals from the provinces, and their main dance in front of the provincial authorities' ribbed tower, which looked like it was squinting from a jolt of sun, might have been a talent show.

Klumba, though, her attention averted from public activism to performing her direct responsibilities for the benefits office, did not feel the struggle's decline. Feverish excitement drove her from address to address nearly at a run. The firm snow chipped and grated under her sturdy heels, and her short shadow raced across the snowdrifts like a hyper little dog. At every pensioner apartment she descended upon, stamping loudly from the cold, she was awaited by yet more eloquent proof of Krugal's baseness; the poverty and germs that had gone hog wild and spilled out everywhere like flickering sand worked her into a state of morbid amazement over and over again. She didn't understand how she could have been so outplayed. Two hundred forty-eight disabled people, all with documents, had received zero and had not played their proper role; they had simply been ignored. Nonetheless, they had pushed their candidate through, a mangy artist with a crooked jaw that made his face resemble a *left* boot. Today's pensioner rounds were for Klumba a way of reinforcing her own sense of correctness. Once again, she was convinced of the reality of her team of invalids: the trembling, *open-ended* scrawls endlessly drawn by the eighteen-year-old girl idiot and the pathetic kitchen utensils of the lonely old men touched her as never before. For some reason, for the first time in her benefits career, it broke her heart in two. Klumba was almost certain that this highly unexpected turn in voter affairs concealed some especially crafty machinations. She couldn't wait to get to the apartment of this Marina Borisovna, who had run the headquarters for Klumba's foe and was probably complicit in her candidate's behind-the-scenes machinations. Klumba hoped to discover some major evidence of foul play there.

Meanwhile, Marina was once again languishing in the waiting room, which over the past few days she had studied better than during all her years of working at Studio A. Demoralized to the nth degree such that even she found herself repulsive, she couldn't take her eyes off the director's door and kept wiping her damp palms stealthily on her synthetic skirt, which only made the stiff fabric greasy. Finally, the voices in the office got louder as they rose from their seats, and when the beaming director ran out on his short legs, which seemed to slip a little and lag behind his body as he saw his visitors out, Marina leaped up. She immediately became unbearably ashamed, but it would have been stupid to sit back down on her disagreeably warm chair. The director, today wearing a striped, sharply waisted suit, in which the upper part of his massive body dominated quite a bit over his lower, turned his eyebrows, which looked like they'd been mowed with a razor, toward her. For a while he busied himself some more with the tall blonde, who was vaguely familiar to Marina, reminding her of the dissolute literary circle at the *Krasnokurinsk Worker*—while the blonde's companion, a good-looking gentleman with an amazingly fresh face and ruddy bags under his eyes, kept trying to wedge his face between them, like a forty-minute program, ingratiatingly touching the director's massive shoulder. At last the blonde, smiling, her delicate, protruding ears as red as fruit in syrup, waved to the director from the hall, and her companion scurried after her, dragging her grandiose fur coat made of fiery tufts of fox. Then the director, stepping back a little from his office door, made Marina a reluctant sign of invitation.

"So you're Marina Borisovna," he said, informing himself, and slipped nimbly into his chair, rolling to the very middle of his polished, seriously empty desk. Marina, who had taken the small little rolling chair at one side, keenly felt the humiliation of her place on the side, which, according to the logic of *position* the director had created, was beneath his notice. "You know what, I'm going to be frank with you," the director suddenly said in a freer voice, leaning back and throwing his short arm behind his head, revealing his jacket's worn armpit and a loose thread. "I'm a plainspoken man, anyone will tell you that, and anyone who doesn't know me will find out. I know you were promised the job of my deputy, but here's the thing. That position has now been taken by someone else who is close and important to me in both the sexual and the spiritual sense, I won't hide that." "I see," Marina mumbled politely, having known in advance that this was approximately what was going to be said. Nonetheless, her heart felt as if it had been wiped with a cold cotton ball before an injection. "Basically, Sergei Sergeich, well, you know Sergei Sergeich, he asked me to give you a job at the studio," the director went on, giving his cropped head a hard jerk, which sent his hacked bang rearing back. "Actually, I'm prepared to take you on your former terms, which I know. You could even start today."

"On contract?" Marina asked quietly, not trusting her own voice, which was shaking treacherously. The day before, she had glimpsed her old desk moved over to the wall and covered with dirty mugs that had the iridescent remains of some sweet tar, two rock-hard sugar balls, and some defiled greasy napkins under a mound of cafeteria meat patties that looked like something from a kiddie sandbox. "Well, yes," the director confirmed, fondly stroking his round nape. "For you that would be an option. Sergei Sergeich said you're a good commentator, but I asked your coworkers, and they said something different. Actually, I could be wrong. But if I am, you'll easily find a job at another TV studio, so what do you need this contract for?" The new director may not yet have known that, under relentless pressure from graduates of the school of journalism, vacancies at any decent media outlet didn't last ten days; however, he couldn't help but understand that Marina, with her current political dowry, could work only for her own people, that none of the more advanced TV companies (which had far outdistanced freelance Studio A in the quality of their highly varied and decently paid projects) would take her on. Nonetheless, the director looked straight ahead with his perfectly calm, quietly shining little eyes, the color of damp coffee grounds. "As I already said, I'm a plainspoken man," he repeated, abruptly reorienting his impressive pose toward and looking straight at the central, business point on his desk. "I will say that I would rather not hire you. Your presence would upset the person close to me, a person I respect and treasure. All of you who live here can find jobs somewhere through acquaintances. But I understand the meaning of compromise. I am warning you honestly that you won't be getting promoted because my person has to be shielded from you. You yourself may leave eventually. Then you'll write your resignation. That's all."

At these last words from the focused director, who had been tapping a few pencils against the table, Marina figured out what had been bothering her the past few days. A contrived *Party spirit*, which had accumulated much more power over her than had been in evidence at the beginning of this strictly in-house game, now assumed her incomprehensible but incontestable guilt before the Party—and Professor Shishkov's total absence of guilt before her, to say nothing of that actor Krugal's. Marina could *stick to her guns* and put her symbolic Party ticket on the desk of one of her benefactors. Doing so—in the absence of Klimov, who could never be discounted—meant such intense loneliness that its perfection almost entranced Marina, who had one sole talent: striving for the absolute. However, fear, garden-variety fear, held her at the edge of the abyss and the chair she was on, and with her hands pressed between her knees, she started rocking mechanically. Actually, rather than detain the director, she ought to slide over the old piece of paper he'd pulled out from somewhere, which looked singed along the edges, write her resignation, and go clean out her desk. But Marina's hands were so damp, she was afraid of leaving greasy spots on the paper, like from those disgusting brown meat patties, and worst of all she was afraid of making grammatical mistakes, which would serve as the first proof of her poor qualifications. In her mind, this resignation, which would now be nothing but an obvious demonstration of her shameful weakness, set out on a blank sheet of paper, got mixed up with the work contract, which evidently would have to be signed separately. The director was silently, mockingly patient, smiling with just his cheeks, where his unshaven, splintery stubble had become noticeable. It was her self-loathing, and not just the simple thought that she had essentially nothing to fear given her stepfather's pension, that decided Marina's fate. Intuitively, she realized what should not under any circumstances be done in this office and knew that this was exactly what she was about to do.

Still on her rolling chair, Marina pushed off from the carpeting with her boots, her sharp heel crackling as it caught, and abruptly found herself directly facing the director—who hadn't even thought to put his short legs and shoeless feet under his desk and was gripping the crosspiece like an ape. Marina was blocking the door, so that now they seemed to have suddenly switched places. Moreover, the office's owner and situation were suddenly pushed against the wall and drawn on it as distinctly as on a cinema screen. "What kind of tête-à-tête is this?" the director, who did not like this new situation one bit, said irritably. "You and I aren't in some café now." "I'm not interested in your contract," Marina said. It felt to her that the office and all its contents were slowly tipping on their side, toward the tall window that had pulled the sunshine slantwise across the gray carpet. "Are you going to run to Shishkov and complain?" the director asked, slamming his hand down on the slipping piece of paper and rolling the chattering faceted pencil. "You can tell the professor," Marina said distinctly, feeling a smooth tilt in her head, "that I'm sick of covering his respected ass. He can use your close friend now. I don't care. You can tell him he's a punk and a scoundrel."

Someone else in Marina's place symbolically flinging down her Party ticket would have found substantially more stinging words— but for her, even this was too much. Her legs were buckling and she needed to leave the office and not be terrified. "Hey!" The obviously upset director called to her, having jumped up, to judge from the way his chair creaked. Evidently, he'd realized that this Marina Borisovna, in inflicting these outrageous words on him, words that one way or another had to be conveyed to Shishkov, had unexpectedly placed him in the way of the professor's ambitions, whose limits the director didn't know. Marina didn't stop, though. She just caught her heel again, pulling some white threads from the carpet's synthetic curls. What did this remind her of? It reminded her of the way she, as a university student, had entered an auditorium, having failed to cross paths with the divine Klimov running out of his lectures, and had seen before her a stale emptiness and faces she didn't need. Only now Marina couldn't go back and chase down her retreating love. The emptiness before her was infinite, and she could only wade into it further and overcome the familiar resistance of a dimension without qualities. Now she probably could not say, "My entire life is up to me." Having failed to cross paths with her true life somehow—now time, which never went backward, was part of this movement—Marina put on her coat. At last she understood why she'd been saving up money in the battered, shell-covered box. "Marina Borisovna, are you leaving for good?" a surprised Lyudochka tore herself away from the spluttering explosions and croaking commands of her computer game.

That very same moment, a flushed Klumba plopped her heavily sighing bag on the stool and saw the philanthropic lists on the windowsill.

■ □ ■

At first, when the half-unbuttoned benefits rep materialized in the front hall, sniffing and making decisive gestures, it had occurred to Nina Alexandrovna that Klumba was drunk. But she didn't smell of alcohol, and the strong Cahors of her bordeaux flush was probably the result of the cold and walking fast. Still, Nina Alexandrovna clearly sensed something abnormal in Klumba's behavior. As Klumba pulled off her long Turkish sheepskin coat, she sought something with feverish little eyes, as if she'd never been in the apartment before, and even secretly pinched the thick clothing that was hanging up. Nina Alexandrovna was embarrassed that the night before, after she took that trip to see her nephew, she hadn't swept the spider web, which had collected flakes of grout, from the front hall, or the crushed eggshell in the corners. Now she thought that before giving her her money, Klumba was going to give her a good scolding.

But what did happen was even more surprising. On her way to the kitchen, Klumba swiveled on her axis a couple of times, as if she were on a tour, and the enthusiasm on her flushed face was gradually mixed with disappointment, as if they'd watered down the wine. But suddenly her hot, catarrhish mouth opened and she stared at the well-wiped windowsill, where next to the light pyramid of washed kefir packages, the modest stack of Marina's papers was drying out, spots faceup. Klumba looked like a woman who could not believe her own luck. And so, in fact, it was. In suggesting she take a good look around at this Marina Borisovna's, Klumba had expected to discover new furniture, say, or an ostentatious mink coat with a fancy top button as big as the saucer in a gilt tea service. What she had found, her gaze having crashed into the familiar lines and worn comments in her own hand, exceeded her boldest speculations. In essence, Klumba had in her hands direct evidence that this Marina Borisovna had taken the invalids' money and, moreover, had taken the database so that later she could use Klumba's social instrument in her own interests. "Excuse me. Is that yours? Did you lose it?" Nina Alexandrovna asked, uneasy, not knowing how to take the ill-starred papers away from the benefits rep, papers on which she suddenly noticed a shriveled bit of chicken fat. "I'll tell you what this is right now," Klumba replied, gasping for air, and something in her exultant voice made Nina Alexandrovna turn to stone and take a seat on the stool.

. . . What she heard from the benefits rep over the next quarter hour was so horrific that an awkward smile kept appearing on Nina

Alexandrovna's face, the kind of smile on polite people suffering through improbable tales. Her pale, screwed-up grimace, which also betrayed the pain that gripped Nina Alexandrovna under her shoulder blade harder and harder, must have enraged the already agitated Klumba. Nothing remained of her exultant mood but a scream that shook the building. Nina Alexandrovna knew that Marina wasn't working at the TV studio anymore. The photograph in the newspaper said clearly that her daughter had gone from being a correspondent to an object of interest in a scandal sheet and had landed in some incident. But these fraudulent elections with their general subornation and thievery and their spending of philanthropic money intended for old people were much more eloquent and worse than those odd-numbered campaign-period scenes that Nina Alexandrovna had attempted to draw for herself, simultaneously relieving and feeding her alarm.

Meanwhile, with the part of her long-distance hearing not completely taken up by Klumba's decibels, Nina Alexandrovna sensed that the door to Alexei Afanasievich's room was *open*. The saga of the criminal elections, which could not compare to the benefits rep's dangerous comments and contradicted everything the paralyzed man had been told and shown over the past fourteen years, was penetrating there quite freely. It was as if some solid membrane had burst and Nina Alexandrovna clearly heard the sick man's quiet, guttural bursts, as she did the slow creaks of the chainmail mesh that suddenly had tensed with an abundant clank, as if Alexei Afanasievich had risen from his bed. That was impossible, of course, but his event-free time had obviously not withstood the press of events conveyed to the damaged Red Corner, leaving no hope whatsoever of restoring that bubble of immortality. Feverishly casting about for how to deal with this situation now, Nina Alexandrovna had the cowardly thought that Alexei Afanasievich wouldn't be able to *ask*— and the simplest thing would be to hush up this kitchen row between women without going into explanations. But then she realized that then she would have to treat Alexei Afanasievich like an inanimate object. Never again would they be able to speak in the language of floating electrical figures, never again would that wordless physical understanding be restored that is known only to people who have cared for the half-alive bodies of paralyzed and comatose partners for many years and have learned a thing or two about the characteristics of their *invisible* presence independent of the body. Evidently, Nina Alexandrovna would somehow have to find the words and overcome the shame of her years-long deception, so insulting for the veteran, and chronicle the changes for Alexei Afanasievich. She could not imagine a situation in which Alexei Afanasievich, who had never faltered before anything in this world, including street thugs and capricious bosses, would forgive this cowardice of saving the Brezhnev portrait and hanging it up for him as a symbol. Looking at Klumba, who had rifled all the way through the lists and held her nail firmly on a line she'd found, Nina Alexandrovna mentally saw the dust of immortality, like poplar fluff, being removed from the match that had finally burned down and fallen from the veteran's fingers. The transparent flame, eating a clean, sootless hole in the white substance, bared *what was there in fact*: old furniture cracked and filmed over from long years of polishing, the crazy little TV set, the broken spider toy no longer capable of jumping but only wheezing dull rubber air, and the worn baby doll lying in wait in the blanket's folds.

"So you mean you don't believe your daughter stole twelve thousand rubles?" Klumba's harsh voice snapped Nina Alexandrovna out of her reverie and brought her back to the kitchen. "It's supposed to be distributed according to these lists, but the lists, it turns out, here they are, and you're wrapping herring in them. Look: number ninety-four, A. A. Kharitonov. Your old man is supposed to get a subsidy, too, and they brought him food, and they would have brought money, only Marina Borisovna had no shame. You have to look for it. Dig through her closets! Not just twelve thousand, you'll find even more! There's a good reason the people at headquarters kept beating around the bush and slipping money up their sleeves. People stood in line for days to get their due, and these people probably signed for its receipt! Now the canvassers are supposed to get a bonus and the headquarters isn't paying out anything, while your daughter has hundreds of thousands under her panties and beads, so you go look, just to satisfy yourself, or you and your old man aren't going to get anything!" Pain pulled tight on Nina Alexandrovna's entire shoulder, like a sturdy belt fastened on the last hole; her left arm, lying like a log on the table, went totally numb to the point that there was just a weak Morse code being tapped out in her fingers. Looking at line ninety-four, where Alexei Afanasievich and their home address and telephone had been written down in an unfamiliar, cramped handwriting, Nina Alexandrovna felt this whole story—heretofore abstract with all its headquarters, politicians, and invalids—suddenly take on an incontrovertible reality. "Your apartment is stuffed with money, but I'll give you your pension. I'm not a thief," Klumba stated sarcastically, jamming the scattered lists into her bulging bag. "I'll look in on the old man and tell him separately how his subsidy was stolen from him. Maybe then Marina Borisovna won't have the gall to spend it all on herself and there'll be at least one invalid her philanthropy will reach." With these words, the benefits rep, her lips drawn into a tube and her printed roses getting closer together and farther apart in the agitation of her bodily folds, headed for the hallway. The way before her was perfectly free—so free that Nina Alexandrovna even thought Klumba might fall through that freedom as if it were an open hatch. In any event, she heard the unmasker stumble and gasp and slap her hand hard against the wall.

Nina Alexandrovna had to follow her—if not to avert her scandalous monologue then at least to be present. But right then, for the first time, she experienced a physical pain that wouldn't let her stand up. A strap was strangling her left shoulder, as if some very heavy weight were hanging from it—and every attempt Nina Alexandrovna made to stand on her buckling legs led only to her head tightening up, peeling and ringing, like a firmly inflated ball being struck. So that meant Marina was going to be tried. Of course, she didn't take the money. Of course, all this would be cleared up. She just had to sit here a bit and then stand. Suddenly a scream reached Nina Alexandrovna—not even a scream but a triumphant wail broken by snatches of independently babbling, hottish air, that even on the inhale continued, inhuman sounds like the hollow vibrations of a water pipe. In that first moment, Nina Alexandrovna thought she was the one screaming, with both her hands pressing on her ears, listening to the bubbles whooshing. Then she realized that the scream was coming from the paralyzed man's room, and she jumped up on light feet, as if she were young again.

The hallway led in an unfamiliar direction, as if Nina Alexandrovna were running through a train car listing hard on the turn, and while hurrying through the train on light feet, she inexplicably lagged behind its speed of motion and was thrown into the small table as the telephone started ringing softly. At last she struggled through the half-open door and saw the scene she seemed to have had in her mind a second before. Klumba, unrecognizable, was screaming. She had nearly collapsed. Her mouth, sucking in air, was open in idiotic astonishment, and she couldn't take her eyes—disturbed and cloudy, like water in a glass just used for rinsing a watercolor brush—off Alexei Afanasievich, who was lying inert in a freely thrown noose. The vital color had drained very quickly from the veteran's face, which was oddly heavy, his eye sockets sunken. Even though the rope hadn't pulled tight and, impregnated with tar, was bulging under his chin, Nina Alexandrovna suddenly realized that she did not see the watermark that signaled life in her husband's myopically blurred face. Instantly she was at his bedside throwing back the blanket. A limp rubber toy jumped out and slammed to the floor with a bruised squeak. Putting her trembling hand where the scout's unfailing heart had always beat, like a simple two-stroke engine, Nina Alexandrovna felt nothing. There was only a final minty pain that licked her palm and dissolved into emptiness.

If in the next few minutes someone (not Klumba, who had sunk to the floor with a moan) had observed the room from the heavens, say, he would have been amazed to see a disheveled old woman straddling a long old man on her bared bluish knees, jumping frenziedly and periodically dropping to his bared mouth. Nina Alexandrovna didn't know the rules of artificial respiration or CPR. She pressed down on his slippery basket of ribs with the same desperate strength she used to plunge blocked toilet lines. After a few presses—she couldn't count them—she breathed a hot bubble into his slimy gray mouth, which was already sticking to his firm teeth, but the bubble disappeared behind the veteran's cheek. The more force she applied, the more clearly she felt that she and Alexei Afanasievich were communicating vessels and that the tightest stopper was in her head. Finally, it became clear to her that the obstruction couldn't be breached. Slowly, Nina Alexandrovna tumbled over on her side and lay on her husband's pillow, staring very closely at his elongated profile, at the firm little scar of unknown origin, white on the veteran's neck, at the sharp wrinkle under his dangling tuft of gray hair, like an important line drawn by a nail. All this, infinitely precious, was already disappearing, melting away, becoming the past. Cautiously holding his head, which had become heavy and hard, like a sealed vessel filled with treasure, Nina Alexandrovna removed the worthless noose. So there had been no artificial death. At that moment she heard the woman who had kept the veteran from suicide fumbling around on the floor and shuffling her soft feet, in an effort to sit up.

"Get me something to drink," Klumba rasped quietly with her flaccid vocal cords as she climbed, like a fat grasshopper everted every which way, onto the armchair with the knitting and needles. Beside the bed, for Alexei Afanasievich to wash down his medicine, was a faceted glass of boiled water; Nina Alexandrovna hastily straightened her ridden-up robe and brought the glass, which seemed to retain a weak dilution of his vanished life, to that strange being half-recumbent in the chair. Instead of taking what she'd been brought, Klumba grabbed Nina Alexandrovna's hand hard and began disgorging a soft milky bile into the offered water. This wasn't Klumba anymore. Her small, symmetrical eyes had become inhumanly identical (the left and right could have switched places without any disturbance) and looked as if they were seeing several layers of the things around her. Her features were strangely smoothed out, and her fluffy curls, which her fingers kept getting stuck in as if she were doing this for the first time in her life, looked like a wig.

Nina Alexandrovna now almost understood what had happened. In order for the man who couldn't die to die, there had to be a *reason*—which was not just the broadcast from the kitchen. Alexei Afanasievich's heart clearly wasn't as strong as everyone had supposed. His attempts to get into the noose (and those tarry laces that had appeared on the headboard from out of nowhere undoubtedly *held death*) had pretty much worn out the perishable two-stroke mechanism. When Alexei Afanasievich finally curtailed the millimeters separating him from the finish line, his heart, which was human after all, probably fell morbidly out of sync. Today, when it all came together—the obedience of his loyal instrument unexpectedly seized by his fingers, the proximity of the beauty in the hood looking at him not sideways, as once to the merry Bengal-fire crackling of a German submachine gun, but straight in the eye, and the sudden discovery of a different, outrageous reality that the veteran could no longer connect to his own *authentic* life, where he was always and eternally alive—a burning nettle had lashed his heart. The female scream that had come out of that fuzzy being who didn't look like his stepdaughter or his calm wife, who always warned of her appearance with a shining message from her guileless brain, had given him the push he needed to complete his adrenalin leap into nonbeing.

But that wasn't even the whole picture. There was still one last, almost incredible coincidence that enabled the veteran to surmount the elastic wall separating him from death and to pass through the only needle's eye that fate had left him. The moment the agitated Klumba saw the "old man" in the noose and ready to head off to heaven's pastures, her scream was the hysterics of a public-spirited woman in whose mind symbols and "literature" coincided very poorly with reality, which had suddenly declared unjust war on Klumba.

The mechanism of someone else dying, which had already been set in motion and made its test run, suddenly echoed inside her in a rush of harsh and tremendous darkness—and after that, everything went smoothly. There were no further obstacles to Alexei Afanasievich dying. The rare, blessed gift of *empathy* made Klumba (who was Klumba no longer) the immortal man's last helper, and in a way her visceral awareness of what was happening helped the veteran retain his authenticity to the very last moment and to move along intact to where he was met by a waiting God and a military band. Now the quaking woman, who had been splashed by the water in the glass the way a dancing ripple splashes a clumsy swimmer, was possibly the sole person in the world to have been honored with the knowledge of what death is. Finally, she stretched her neck up as if over the surface of the ripple and swallowed. "He died," the woman said, gasping for breath. "Yes, I know," Nina Alexandrovna replied, wiping the woman's face and wet chest, where crystalline drops of saliva sparkled like dew. Now she understood that *all was well*. Alexei Afanasievich's motionless eyes, clouded by the white powder of immortality, were staring at the ceiling. Trying not to press too hard, Nina Alexandrovna closed her husband's viscous, not quite shut eyelids, which left a very small amount of cold, prickly moisture on her fingers.

A fine white dust lingered here and there in the bared room—on the floor under the trophy bed, on the metal frame of the official portrait where medal-bearing Brezhnev was half-covered with a burning gleam in the broken glass—and now she suddenly noticed how the sturdy Soviet cardboard had yellowed and desiccated over all these years. There was a little more dust in the sunbeam. It stratified there, dry and whitish, like strong smoke from cheap tobacco. In order for everything to appear *the way it really was*, the modest participants in this story had to learn just a few things involving the lost pension, the lost nephew, and something else. As for Alexei Afanasievich, he had already found out much more than Nina Alexandrovna could have informed him of in human words, and so there was no call to doubt his forgiveness; his invisible presence was felt in everything.

Suddenly, Nina Alexandrovna understood. Alexei Afanasievich had been standing behind her reading the copy of the newspaper hidden behind the breadbox; he had been listening to the radio without a radio and watching a TV show; and he had been awkwardly touching her soul–with the exact same rough touch of the back of his hand with which he had once touched a yellow, badly staining bouquet and stroked Nina Alexandrovna behind the ear the day she first discovered his noose on the headboard of his trophy bed. His *presence* was so pervasive that at first Nina Alexandrovna took fright, turned around sharply, and saw only a light flutter of dust blissfully transfixed in a powerful, cinema-like beam that cast a fluorescing square onto the room's wall. Then and there she realized there was nothing to fear. This phenomenon, like any other, undoubtedly had its cause. Evidently, in the fourteen years of their nonverbal communication (Nina Alexandrovna's daily monologues didn't count), husband and wife Kharitonov had worked out an *understanding* that even now for some reason had not gone away. Evidently, their existence at death's side had been their training. Now the veteran's heavy body, with his big bones, a body that Nina Alexandrovna, folding the dark, slipping arms over the white ribs, covered with a sheet, bore no direct relation to this *understanding*—not that that mattered, either. For Nina Alexandrovna, it was clear that when she began visiting Alexei Afanasievich at the cemetery it would be more or less the same as it had been all these years alongside the paralyzed body, this flowerbed of tortured flesh whose juices had merely fed the large cardio root vegetable—because the *authentic* Alexei Afanasievich continued to exist.

Meanwhile, the woman in the chair, shifting from side to side, pulled out something soft from under her and with sickly astonishment looked under the bed, where a wobbling ball of yarn had rolled away, flicking its tail. She was gradually regaining her understanding of the world, and she tried to raise up on her unsteady arm and look at her watch. "Just a moment, hold on, just a moment," Nina Alexandrovna intoned, understanding that she had to call an ambulance—not for Alexei Afanasievich anymore but for him, too, to draw up a death certificate and observe all the other formalities. Almost not shuffling even a little, Nina Alexandrovna hurried to the front hall, where she heard the broken telephone's nasal drone and a key turning in the door with a deep click.